The Long Fall of the Ball From the Wall

A novel

by

Michael Boylan

PWI Books

Bethesda, Maryland

Copyedited by Joanna Jensen
Proof read by Lydia Johnson

Cover illustration: "The Persistence of Memory" by Salvador Dali is owned by The Museum of Modern Art in New York City.

The Archē Novels

Naked Reverse

Georgia (A Trilogy)

T-Rx: The History of a Radical Leader

The Long Fall of the Ball from the Wall

Time . . . the relative dating of events and the lapse of time between them are to be reckoned as different for the instrument in the comet and for the instrument at rest in aither. This is a greater strain on our credulity. We need not probe the question further than the conclusion that for the earth and for the comet spatially and temporally are each to have different meanings amid different conditions such as those presented by the earth and the comet.

Alfred North Whitehead, *Science and the Modern World.*

When we compare the empirical-scientific and mythical worlds it becomes evident that the contrast does not reside in their use of entirely different categories in contemplating and interpreting reality. It is not the qualities of these categories but their modality which distinguishes myth from empirical-scientific knowledge.

Ernst Cassirer, *The Philosophy of Symbolic Forms*

. . . the Renaissance, that age in which the Christian scheme of values was broken in two halves: one Catholic and the other Protestant. . . but thought corresponds to reality only for so long as its logicalness remains undisputed. This applies to all thinking not only to deductive dialectic (all the more as it is impossible to distinguish how much deduction is inherent in any act of thinking). It would be wrong, however, to say that deduction became suspect because people suddenly learned to look at facts with different and better eyes. The exact reverse is the case: things are only regarded with different eyes once dialectic has broken down, and that breakdown occurs not at the point where thought interprets reality, since reality could go on indefinitely submitting itself to such interpretation. But anterior to that, in thought's won province of logic, namely in the face of the problems raised by infinity.

Hermann Broch, *The Sleepwalkers*

. . . . in reality there are not two tendencies, or even two directions, but a self which lives and develops by means of its very hesitations, until the free action drops from it like over-ripe fruit.

Henri Bergson, *Time and Free Will*

Sing to me, Muse, of the many ways of man's devices after he sacked the sacred citadel of Troy.

Homer, *Odyssey*

What Tarquinius Superbus spoke in his garden with the poppies was understood by his son, but not by the messenger.

—Hamann (from *Johannes* de Silentio, *Fear and Trembling: A Dialectical Lyric*)

Then I would not have come

To kill my father and marry my mother infamously.

Now I am godless and a child of impurity,

Begetter in the same seed that created my wretched self

—Sophocles, *Oedipus Rex*

א

I WAS NOT CERTAIN WHAT I SHOULD DO. THERE WERE
RUNNERS ON FIRST AND SECOND BUT THERE WERE TWO OUTS.
BILLY WAS STARING AT MY POSITION. HE STOOD ALERT, ON
THE TIPS OF HIS TOES, HIS KNEES SLIGHTLY BENT, AND HIS
ARMS POISED FOR THE INEVITABLE MOMENT.

MY FINGERS BEGAN TO SWEAT. *It seemed heavy in his
arms. Every moment the weight seemed to increase.* I felt
separated *it was as if he were watching a movie or maybe, he felt
it was closer to a dream that you try to control, but can't. His eyes
were fixed on the hand* THAT MIGHT MEAN EVERYTHING.

As I opened the door and went inside, my mother looked
upset. She pushed me out of the bedroom and into the hall. Her
eyes were red, and her hands were shaking. Soon I understood
why my little sister had been crying and I felt ashamed at having
scolded her.

Mother's eyes had crooked red lines heading across
the white part to the black center. She had been crying. I felt
confused at thinking that my mother had been crying. She
walked me into the hall and knelt so that she could give me a
hug, but instead of hugging me she started crying. I didn't
know what I should do. I wanted to run upstairs and hide or
to 'wake up from my nightmare.' Yes, I wanted to wake up. *He
had lost control of the dream.* "Why are you crying? Mommy,
why are you crying?"

I wanted to say something but I didn't. I couldn't. Instead, I stood perfectly still. I didn't move. I was a statue. My legs were firmly planted to the floor. My fingers no longer sweated *and the trigger was no longer damp.* Suddenly I felt that I had to go to the bathroom. It wasn't just a small twinge, but a terrible pain that demanded urgency. I had known this feeling before when playing wall-baseball. I had often wondered what big leaguers did when, in the middle of an inning, they got the call. There was no way to stop the game---if they did, everyone would know! Millions of people would know! It would be as if they were watching you go. No, a big leaguer would wait until the end of the inning before he went. *Lita called him. This changed everything.*

I didn't understand why Mr. Souposey was so friendly to me when I went home. I cut across his backyard and he didn't even yell like he always used to. Sometimes he would go into the house and get his broom and hit kids on the head when they climbed his fence and cut across his lawn. I'm sure that a lot of kids just cut across his yard to see if they could make it before he got his broom--but today I had a real reason to get home fast.

I suspect that he waits at his window just to trap kids who walk over his beautiful spongy grass. I always wondered how he could keep his grass so spongy. It was lots of fun climbing his fence and jumping down onto the soft spongy turf and rolling around.

When I got to the fence, I put my left foot into one of the wire links and grabbed hold of the metal bar that runs along the top of the fence and pulled myself up, swinging my other leg over so that my right foot was carefully balanced on the bar. Then I brought my left leg up slowly so that I could jump down onto the grass, but as I was lifting my left leg, I slipped. THE BALL CAME DOWN, CAREENED OFF THE CEMENT IN FRONT OF THE WALL, AND BOUNCED WEAKLY OFF THE BRICK. IT WAS GOING TO BE A BLOOPER, A TEXAS LEAGUER. I HAD WANTED A HOMERUN, BUT THE BALL HAD SLIPPED. I HAD WANTED TO SEND IT OVER BILLY'S HEAD, BUT AS I THREW IT, THE BALL HAD SLIPPED. I couldn't bear to look, but I had to, just to make sure

THAT BILLY DIDN'T CHEAT. So, I looked up and saw that it was a mess. The kitchen, which usually was kept so clean by my mother, was messy. Then I heard my sister crying. I wondered where mother was and if she knew that Dianne had messed up her kitchen. For a first grader she could act pretty dumb. I walked up to where she was sitting on the floor, eating a banana. "Did you do this?" I asked.

"Do what?" she said as she looked up. She gave me that innocent look of hers. Those eyes of hers that could hide anything. No matter what mischief she had gotten into, she could always turn on those innocent eyes: those phony, innocent eyes. Those eyes that make everyone think she is so good, so nice—when really, she's just taken your last candy bar out of your secret hiding place. *Those eyes stared at him from the picture on the refrigerator; how he now hated those eyes* at that moment *he knew that it was her fault* she had messed up the kitchen. I was still in a state of shock. I didn't have a chance to recover from it. It was like moving from one state to another, from one shock to another. I couldn't believe what was happening: Virginia's naked body; it's all his fault; I'm a shameless son.

"I DON'T KNOW WHAT HAPPENED AT THAT PARTY. THINGS JUST WENT WILD." F.B.I. AGENT WALLACE NODDED AS HE JOTTED SOMETHING DOWN IN HIS NOTEBOOK.

"I NEVER UNDERSTOOD WHY—" I had to go to the bathroom. But Mother wouldn't let go of me. She was hugging me so tightly and crying. I wanted to wipe off her tears from my neck. They were wet and greasy. They just flowed onto my neck and left it greasy and dirty. "Your father, my Rex, your father, your father. . ." What was she trying to say? Whose car is that out front? I don't recognize it. Who's visiting? I had to go to the bathroom. I wanted to go, but my Mother wouldn't let go of me. The pain was getting unbearable.

"Mommy," I said. She looked up. She didn't understand—she couldn't—I knew she wasn't going to let go of me so I jerked out of her arms and ran to the bathroom—but she got up.

"Rico, wait," she called. I began running faster.

"Rico!" Her voice sounded half angry, half desperate. She was following me, but they couldn't stop the game. Didn't she know that? Now everyone would know. Everyone would watch. I had to go. Why was she following?

I ran faster; she was close behind. Then I tripped and fell, but the fall was made soft by the spongy grass. Mr. Souposey came out. "Who's out there. . . ?" he began, but then he saw me there lying on the grass, his grass—his prized grass. I started to get up, but as I was scrambling, he broke his tone and smiled, "Oh, it's you Rico." I didn't like to see him smile. He never smiled at me before and in fact, I doubt if I had ever seen Mr. Souposey smile. I had never supposed him capable of it. I was up on my feet as he approached me. I was ready to run. This must be some kind of trap. He was waiting to get me. One of his hands was behind his back as if he was concealing something. Maybe he had a club and was going to beat me with it. "Are you hurt?" he asked. I stared at his face, trying to figure out his angle.

A man can be anything,
if he wants to hard enough,
and sets his mind to it.

He had a strange look on his face: a look I didn't understand.

"You're not hurt?" he repeated. I didn't move. As he came within striking range, I backed away.

"Don't be afraid. I won't bite you," he said with that smile. MY RIGHT ARM BEGAN TO QUIVER. *He knew he must steady it.*

"Did you just finish a little wall ball?" he asked.

Wall Ball! How did he know about wall ball? Who told him the name, 'wall ball'? How did he know anything about it? Why was he asking so many questions? His arm that was behind his back began to move. He was probably getting ready to really clobber me. But I already had an escape route planned. He brought his hand around quickly as he leaned forward. I dodged and rolled under him.

"What's the matter, Rico?" he asked as I was rolling. I felt a hand catch the collar of my shirt. I knew that he had caught me and I resigned myself to the eventual punishment.
"Don't be scared. I'm not going to hurt you." A strong feeling of resentment rose within me. I wanted to kick him in the shins and run away. "Did you have a good game?"

"Yes," I said.

"Did you win?"

"Yes."

"You'd better get home, son. I think your mother would like to see you." He took his hand off of my collar, and mussed my hair. My resentment turned to disgust, and I pushed his hand off my head and ran away. What did he mean talking about my mother?

What right did he have uttering her name? As I walked down the block, a black car sped past me going down the street. It was past lunchtime and I hadn't eaten. I was hungry. "And you are fined a dollar for having such a fine boy," said the man at the front of the room. The rest of the men in the room laughed. Their laughter was a hearty laughter. Father was smiling.

Your father, your father

I could tell that he was happy.

"Well, young man, you can be very proud of your father." I nodded. He put his hand on my shoulder. "Yes, indeed, he was some president." I smiled and nodded.

"Ah, c'mon Jim," my father said. His voice was light and happy.

Then the man addressed me again, "Did you know that when your father was president, we had the best entertainment this Rotary's ever had?"

"C'mon Jim," said Father like he half-wanted him to stop.

"Why we had a fellow from the University of Washington once who talked on-"

"He's not interested in entertainment at Rotary," said Father.

"Why shouldn't I tell the kid what a great old man he's got?"

"Jim—" began Father.

"Let him talk, Rex," said another man across the table. "Your boy's got a right to be proud."

"Yeah," said the first. "It's not every young lad who has a father whose business career has shot up as fast as yours has, Rex."

"I don't know how you do it. You must put in fifteen-hour days to get accomplished all that you do," said the second, "a regional president at forty-three."

"You ought to be very proud of your father, he's a big success," said the first, and I nodded.

"Yes, you've got quite a daddy," said the second. I nodded.

"What most young boys would give to have a daddy like yours."

"You'll have mighty big shoes to fill."

I smiled.

"Once you guys get going you really lay it on," said Father. The men at the table all laughed. Then Father pulled me to him so that I was standing against his left thigh. His left arm was around my shoulders when he declared, "Rico's going to be a bigger success than I am, aren't you, little whiskers?" Everyone bounced in their chairs and shook with delight. I tried to smile but really felt like prowling underneath the table. My hands were clenched. My throat was very dry. I couldn't talk.

"Heck, I'm just an insurance man, but Rico here, he's going to be President someday; and I *don't* mean of Rotary." All the men laughed. My father was also roaring with delight. My throat was dry. A rough hand affectionately mussed my hair. I freed myself and moved to my chair so that I could reach for my water, but my cuff caught on the glass. Father lunged for the glass and grabbed it so only a little water was spilled.

"Pretty quick there, Rex."

"Didn't know you could move that fast."

"With hands like that you should have been a great football player."

"Or a great lover." Everyone laughed loudly. Everyone except Father's friend, Mr. Hansen, and Rex didn't laugh at all.

"I leave that game to you Jim—you're the bachelor— I've got my hands full with Jackie."

"I'll admit she looks like quite a little handful," laughed Jim. All the men doubled over. They guffawed almost uncontrollably and my father brayed the loudest. All the men laughed—that is, all but one.

William Bonnavert. I'm roomin' with a Bill Bonnavert, a hick from Idaho!

The men ate their meal quietly, as they listened to a man talk about the alarming rise in teen-age delinquency. He said that the root of the problem was that parents are too easy on their kids. My roommate is going to be Bill Bonnavert

Father and the other men just ate in silence, nodding their heads occasionally. I never really wanted to go to college. I had no interest in it but Father had never been to college and he had wanted me to go, so I went.

"The trouble with kids today is that they have no idols they can look up to. When I was a boy, we had Ted Williams, Stan Musial, Bob Feller, ah, you could go on and on. Ball players that weren't just great athletes, but fine examples as Men as well. Did you know that Rogers Hornsby never made an ad for alcohol or cigarettes in his life?" The speaker was a short, thin man with close-clipped hair and a receding hairline.

My father cleared his throat. "It wasn't that he was rich either, but because he figured that being a big leaguer meant something. It meant that a man had a responsibility to all the youngsters that watched the games. The kids that would copy anything the stars did."

Short-hair looked around at the others. They nodded their approval.

"Yes, it used to be that kids had a lot of men that knew the responsibility of their positions as stars and therefore they set good examples. They were idols—heroes—that kids could emulate. And kids picked up a lot of plain, simple moral habits that could keep them in good stead for the rest of their lives. But just look around today. What kinds of idols do kids have today? Robinson, Campanella, Aaron, Mays—can kids identify with a bunch of coloreds? Is that what you want your son to take after?"

The other men shook their heads.

"I tell you," said Father as he put his hand on my head. "I don't think my kid could identify with those blackies." He mussed my hair with his hand while all the men nodded their approval.

I tensed my neck. My head was being bobbed about. My brain began to hurt. It was like I was a rag doll, and I was being shaken about. Each hair felt like a nerve. I wanted the meeting to stop soon I would graduate from high school; it didn't mean much to me; in fact, I couldn't care whether I graduated or not. It didn't matter to me at all.

"A person can always tell," began Father, "what type of person you are and your condition by looking at you carefully."

It wasn't often that I had a chance to get into town. I jumped at the chance. Mother was taking me along to buy Christmas gifts. I didn't have a lot of money, but I had planned how I was going to spend it: three dollars on Mom, three dollars on Uncle Adam, and five dollars on Dianne.

Our car was parked in the street. I sat inside waiting. It took a long time. Mom said she'd be just a moment. The car was cold. Where was she? Why didn't she hurry up? I've been waiting in the car for twenty minutes. Where is she? *Then Lita came into the room.*

WALL BASEBALL IS A VERY COMPLECATED GAME. I LIKE IT A LOT. IT'S LOADS OF FUN. I LIKE PAYING WALLBALL. I PAY IT WITH BILLY AND ALWAYS HE BEATS ME, BUT THAT'S OK CAUSE THE PRESODENT DOESN'T HAVE TO PLAY WALLBALL.
RICO PATRICINI

"Rico, Nice handwriting," began Miss Smart, my teacher. I smiled. Few people complimented me on my handwriting. Then Miss Smart leaned down over me until her breasts bumped into my face. I moved away.

"But Rico, you need to explain just what 'wallball' is. You assume that everyone knows. This is a problem. Also, you have three misspelled words: 'playing' [not paying], 'complicated' [not complecated], and 'president' [not presodent]. Look these words up and learn to spell them correctly."

When she finally came out, Uncle Adam was with her. They were smiling and laughing. He had his arm around her waist. We all sat in the front seat while Uncle Adam drove. The car smelled peculiar as the heat came on. Uncle Adam's thick breath mingling with the car heater made my head spin. Outside, it was cold. I always liked the stores at Christmas. They reminded me of when I was very young when my mother used to take me to Toyland to see all of the Christmas toys. They were so exciting. And then she'd take me to the store where Santa Claus was. Even though I didn't really believe in Santa, it was fun anyway.

Uncle Adam was driving too fast. He was a poor driver. He didn't move into the proper lanes when he made a turn, but simply went wherever the car took him. He never used the turn signal to warn motorists of his dangerous dartings. Besides, I think he had had too much to drink. I hated it when, after I had come out of the bathroom, he was hugging Mother. He was talking softly to her, "That's all right Jackie. Everything will be all right. This isn't the end of the world. Everything will be—"

"What will I do Adam?"

"Don't worry."

"But it's just so terrible. How could he have—" she began crying some more. Uncle Adam stroked her back.

"Don't worry, Jackie. I'll come over for a few days while all of the details get taken care of; I'll see this out with you. What's a brother for, if he can't be of some help?"

Then he must have seen me, because they got real quiet all of a sudden and turned to look at me.

"Come on out Rico, I've got something to say to you."

I didn't want to come. I was afraid. He seemed so menacing. Then he started walking towards me, and I screamed. I screamed so loud that I woke up. The room was dark and my arms began to shake. I was shivering. Everywhere I was surrounded by a dark cold. Then Father came into the room.

"What's the matter Rico?" he asked gently. His voice was soft. It always soothed me. His big hands seemed so gentle and warm.

He covered me up and said, "What's the matter, little whiskers? Bad dream?"

"There were monsters and they were after me and I was running and I was so tired, and they were going to eat me."

"Well now, that's not a very nice situation to be in, is it? But next time the monsters come, just pull out your silver sword (like Rico the Great) and kill them."

"I'm afraid."

"There's nothing to be afraid of. You can take care of those monsters. There's nothing you can't do if you want to hard enough and you set your mind to it. Now you go back to sleep, okay?"

He started to leave. "Daddy?" He turned his head. "Stay in here."

"I can't, I have to sleep with Mommy."

"Can I come in and sleep with you?"

"Big, brave boys don't need to sleep with their fathers."

"Daddy—"

"Now, you're Daddy's big, brave boy, aren't you?"

"Yes."

"Well, then you can sleep in your own bed tonight and kill those dragons yourself. Now, go to sleep."

"Nothing's going to hurt you. Are you going to be all right?" he asked. I didn't say anything.

"Rico?" he said again, a little more firmly.

"Yes?" I replied.

"Good. Now be a brave boy and go to sleep. Goodnight," he said as he shut my door.

My room was very dark. *The cold steel stuck to his hand. The butt of the rifle was jammed into his shoulder.*

"You'd better get home son. I think your mother would like to see you," Mr. Souposey said. His breath smelled funny, like Uncle Adam's sometimes—like he had just had some cough syrup. Why was he being friendly all of a sudden? I wanted to kick him in the shin.

It says he's from a hick town in Idaho but that innocent expression didn't fool me. "Only women and children are easily fooled," my father said. "That's why there aren't any women presidents or any heads of countries."

"What about a queen?" I asked.

"There aren't any real queens today, but when there were, they usually had men to act as their ministers in order to rule the country." My father lit his pipe and began puffing sweet smelling smoke. I loved the smell of that smoke.

"Has there ever been a woman ruler?"

"Not a good one, to be sure. Frankly, women just don't have the hard-nosed sense that men have. They're too emotional."

Uncle Adam stopped hugging Mommy when he saw me coming out of the bathroom. He walked over to me. "Come on Rico, I've got something to say to you." His breath smelled funny, like he had just taken some cough syrup.

"I want to talk to you about your father."

Man can be anything he wants to if he sets

His mind to it

This year, however, the stores didn't seem as exciting or as decorated as they used to seem. Every year it seems that they spend less and less effort to make Christmas really nice. I guess when a guy gets into high school, things aren't the same as when he was just a kid.

"I DON'T KNOW WHY. IT WASN'T OUR FAULT. HE WAS RAISED PROPERLY."

"WELL, DID HE HAVE ANY UNUSUAL INTERESTS OR HOBBIES? ANYTHING THAT WAS PECULIAR?" AGENTS WALLACE AND FRIEDMAN LOOKED UP FROM THEIR NOTEBOOKS. THEY WERE AROUND THE SAME AGE (MID-FORTIES), AND BOTH WORE BLACK, HORN-RIMMED GLASSES.

"HE WAS A QUIET BOY—REALLY VERY QUIET. IT WAS HARD TO UNDERSTAND WHAT HE WAS THINKING ABOUT. HE NEVER TALKED MUCH ABOUT ANYTHING EXCEPT HIS FATHER. HE USED TO HAVE LONG WALKS WITH HIS FATHER WHEN HE WAS LITTLE."

"HOW OLD WAS HE WHEN HIS FATHER—"

WALL BASEBALL IS A SIMPLE GAME. ALLS YOU HAVE TO DO IS THROW THE BALL AGAINST THE SEMENT IN FRONT OF THE WALL AND THE BALL BOUNCES OFF THE SEMENT AND ONTO THE WALL. THEN IT HITS THE WALL AND COMES BACK AT YOU. IF THE OTHER PLAYER CATCHES THE BALL ON THE FLY, THEN IT IS AN OUT. IF THE OTHER GUY GETS THE BALL ON THE FIRST BOUNCE IT'S A SINGLE; TWO BOUNCES IT'S A DOUBLE; THREE A TRIPLE, AND FOUR OF MORE A HOMERUN. SOME PLAYERS ADD A COUNTING TO THIS: (THREE FOR A SINGLE, SIX FOR A DOUBLE, AND NINE FOR A TRIPLE). FOR A SACRIFICE, THE GUY UP TO BAT YELLS 'BUNT' WHILE THE BALL IS IN THE AIR AND IF THE GUY CATCHES IT, HE THROWS IT AGAINST THE WALL BEFORE THE COUNT OF THREE—SAME WITH A TAG-UP. YOU GO NINE INNINGS WITH THE SECOND-UPS GETTING THE LAST LICKS.

RICO PATRICINI

"Well, wall-baseball sounds like an exciting game. You misspelled 'cement,' and you used expressions that aren't proper English, like 'Alls you have to do,' and 'last licks.' Try and be more precise with your expressions. Also, there are quite a few 'ifs'—this shows me that you're not certain about what you're talking about."

It took me three tries to pass my driver's test but I was glad to get my license now. I only hope Uncle Adam will let me drive the family car. I hate driving with him because he's such a bad driver. YES, MR. FRIEDMAN, RICO DID HAVE A GIRLFRIEND. SHE WAS NAMED, AH . . . VIRGINIA. YES, THAT WAS HER NAME: VIRGINIA. BUT HE TREATED HER WRONG—REALLY WRONG. We let Mom out in front of the department store, but I had to drive with Uncle Adam to a parking place. The car was too hot for my comfort. I didn't like driving with Uncle Adam, but I was somewhat comforted by the thought that next year I would be old enough for a driver's license.

A Man can do anything he wants to if he really wants it bad enough

We parked about three blocks from the store. It had begun to snow. That's really rare in the Seattle area.

"Look at that damn snow. We'll have to drive back over these damn streets. They're so slippery when this damn snow falls." He struggled with the door handle, which was sticking. "Damn it all. This damn car never does a damn thing. Damn it all."

"Just push up and out," I said. "When it sticks you have to push up and out for it to open."

"Shut up, damn it. Don't you think I know about my own car? I drive it enough. I don't need the likes of you to go telling me how to open a car door."

He pushed up and out and the door opened.

"Damn door."

What was that car doing in front of our house? The car was all black with white wheel covers. I ran inside.

The snow was really coming down heavily. I liked to watch the large flakes falling, carefree, from the sky. They just floated back and forth slowly drifting—like they were in no hurry to get to the ground—lazily sailing—free in the wind— sparkling in the dim light. My lungs were filled with cold air. I felt something fresh and tingling pulse through my body.

"Hurry up Rico," called my Uncle Adam. "We have a walk sign." I saw a snowflake and ran to catch it. It was dancing merrily—just waiting to be caught.

I reached for it with my right hand, but it hopped to the left. So, I grabbed at it with my left hand, but it popped up- wards; laughing gleefully at my futile attempts to capture it. Then I jumped and reached for it with both hands, but it again spun out of my reaching hands as I, grasping wildly, came down abruptly upon my bottom on the ground. I looked up as my flake (which giggled momentarily at my distress) came to rest on the end of my nose.

Father's fingers were thick, but they could quickly soothe me to sleep.

"Rico! Get up."

The flake was melting—

"Rico!"

The water from the flake dripped down both sides of my nose, but more on the right side, I think. It slowly rolled down my face, just as it had descended from the sky. With the edge of my tongue, I caught part of the droplet and escorted it into my mouth. What a fitting way to treat a friend, I thought. Very proper. Quite. Yes, very proper.

"Rico, come on," said Uncle Adam. "You damn little brat. I'll teach you." I looked up, and there he was bringing his arm out from behind his back to hit me as he had so many times before. I dodged and rolled under him.

"What's the matter, Rico?" he said as I was rolling. I felt a hand catch the collar of my shirt. "Don't be afraid, I'm not going to hurt you." A funny smile appeared on that face. I didn't like Mr. Souposey when he was angry, and I didn't like him any more when he was smiling. As I was running down the street, a black car sped past. The car was all black except that it had white wheel covers. Guess what Mom? I met this girl today, and she's named Virginia. She's really a pretty girl and so much fun to be with.

"You know it's the *type* which is important. They can always determine your condition by the type—"

I ran down the sidewalk towards home. I looked down at the cracks in the sidewalk and tried to remember not to step on a crack. The day was pretty hot, and I was beginning to sweat. Then I saw Rick; he was going to go swimming, I guess, or at least he was dressed for it. He had a pass to go to the city swimming pool any time he wanted to go. I wish I had such a pass. Then I could learn to swim and meet some of the neat guys. *The sun was hot and his fingers began to sweat as he held the gun in place.* Pretty soon I could see our rose bushes. My teacher says I'm pretty good in pottery. He says that I have a lot of potential. He says that I could become a good artist if I worked at it.

"You know what I think of that?" queried Uncle Adam with a smile. "I think pottery is for fags. It's for those swishes who can't make a living any other way. If your father could only see you now, he'd certainly be ashamed."

"WE BOTH LOVED HIM VERY MUCH, AND I THINK YOU'D HAVE TO SAY THAT HE WAS A HAPPY CHILD."

As I turned over, I felt the sharp arrows of sunlight shooting through the holes in the curtains to wake me.

I opened one eye slightly to make sure the sun was really rising and that it wasn't just an aberration. From the corner of my eye I could see the brilliant orange majesty of the sun rising from the horizon. Then I opened both eyes and propped up my head by doubling over the pillow. I was wide awake. *Virginia, Virginia,* what a beautiful name.

I pulled the curtains open and hopped back into bed. My bed was so warm and cozy. I didn't want to get out from under the warm covers and re-enter the cold outer world which was my room in the mornings. My bed was so warm. I just lay there comfortably watching the sun rise. It was so bright and regal as it rose: very slowly, but with a detectable motion. Silently and deliberately it ascended, taking its rightful seat in the sky. *Virginia, how I wish you were here with me watching the sun.* It seemed appropriate that something so important was so silent. It didn't need to be loud or obtrusive to make its presence known. It just existed and, as such, it was the source of all life on this planet. We all depend on the sun. It was the sun that was the source of life. If it stopped rising one sad morning, then we'd soon die. Artificial light could grow some crops, but we couldn't generate enough electricity to adequately light thousands or millions of acres of farm land. All the plants would soon die and then following them the animals, including Man, who depends on the ecological food chain to survive. The world would slowly die.

Virginia, don't you see how important the sun is? Within the sun is all of life— everything. The ancients weren't so foolish. After all, they worshipped the sun. We owe everything to the sun. Without the power of the sun we wouldn't exist. Why then doesn't somebody talk about the sun? Why can't they see that it is through the saving grace of the Son (Jesus) that we are allowed to be?

Yet no one discusses the sun. All is taken for granted. For granted. The strong silent sun doesn't need us to survive. It goes on with or without people. It is independent of us. The sun's greatness transcends any glory that we can bestow upon it. Yet, why doesn't someone sing out to the sun and admit our utter and complete dependence upon it? I love you Virginia. I love you love you love you love you love you love you. Oh yes love you

And   I   do   but

you

    don't   *even*   *know*   *my*

        name

Sometimes I used to think that the sun was like the President. Nobody ever sees the President, but that doesn't make him any less the ruler of all people. The President doesn't *have* to play wall ball.

He knows the real value of a dollar. Money comes dearly and shouldn't be thrown away on frivolities.

What is *frivolity?*

"That's spending money on something that you really didn't need." I DON'T UNDERSTAND. "For example, if you had twenty cents and wanted to get something to eat, you could buy a piece of beef jerky or an ice cream cone, which would you choose? Now, jerky stays with you longer and is better for you, so you should buy the jerky." BUT I LIKE ICE CREAM. "That's not the point. You see, suppose the jerky cost ten cents and the ice cream cost twenty cents. If you bought the ice cream, then you would have used all of your money. And say, for example, I was dying and needed ten cents to save my life. If you had bought the jerky, I could have lived, but by buying something frivolous, I died."

I BEGAN TO CRY.

"Rico, don't cry. What's the matter? What's the matter? It was only a story. Rico? Rico?"

There was something about getting up in the morning before everyone else that always made me feel special. It was like I was better than they were because I could get up while they were enjoying the excesses of surplus sleep. The whole house was quiet. Everything was so still. I wondered what the President was doing. I was certain that he was also up before everyone else. Somehow, I felt I knew the President very well, though I didn't even know his name.

"THEN THERE WERE THOSE PERSONALITY TESTS THAT HE TOOK NEAR THE END OF HIGH SCHOOL."

"WHAT DID THEY SAY?" ASKED AGENT WALLACE (HE WAS A PSYCHOLOGIST).

"I DON'T REMEMBER, EXACTLY, BUT THEY CALLED ME IN TO TALK WITH ME."

"WHAT DID THEY ASK YOU?"

"I DON'T REMEMBER, EXACTLY. BUT THEY ASKED ME IF I WAS MARRIED, AND WHETHER OR NOT I THOUGHT RICO LIKED HIS UNCLE, MY BROTHER, ADAM. CAN YOU IMAGINE THE NERVE OF THOSE NOSEY PSYCHOLOGISTS? THEY THINK THAT JUST BECAUSE THEY'VE BEEN TO FOUR YEARS OF COLLEGE THAT THEY CAN BUTT THEIR NOSES INTO OTHER PEOPLE'S AFFAIRS."

"WHAT DID YOU TELL THEM?"

"I PICKED-UP MY BAG AND TOLD HIM I WASN'T GOING TO ANSWER ANY MORE OF THOSE SORTS OF QUESTIONS AND THAT I WAS PERSONALLY INSULTED. THEN I TURNED AROUND AND WALKED OUT."

"SO, THE PSYCHOLOGIST WAS A MAN?"

"NO, THAT'S NOT RIGHT. IT WAS A WOMAN WHO CALLED ME IN. *IT WAS A WOMAN I TALKED TO.*"

The room was so quiet and calm. The warm rays of sunlight relaxed me under the covers. Somehow this time of the day was the happiest for me. On Sundays it always lasted an extra two or three hours. Then I heard footsteps and I knew that my sister was up. The quiet and peace were gone. The moment had vanished. It would be time to watch television. Yes, it would be time to look at the tube until Father woke up.

The door of my room opened slightly. "Rico, are you awake?" asked my sister in a medium-loud voice. I shut my eyes and was pretending to be asleep. I didn't want Dianne to see that I was awake.

"Are you sleeping?" she asked, this time walking into my room.

"Yes," I said.

"You want to watch TV?" she asked as she sat down on the far corner of my bed. She stared at me for a second and then moved forward and slid under the covers.

"What's on?" I asked.

Instead of answering she began tickling my feet. I crawled under my covers and grabbed her hands, but she slipped out of my grasp. Then I reached for her again, and this time I caught her Virginia was on the floor naked Dianne looked at me with that expression of hers like I was at fault, I don't think she was even embarrassed or ashamed I looked at her naked breasts which were very full despite her only being still a teenager and she looked at me but I wasn't going to fall for that again— no never again. I couldn't believe my eyes

So I squinted so that I could see *the sun was bright in his eyes as he looked down to the street. He knew that it wouldn't be long now. He leaned forward against the white half-wall and lifted the black imitation leather case and carefully unzipped it. The sunrise was bright, but he knew that it would still be another six hours before the motorcade would*

"C'mon Dianne," I said, but she continued to wiggle. "Di," I said as sternly as I could. "If you make too much noise, you'll wake up Father." She continued to wiggle. "Di, Father will be mad if he gets woken early on Sunday morning." Then she stopped and did a backwards somersault, pulling all the covers with her. My bed was a mess around her blue pajamas.

"Janny's brother plays a lot with her."

"Well, I'm not Jake Murdock."

"C'mon Rico, let's play cestin," said Dianne.

"I don't feel like playing cestin just now."

"Please," she entreated.

"No, let's go watch TV."

"*Please*," she said as she looked at me in her appealing, innocent fashion.

"Di."

"Rico?"

Why was she trying to upset the order of things? We always watched TV on Sunday mornings. She had woken up too early. Why couldn't she have just stayed in her room? Why did she have to come and bother me? I didn't want to play with my little sister. 'Cestin' made me sick. She was such a baby always whining when she didn't get her way. And then she would give me that stupid look of hers. She thought that her dramatics convinced people, but really all they did were to set me against her.

"Now I mean it, Di."

"Just for a while?"

I was very irritated. I wouldn't give in to her demands. Father never gave in to Mommy's demands. He was firm with her.

Women are just emotional.

I didn't see any reason to give in to a six-year-old-girl.

"Now, I don't—" I began, but it was too late. She was off to the bathroom for the wet washcloth. I couldn't run after her because it would make too big of a fuss, and that would upset Father. Then he would be really mad and blame me. No, she would get the washcloth and there was nothing I could do about it.

I just sat there waiting for the inevitable. And his hand came down and hit me on the side of the head. It was a powerful blow and knocked my skull to the cement where all the other snowflakes had fallen. All of a sudden, I felt like he was staring at me. Watching me with my melted snowflake, which he didn't like. For some reason he had entered my world. The snowflake was gone. I began to cry. Everywhere there was just cement and cold: cold mushy snow. I was crying loudly but no tears were coming from my eyes. He hit me again; this time I rolled over on my back. He was talking, but I didn't hear what he was saying. It didn't matter. He had interfered with something private. He had entered my private happiness. I felt violated. My muscles recoiled as my body scrunched up into a little ball that was tight and secure. Now any blows would bounce off, and I couldn't be touched—I was safe inside my little house; protected from everyone. I could *hear* sounds, but I didn't try and discriminate between them. I didn't want to hear anything that was said—I didn't want to feel—I only wanted to be left alone so that I could sing, without an audience—sing to myself, sing to nothing. I felt like singing to no one at all.

He looked at the book depository building. Then he saw nothing.

But it wasn't 'no thing' in the sense that there wasn't *any* thing

A Man can be anything...

"Will you let me just be your—"

She just stood there.

"Lita! I need to act!" he said.

Then she went to him.

At that moment I felt myself being lifted up and carried. There were buzzing sounds. But I heard my name. Rico. Rico Rico Ricoricoricoricoooo. I was only murmuring.

I opened my eyes expecting those gentle fingers of my father, but instead I only saw my mother.

It was warm. There were many colors. People were walking around. Then I was standing with my head against something scratchy. It was a dress.

Uncle Adam said, "Rico, I have something to tell you."

A sinister, fire-breathing monster. And I, with my sword, will smite you all and free the land from your evil scourge. I will free you all. Step back and let me slit the gullet of this repulsive vermin that is slowly killing us all. The time of indecision is over. The seventh seal has been broken, and we are warriors who have lost our way. Death to the unbelievers! Judgment has come upon you all. . . And you shall dwell in the House of the Lord forever. Let us pray. Oh, great and merciful Father, forgive us for we have sinned against Thee and Thy people. We recognize that we are wicked creatures that have no right to even gather the crumbs under Thy table, but we know that Thou art a kind and merciful God and has forgiven us already through the death of Thy son, Jesus Christ, our Lord, whose birth we now celebrate. Help us and give us strength now and in the coming year. We ask in Jesus' name we pray, Amen.

Then we all got up and began to sing a song I didn't know. I felt easy as all the voices blended into one. Only my little sister tugging at me kept me from becoming lost in Father Weal and the body of the Holy Church. It's remarkable how a four-year-old can make so much noise. But I quieted her as best I could, while everybody sang a song.

It was strange to be with so many people, losing myself in the corporate body. It was as if everyone and everything were subsumed within the confines of the large room. I always looked forward to each Sunday when I could again lose myself to the magical mystery of the dim lights, strange smells, smooth wood, and soft prayer cushions. Early each Sunday I would anticipate Father's booming voice: "Church everybody, let's hop!" I would then turn off the television and push my little sister into the bathroom so she'd get ready. Generally, she'd put up an argument; but I'd always win, because she knew that I had Father on my side. It was a good feeling to see my little sister obey me for once. I was the only one who was wise to her little tricks. Then she turned and looked at me shamelessly. She wasn't even embarrassed. The little minx didn't even care. She didn't even care.

The faces of the people were all fixed upon their books, except when they looked up. I stood as straight as I could, holding onto my little sister's hand so she wouldn't cause any trouble. Somehow, I felt taller when we were in church. I felt like giving a speech like the priest and having everyone listen attentively. I remembered the story of when Jesus was a boy and all the important men listened to him and what he was saying. I wonder whether Jesus was ever President. He must have been, because everyone seemed to like him so much.

I liked it when the priest talked sternly to all the people. I would look up to my father and watch his face. He was a statue, hard and immoveable. I felt a deep relaxation, and wished that this time would never end but melt away to endless wandering toward nowhere.

Sometimes I wondered what would happen if I ran up to the front of the people and stood on the railing and began talking sternly. Everyone would listen and become very attentive. They would all sit silently and let my words bounce around the room. And I could play catch with my own words, kind of like that game wall baseball that Father promised to teach me. And when I lifted my hands everyone would hang their heads down and be extra still, and then I would be holding all the people in my arms and I could put them into my pocket if I wanted to and then I could talk to **mu**.

WHEN I WAS LITTLE, I USED TO PLAY ANOTHER GAME BESIDES WALLBALL. THE GAME IS CESTIN. IT'S A SILLY GAME. IT IS WHEN YOU GET A WET WASHCLOTH AND YOU TRY TO PUT IT UNDER ANOTHER PERSON'S CLOTHES (GENERALLY UNDER THE SHIRT). IF YOU ARE SUCCESSFUL, THEY GET REAL WET. MY FATHER MADE UP THE GAME WHEN HE DID IT TO

MY MOTHER ONCE. MY SISTER MADE UP THE NAME WHEN
SHE COULDN'T PRONOUNCE CHEST AND SAID 'CEST.' YOU
PUT THE WASHCLOTH ON THE CHEST. IT ISN'T VERY FUN,
AND I DON'T LIKE IT VERY MUCH. I DON'T PLAY IT VERY
OFTEN EXCEPT WHEN I HAVE TO.
         RICO PATRICINI

"Your spelling is improving, but you are having trouble with
the tenses of your verb forms, past, present and future. Also,
you can combine your sentences. For example, your first two
sentences could read: When I was little, I learned another game
(besides wallball) called 'cestin.' Cestin is a silly game in which
one participant gets a wet wash cloth and attempts to drop it
down the other's shirt. This wet fun was invented by my father
and named by my little sister (who couldn't pronounce the
word 'chest' correctly, saying 'cest' instead).

         "On the whole you are getting a better sense of
communicating your thoughts to others. This means you are
developing a sense of audience. This shows real improvement.

         "If your papers continue to improve as they have been
don't be surprised to find a w e t w a s h c l o t h d o w n
y o u r s h i r t o n e o f t h e s e d a y s ; C e s t i n !"

         Riding home in the car was different on Sundays,
because everyone was silent. Then Father would break the
stillness and comment on what the preacher said in his speech.
My mother would usually agree with Father and then there
would be silence again.

         I liked the silence, but my little sister hated it. She would
squirm around in the back seat and it was my job to hold her
down. "*'G e t u p, ' I s a i d. B u t t h e y d i d n ' t p a y a n y
a t t e n t i o n ; t h e y i g n o r e d m e. I t w a s i f I w a s n ' t
e v e n t h e r e. H e r e t h e y w e r e a n d t h e y — t h e y*"

         *He looked at the brown building. It was very solid
looking. It was a 7-story building facing Dealey Plaza. "I'll bet
that was built around the turn of the century," he thought. He*

stared at the old structure for a moment before crossing the street to the bus stop, which would take him back to work.

When she came back into the room with the wet cloth, I was ready for her. She ran through the doorway expecting to find me where she had left me. She never thought anyone else had a mind of his own. In her world, everyone acted as a sort of echo to her—but I didn't. No, when she came through the doorway, I was behind the door waiting for her. Usually, when I wasn't in plain view, I was hiding in the closet, so that's where she looked first. When her back was turned as she looked in the closet, I slid out from behind the door, shutting it with my foot as I went past. I quickly came up behind her and grabbed the washcloth from her hand and, before she had an opportunity to turn around, I pulled her over to the bed and dragged her down. There wasn't anything she could do.

She was good at cestin because she was so quick, but this time I showed that intelligence counted as at least an equal commodity to mere animal reflexes. I pulled her down to the bed so that she was on her stomach and then I took the cloth with my left hand and stuffed it down her pajama bottoms.

"Rico don't!" she squealed.

The cold water made her jump.

"Rico, that's not fair. Down the pants isn't fair," she said as she was rolling around the bed. I wouldn't let her take it out.

"I'm going to get you," she said, "just wait. Down the pants isn't fair."

"You can't get me. I'm too good for you. Look at your pants; they're all wet. Did you wet your pants? Di wet her pants. Di wet her pants!" I was laughing so hard that she got up and slipped out of the room. I knew where she was going. She was going to get the washcloth real wet and cold and try and get me. But I knew that she didn't stand a chance. She didn't stand a chance against me.

The dormitories at the University of Washington have a kind of sterile atmosphere that made me feel uneasy. I was in 342 so I took the elevator to the second floor because there was no third floor listed, and I got out and looked for the third floor but I couldn't find it. I went out to the staircase and walked up and arrived at the fourth floor. I didn't want to ask anyone because they would know that I was a freshman, and not only a freshman but one who couldn't even find his own room. So, I walked down to the second floor again and looked around, then I saw a fellow who was sitting in the lounge.

"Hi," he said.

"Hi."

"You livin' here?" he asked.

"Yeah." I was carrying a suitcase in my hand. And I had a trunk downstairs.

"What's your name?" he asked.

"Ah, Rico," I said. I was taken aback by his forward style. I didn't want to talk with him for fear that he might find out that I didn't know where my room was. I could imagine him laughing at me for not being able to find my room: the typical dumb freshman. Then he would tell his buddies that I couldn't even find my room.

They would all laugh and later come and knock on my door. When I would open it, they would point and laugh at me for not being able to find my room. I was the archetype of the dumb freshman.

Then the guy who took me to my room would proclaim that if he hadn't taken control of me that I'd still be wandering around (classes having been going on for two weeks). That I was not "college material."

Maybe I should join the cleaning staff. That's the only role in college that I was fit for.

Then the guys would rag my "protector." They would say that he'd helped in the pollution of the dorm. "The new guy even smells," one upper classman would intone.

Father always wanted me to go to college.

"Hey, you sorry-fuck-dago. In this country we take showers to clean ourselves. I have half a mind right now to take you into the lav and make you wash your ass. You sorry fuck."

"Nice dorm you have here, gentlemen," was my reply.
I thought that they'd laugh at that, but they screwed up their faces. My tormentor spat at me, and the crowd dispersed. When my tormentor was almost out of sight he turned and said, "We'll be watching you."

Then he got his trunk and headed to his room.

My tormentor was a skinny guy about my height. His face was broken out in acne. I tried to think about whether I could take him in a fight. I had learned to fight in primary school and had continued to do so all of my life when people disrespected me.

I decided that if pimple-face confronted me again there would be a price to pay.

"Rico Patracini? Is that your name?" asked the guy who I took to be the RA, a student who was in charge of the dormitory floor.

I grimaced, but refrained, "Why yes; why do you ask?" The RA was a short, stocky guy with closely-cut dark hair. I didn't ask him how he almost knew my name when he had never seen me before.

"I don't care what the bastard said. He doesn't know anything," said Uncle Adam.

"I've been waiting for you. I'm your roommate, Bill Bonavert."

I was confused. I thought that this fellow before me was my superior, but he was just my roommate. I didn't know how that made me feel.

"So, what do you think of our room?" asked a jovial Bill. I wondered whether Bill was of Italian ancestry, like I was.

I really hadn't had time to inspect the room, after being shown where to go and having tried my key in the lock. I realized that I had been distracted.

"Very nice, Bill. What do you think?"

Bill scrunched up his face so that his lips made a circle that almost touched his nose. "Too small, if you ask me. I think we should go for bunk beds and open up some space." Bill slanted his head as if to elicit a response. I didn't know what to do *the gun was heavy in his hands. He had practiced at his make-shift rifle range in the abandoned railroad yard for this moment, but now that the big event had arrived, he wondered whether he would be ready for the execution. He just had to have faith:* "Sure, bunk beds would be fine. How do we make that happen?"

"No problem. I talked to our RA and he has some frames in the basement. If we act right away, we can snatch one. If we wait, they may be gone."

He had to act right away. As soon as the motorcade came by there would be no other opportunity. He put his hand on my shoulder

"Don't be afraid. I won't bite you," he said with that smile — my cuff caught the glass— *His right arm was shaking almost uncontrollably.*

When Di returned, I was in the center of the room waiting. She was going to learn that when I said I wanted to go right away I meant right away. Sometimes, when l felt like it, I might let her win a few times, but when I told her we're going to watch TV, then I expected her to follow my wishes. After all, she's my little sister and should do the things that I say.

Then I saw her face, she was looking around the corner from a kneeling position. "Come on in, Di," I said. She didn't say anything, but got up slowly and walked into the room. She was holding the washcloth in her left hand in front of her. I watched her hand carefully.

THE BALL WENT DOWN AND HIT HARD. IT WAS A LONG FLY. BILLY BOUNCED IT PERFECTLY. I MADE A RUNNING TRY FOR IT. BUT I WAS NERVOUS. I KEPT MY EYES ON THE ARC. I LEAPT AT MY OPPORTUNE MOMENT. THE BALL HIT MY FINGER-TIPS, STICKING ON THEM MOMENTARILY, THEN BOUNCING OFF AND FALLING TO THE GROUND.

"AND THE RED SOX WIN AGAIN!" YELLED BILLY.

I WAS ON MY BACK LOOKING UP AT HIM. THE BALL ROLLED INTO THE ANDERSON'S YARD.

Di wasn't as excited or flustered as she had been when she left the room. She entered deliberately, then made a fast break towards me. I stepped to the left, pushing her down, and grabbed the washcloth. She went to the floor. I picked up the washcloth, but it was warm! She had gotten a lukewarm towel.

I couldn't understand why—then she squirmed up. I didn't understand why she—she ran out of the room quickly. I was kneeling with the washcloth in my hand. Then she was back. I looked up and almost instantaneously felt the cold of a washcloth on my neck. She had used two towels! I tried to get her arm, but she was stuffing the towel down my back.

"Cestin, Cestin, Cestin!" she proclaimed.

Then I caught ahold of her leg. She went down. I got on top of her and took the towel out from my shirt. "Ha! Ha! Cestin! I got you. Ha! Ha! I got you."

I struggled to subdue her. She didn't like it.

"But Rico, I got you. I got you first, Rico."

I pinned her arms down.

"That was a pretty good trick. Wasn't that funny? Didn't you think that was funny, Rico?"

Then I retrieved the washcloth and pulled down her pajama bottoms. She was lying on her back.

"Oh Rico, that was the best cestin I ever saw. Ha, ha, ha ha ha ha ha ha ha ha ha ha ha."

I pulled down her pants real far, almost to her knees and stood above her with the towel.

"Ha ha ha ha ha ha, oh Rico, ha ha ha ha," she just kept laughing. Then I got up and walked over to the door. I picked up the other towel and held one in each hand.

"Let's go and watch some television," I said.

She looked at me and stopped laughing. Then she rolled over on her stomach and pulled up her pajamas. I walked down the hall to the living room. The tiles of the floor were warped. I had always wondered how they got that way. They were discolored, brown, and almost fit in with the darkness of the hall.

Upstairs, Father and Mother were asleep. All was quiet for a moment. Then I heard my mother say, "What's the matter with him?"

"What's ever the matter with him," said Uncle Adam. "He's a little dreamer; he's got his head in the clouds."

"But what was he doing on the ground? Did you hit him?"

"Jocasta!" intoned Uncle Adam sharply to Mother. I looked at him directly. I wanted to kick him in the groin and run away but instead I just looked at him and frowned.

"I don't want to hear you accusing me. I will not stand for it."

"Well, how did he get a cut on the side of his face?" asked Mother.

"He hit his head on the cement."

"And how did his head happen to hit the cement?"

"What do you mean by that?" Uncle Adam was struggling to find the right lie.

A crowd of people was gathering around. Everyone was BUT WHAT HAPPENS WHEN A MAJOR LEAGER HAS TO—YOU KNOW. ALL EYES ARE AROUND. EVERYONE IS LOOKING.

"Are we going to stand here in front of the store discussing this?" he asked. "Let's either go inside or go home. Take your pick."

"Now, Adam."

"Which will it be?"

"Adam, please."

"Let's go inside."

So, we went inside and all was forgotten as we made our way to the second floor.

"Now let's synchronize watches and we'll go and buy whatever we have to and in, say, eighty minutes we'll meet back here," said Uncle Adam.

So, we split up. I decided to try the fence. I was hungry. We finally got to eat. When I reached for my glass *he didn't like the confusion. Every day he would pass that brown building as he made his way to the bus stop. There was something pathetic about it yet somehow, he could understand, yes, even love, that building. It had stood the test of time. It was reliable.*

There's no substitute for fine construction and workmanship.

A car rushed past us down the street. It had white wheel covers. It was the first time that Uncle Adam had let me use the car. The roads were dry and the sun was out. I started it and pushed in the clutch. Then I remembered about the emergency brake. *He let it off gently, resting the barrel on his hand.* Then I shifted into reverse and let up easy on the clutch. The car began to move as my foot gently depressed the accelerator. I cramped the wheel and hit the brake. Then I put it into first gear and was off. Virginia. 35mph. Doing the speed limit—exactly. Virginia. Why was she asking? No, I could walk home.

We sat watching in front of the TV. *"HE WAS ALWAYS QUIET."*

"DID HE HAVE ANY UNUSUAL INTERESTS?"

"NO, HE WAS PRETTY NORMAL. HE WAS ALWAYS SO PATIENT."

Then I heard the toilet flush. Father must be up. He started walking downstairs. When he got to the kitchen, he called to us, "Church everybody; let's hop!"

I ran upstairs to help him with the meal. On Sundays we always made breakfast for Mother. I wanted to do something for her, but I wasn't sure what to do. I had to go to the bathroom.

"Hi Daddy," I said as I walked into the kitchen.

"Hello, little whiskers," said Father as I sat down.

"Want to help me make the breakfast? Come over and put in the toast."

I got out the bread and put in two slices. Then I turned around and watched Dad, who was making scrambled eggs. He was adding the milk when something began to smell.

"What's burning?" he asked. I shrugged my shoulders. "It's the toast." He ran and pulled out the plug, then picked up a fork and pried up the pieces of burnt toast.

"Didn't you check the regulator button?"

I shook my head, and looked down.

"That sister of yours has been playing with the toaster and caused us to burn the toast. Isn't that something? Two wasted pieces of toast. Such an unnecessary extravagance. Now I'm going to have to throw them away."

"Why will you have to throw them away?" I asked.

"We can't have people eating burnt toast."

"I wouldn't mind. I like burnt toast." I looked up again to Father.

"You've never had burnt toast, and you know it. You're just covering for your sister."

"I did, too. At Billy's once I had a burnt hamburger bun. That's just like toast."

"Well, if you want to eat it, that's all right with me."

I took the toast and buttered it and placed it on my plate.

"Next time I'll watch the setting on the toaster. I'm sorry, Father." I looked down at my plate.

"Hey," Father turned around and walked over to me. "There's no real harm done. It's just that sometimes we have to correct the mistakes that the women folk make around us. They don't think about a lot of these things, you know."

I nodded. We started eating.

"Hey, you're still Daddy's best helper, right?" he asked. I nodded.

"There, that's right," he said, shaking my hand.

He had a firm, affirming handshake that made you feel like getting back to work. The sun was bright in the sky. I was running as fast as I could. Pretty soon I could see the roses. There was a strange car in the driveway. White hubcaps.

Everyone came down to eat after Father called, "Breakfast!"

Dianne was still in her pajamas, but Mother had already dressed. She looked tired. She didn't like getting up as early as Father. My fork was runny with smooth, yellow melted butter sopped up with charred bread.

Church. Singing. **Mu**.

Clip, clip, clip

"It's the clip: number of rounds," he said. "The clip capacity."

I was out clipping the front bush. "Be careful," he said. "You can cut yourself. Roses have thorns."

"Di," I said. "Roses have thorns."

As we were riding back from church I sat in the backseat, quietly humming to myself. Everyone was silent.

"Say Rico," said Father. "Do you want to go to the park after lunch and take a walk?"

I nodded.

"Rico?"

"Yes, I sure would."

"All right. We'll go right after lunch. Maybe I'll have time to teach you wall baseball."

I looked up at him. The sun was shining through the windshield.

To work hard and always be true
And with God's help you'll get your due.

The car was moving along at a good,

but unhurried pace. Virginia's house was

the third from the corner. I pulled into the driveway and got out.

Listen my son and understand just what it is to be a man.

"Hi Rico," she said, as she greeted me at the door. Virginia was wearing a red dress with a high neckline and a silver belt around her waist.

"Hello," I said, possibly a little too formally. I was wearing a white shirt and a thin black tie. The top button made my neck feel uncomfortable. I felt as if I were being strangled.

"Come in and meet my mother and father." She moved her hand with a wave as if she were the guardian of the door. My eyes hadn't adjusted to the dim room from the bright sunlight. The hallway seemed very dark.

"Don't they have any lights or don't they believe in investing a little money in the cause of safety?" I asked.

"It is a little dark in here," said Bill as we looked for the bunkbeds.

"Is there somebody in charge around here who can get this fixed? I don't like walking down hallways where I can't see. A fellow might trip and break his neck."

"It's not *too* bad once your eyes get adjusted to it."

"I'd like to tell someone about it just the same."

"Did you say your trunk is in the lobby downstairs?"

"Yes, it's downstairs," I replied.

Bill was certainly skinny. It seemed strange that he was so thin. I had pictured him as huskier—but thinness suited her figure well. I suppose she got it from her mother who still had a good figure despite the fact that she must have been almost fifty.

Virginia steadied my arm as I stood erectly at the entrance to the room where her parents sat, seemingly relaxed while staring intently at me as if I were a product they were considering to buy. When the inspection was finished, we exited to the car where I opened Virginia's door for her.

"How are you coming on that paper?" she asked.

"Haven't started yet. Have you?" I asked.

"Well, I've done a little reading."

We drove on.

"Did you go to the football game Friday?" she inquired, breaking the silence.

"No, who did we play?"

"A team from Ingram."

"Who won?"

"*They* did, of course. We never win."

I pulled the car over to the ordering window of the hamburger stand. We made our orders, picked-up our food on the other side, and parked at the far end of the lot—in an obscure point of darkness.

"Was it a good game?" I ventured, a little more relaxed now that we had almost finished our burgers and fries.

"Oh yes, Julie and Beverly were there. We all sat together, and we were throwing popcorn at Sam Pihah. You know Sam, don't you?"

"I'm not sure," I replied.

"He's a smallish guy—maybe a half inch smaller than you, with curly black hair. He has real big lips and talks kind of funny."

"I guess so."

"You know him?"

"Ah, oh yeah, Sam. I know him, Sam." Virginia turned away. Did she know that I was lying to her? I didn't have any notion of who Sam was— nor did I even care. I wanted to ask her some questions about her life so I could get to know all about her. I longed to know what things she liked to do: what books she liked to read; what cereals she ate in the morning. . . Why did she go out with me? That's something I didn't understand. Why did she say "Yes?" Did she find me attractive? What drew her to me? Was she in love with me? No, that was too much. But did she *like* me?

A man can do anything if he sets his mind to it.

I wondered what I could ask her? There were so many questions that I didn't know quite where to start. What could I—

"Do you ski?" she asked.

"No, do you?"

"No, isn't that funny? You know, so many people in the Seattle area ski that I didn't know for sure. You have to ask each of your friends individually whether or not they ski."

For some reason I wished I could ski.
I wished I had gone to ski school.

YOUR FATHER DIDN'T BELIEVE IN FRIVOLITIES AND NEITHER DO I. YOU CAN GET ALONG FINE.

On the other hand, while everyone's at the ski slopes, I'll be able to see my Virginia without any competition! *He lay on his bed looking at the walls, which were a crazy off- shade of green. He wondered whatever got into their heads, to make that shade of paint? It reminded him of an institution. Was he really in an institution? An institution for the insane?*

He turned his attention towards the window, wishing that his bed looked directly out of it. It was dark. That was his favorite time of the day, yet he had to prepare for the sunlight and work.

I felt that Bill had tricked me by asking me which bunk I wanted. By the time I had gotten into the room, he had already had some time to look the place over to decide what *he wanted.* That was very clever of him. Very clever.

What was that car—the side of my sweatshirt caught on the roses. I had to stop and carefully free myself, before I went into the house.

White wheel covers.

Inside the kitchen there were pots and pans strewn everywhere. It was Dianne playing house again. If it's not cestin; it's house. That's all girls are interested in, cestin and house.

"You mean Patricini?"

"Sure, no problem." That's what Virginia was reputed to have said.

"I don't believe it," Rollo told me he replied.

"I can get anybody including—" was his account of what she said.

My father. I was waiting for my father to get ready. I liked the idea of going to the park. I got one of his tennis balls as he had instructed.

"She made a bet about you," said Rollo.

"You're lying to me," I said, as I started breathing hard.

"No, that's really what she said."

"I don't believe it. Tell me the truth," I replied.

"I am."

"I don't believe you." I was again in control of my breathing.

"Don't, then. I was only trying to save you some trouble." Rollo left me with a sneer on his face.

"Well, go find somebody with a problem," I chimed back.

"Go away, Di. Father and I are going to the park."

"Can I go too?"

"This is just for men. You're just a girl."

"So?"

"So, girls can't come along. Why don't you go and play house with yourself?"

"I don't feel like playing house. I want to come."

"Well, you can't. So, go away." Then she started crying.

"Now don't start crying. I know that trick, and it's not going to work."

She began crying loudly. I knew what might happen if I didn't hurry. *He had to hurry. He could see the car coming. It was a black limousine. He had to act.*

"Go over everything carefully. Be steady," he told himself.

I could hear Father walking out of his room.

"Di, do you want to go?" I asked.

She stopped crying instantly. She looked surprised.

"If you do, you'd better pick up your doll house that's scattered all over the basement."

"Why?"

"Because Father's going to get the ball, and it's downstairs. And if he sees that mess you'll be in real trouble."

She got up and went downstairs as Father was descending the stairs from his upper level.

"Ready to go?" he asked.

"Yep."

"Got the ball?"

"Yep."

"Well then, let's go."

We walked to the door. I could hear my sister trying to get everything together downstairs. As I shut the door Father asked me, "Did I hear Dianne crying?"

"Yeah, she was bawling a little."

"Why?"

"She wanted to come along, but I told her she'd have to clean up all her mess that she made this morning."

"And she started crying?"

"You know—she didn't want to clean up."

"Well, is she coming with us?"

"No, I think she went outside and pouted."

"Maybe I should go and see."

"She's all right, really."

He started towards the back door.

"I thought this was just going to be you and me," I said. He stopped.

"That's right; it'll be a good time." He turned and started for the car.

"Girls sure can bawl," I said as we made our way to the Buick.

"That's how they get what they want," he said as we got into the car.

I opened the door and saw them on the sofa together. The entire evening was spinning around in my mind. "Formal dance?" I said scornfully to no one. What was happening?

Suddenly the procession slowed. Would the President get out of his car and begin shaking hands? This would cause a problem.

Art History—FA 101 Room Change to Undergraduate Library 109

As I was riding in the car with Father, I thought about recess and all the guys who played wall ball. There were two places that you could play wall ball at school: one was against the gym—which was the best spot because the wall was smooth and most of the area around it was grass, so that you could go for diving catches without skinning your knee. The other place you could play was in the front of the school near the flagpole. There were several disadvantages to this location, due to the many obstacles that were around like the flagpole and its elevated, concrete base. Also, there were the metal bike rack holders that were never completed. What was there instead was a dangerous, low wall that was surrounded by a moat of sharp gravel.

CHANGES IN ROOM ASSIGNMENTS FOR FINAL EXAMINATIONS

During recess everyone runs to the places where you can play wall ball and get into games. On the gym wall you can play three or four games, while on the other side you can play only two games. Then the rest of the kids either watch or go and play with the girls.

I generally watch the games between Richard and Rollo, the best guys. Sometimes there is an opening on the other side and I would almost get up, except I didn't want anyone seeing that I didn't know how to play. Richard and Rollo are the best players.

"Let's go to the party," suggested Virginia.

"No, I don't want to."

"Why not?"

"I just don't like the things they do."

"What are you talking about?"

"You know, the beer and everything."

"Who told you that there was going to be beer?"

"Oh, knock it off. You know as well as I do that it's going to be a real wild party."

"I don't know anything of the kind."

"I don't believe you!" I cried.

"Rico honey, Uncle Adam's—"

"You're lying; both of you."

"Rico."

"I want to see my daddy."

Uncle Adam held me so that I couldn't move. I wanted to get into his bedroom, but they wouldn't let me. Why wouldn't they let me get in to see my father? Why were they stopping me? "Let go of me."

"Oh Rico, honey," said my mother as she began again.

It wasn't going to work. I knew that trick. Downstairs I could hear my sister yelling and banging with the pans. Her laughter bounced around in the kitchen like a tennis ball jumping off a face of red bricks: it was free and unworried. I grabbed Uncle Adam's arm and began twisting my elbow with all of my strength. Laughter and glee—pots clanging--I turned harder on his arm until my hands began *sweating. It seemed heavy in his arms.*

What happened to the dream? He wondered whether it was intermission. He turned to Lita.

"Ow, damn it," yelled Uncle Adam as he pulled his arm free. Mother looked up. "What are you trying to do? Take my arm off?"

"Now Adam," began my mother.

"This little monster's trying to take my arm off."

"He's only frightened," she started, when I kicked Uncle Adam in the shins and broke away momentarily. I was free.

Breaking through

   to another place, to another side

         maybe only an inch away

           but clear of that prison

              of seeming lies and absurdity

           blurs even the round stadium

         About which none can escape

           but simply endure

            necessity

          yes

     I broke

   through

 yes

I

The hand came and caught my shoulder. It was Mr. Souposey. Rollo turned away about to go to class, "Listen, just remember what I said about her." Then he walked away. I spat at him but I missed.

I turned around and read the anger in Uncle Adam's face but I didn't care. I wouldn't have minded if he had killed me at that moment, but instead I saw the hand come from behind him, in an upward motion towards me. He was tense. I could tell this because the skin was drawn tightly across his face so that his normal wrinkles had disappeared. It was as if he were wearing a mask. A clown's mask? No, another more sinister masque that grotesquely revealed *a cold architecture of the soul that was perversely deformed, not as a gargoyle, but instead as a plain brown building that stands ambuscading above the quiet street. And the grassy knoll with a half-wall atop. Who could have thought that—someone else would choose that very day and from that very building across from him? Still, he waited on a grassy hill, hidden from view.*

I felt like I was a spectator at that moment, and no longer a participant, and even after the hand had struck my face, I could no longer feel as if I were a part of what was happening. I was just a dot preaching into the empty church—isolated. Even my mother's almost hysterical screaming at Uncle Adam didn't coax me from my cenacle of silence that was gently rocking me to sleep as Father used to. At times like these I liked to shut my eyes and listen to his soft humming.

LOOK WHAT YOU'VE DONE TO HIM

Father had such a pretty voice. It soothed my entire body. After a while he would tell me a story, usually about Rico the Great, who lived in a time and place far away. Rico the Great wanted to do good to all the people.

HE CAN'T EVEN TALK! YOU'VE SENT HIM INTO SHOCK!

I always liked these stories. I could imagine just what Rico the Great looked like. Sometimes he was me and sometimes he was somebody else—like a movie star.

"And once there was a crippled boy who had to work to help support his family. He worked all day long and at night he studied very hard. He was very frugal with his money and bought almost nothing for himself. He couldn't afford to be frivolous.

YOU BIG OX, WHY DO YOU HAVE SUCH A TERRIBLE TEMPER? HE'S JUST AN EIGHT-YEAR-OLD BOY—AND YOU HAD TO HIT HIM THE DAY HIS FATHER—OH GOD, OH GOD, OH GOD

"He worked very hard and gave almost all of his paychecks to his father, who was a very harsh man, even though he loved his son very much.

"The son loved his father even though his father drank too much and left much of the responsibility of running the family to the son. The son took these extra burdens without complaint and tried to make do. One day the father got into a fight at the tavern with another man and during the fight the other man pulled out a gun and shot the father. The father was rushed to the hospital and the family was notified. The son raced to his father's bedside and stayed with him until he died. His last words to his only child were, 'Son, I know I haven't been a very good father to you, but I've tried. Yes, I've tried to do what I thought was best. I've had my faults, oh yes, so many faults.

"'I'm sorry for them. I've beaten you for no good reason. And for those failings I beg your forgiveness. But just let me tell you that I—' he began coughing very hard—the boy moved to his father to comfort him. The father sighed heavily, and began again, in a very strained voice, 'I want to tell you that I'm proud of you, son. I'm very proud. I hope you go far. Be frugal my boy, and remember that—' he coughed again. 'A man can be anything he wants to be if he wants to hard enough. You *will* be a success my boy. Yes, a big success, something that I—I never could be'—then he began coughing violently, his body became very tense and suddenly it was over. His father was dead.

Michael Boylan   47

"The boy was heart-broken, and he cried over his father's body until one of the nurses took him away. From that moment on he dedicated himself to fulfilling his father's dying wish: to become a success. No longer would he allow himself any luxuries, only what was essential. All day and into the night he would work, despite the pain he was beginning to feel in his crippled leg. Then when he got home, he studied so that he could get into college, because a man isn't anything unless he can get ahead.

"One day Rico the Great happened to see the crippled boy, who was walking home from work. Being a very kind man, he stopped the boy and asked him his name and whether he might like a ride home in his car. The boy never liked to accept favors because he didn't want to owe anyone anything, preferring to earn his living on his own. He said, 'No thank you,' but the man asked again and he seemed so friendly and his own leg was very painful— 'C'mon,' said the man (Rico the Great). 'I'll make you a deal; I'll give you a ride home and you tell me about yourself. I'm very lonely and I'd like someone to talk to.' When he put it that way the boy accepted immediately. After all, he wasn't accepting charity—he was giving the man something. In fact, he thought, I'm almost doing this man a favor just to keep him company."

ADAM, I DON'T KNOW WHAT TO DO WITH YOU

"'My name's Rico,' said the man.

"'What's yours?' he asked cautiously, for he knew that the boy was very shy.

"'Paul,' the boy said softly.

"'Where do you live?' asked Rico.

"'I'm on Elm Street.'

"'Elm?' said Rico, a little surprised. 'That's a long way from here. What brought you all this way?'

"'My job.'

"'Your job? Why you're hardly old enough to— Did you finish school?'

"'No sir,' said Paul, who was now very ashamed.

"Rico looked over at the boy and instantly knew what he was feeling, and he felt sorry for the boy. It was obvious that the boy was working because he needed the money. Then he got an idea, but he had to ask a few more questions just to make sure that a few of his assumptions about the boy were correct.

"'What school did you used to attend?' asked Rico.

"'Central,' said Paul in an almost inaudible voice.

"'What was your favorite subject?'

"'Well, I liked most of my classes,' Paul began in the same timid voice. 'But most of all I liked social studies and particularly law,' he said in a stronger voice.

"Rico sensed the boy's enthusiasm. 'Law's very interesting and you'll always be sure of clients. What kind of law would you be interested in?'

"'I don't know.'

"'Well, what interested you in being a lawyer?'

"'I'd like to help people. I would defend those people who needed help, but who couldn't afford it. You know there's lots of people who get pushed around because the people with money can afford to do things to anybody and so long as they don't have any money—the poor can't do anything about it. Hundreds of men lie in the streets because there's nobody there to help them, and then they die, leaving families with no one to provide for them.'

"Paul's voice was now strong and firm. He turned and looked Rico straight in the eye and said, 'Yes, Mister, I want to help some of these human beings that nobody else has found the time or taken the trouble to help. I want to be a lawyer.'

"Rico smiled to himself and said to the boy, 'Well, Paul, I know a man at the law school and he said that they are considering applications for entrance at this time, and if your application is accepted then they'll pay all of your expenses.'

"'Really?'

"'Certainly. If you're accepted, they pay your way.' Then Paul was suddenly silent.

"'If you really want to be a lawyer then you could write him a letter telling why you want to be a lawyer. That should do for an application, and if he likes it, you're in.'

"Paul hung his head and stared at his hands folded in his lap.

"'What do you think of that?'

"Paul was silent.

"'Don't you really want to be a lawyer?' Paul looked up. 'Maybe you don't really want to be a lawyer. It's easy to *talk* about helping people, and it's another thing to actually get up the gumption to go and really do something. I assumed by listening to you that you were *that* kind of person, but maybe I was wrong.'

"Rico the Great turned and stared at the road.

"'No,' said Paul softly.

"'What? Did you say something?'

"'No,' said Paul assertively. 'I mean *yes*. I did say something. It was *no*. I said that you're wrong. I *do* want to be a lawyer, and I would write to this man except—except—'

"'Except what?'

"'Who would accept a crippled dropout?'

"'My, don't we feel sorry for ourselves. Listen, Paul, everyone's got his handicaps. We make the best with what the Lord gave us. As to being a dropout, I admit, that will mean a great deal of work, but I had the impression that hard work didn't frighten you. Am I right? Are you afraid of hard work?'

"'No sir.'

"'Well, that's what it'll take; lots of hard work. Let me tell you a poem that my father used to tell me:

"'Listen my son and understand
Just what it is to be a man,
To work hard and always be true,
And with God's help, you'll get your due.'

"'There's a lot of truth in those lines Paul.'

"When Paul got out of the car, he still had Rico's words ringing in his ears: 'you'll get your due.' In his hand Paul clutched the piece of paper that the man had given him with the Dean of the Law school's name. Paul felt happy, yet, underneath all his joy, he was troubled. 'Why should any law school accept me?' he thought. And so, he went inside and ate his dinner of dreams, no longer aware (for the first time) of his abject poverty. Now he had something new.

"Meanwhile, Rico the Great paid a visit to Mr. A.G. Spoon, the dean of the Law School and told him about Paul.

"'He's a good boy, and I'm sure he'd make it if you only gave him the chance.'

"'Well, Rico, I respect your judgment, but you're very soft-hearted (soft-headed was what he was thinking) and have a tendency to feel the pangs of your heart strings on any provocation.'

"'Listen, A.G., I know this is a little out of the ordinary, but if you could have seen the determination on that boy's face—'

"'I'm not in the business of looking at faces, Rico. I'm in the business of turning out lawyers.'

"'Well, you'll be turning down a fine prospect if you don't take this boy.'

"'This isn't a charity I run here, for every young—'

"'Well, who said anything about *every* youngster? I only mentioned one outstanding prospect and you generalize the case to include all of humanity.'

"'Now Rico—'

"'It's now or nothing! There are no ifs, ands, or buts about it. This boy will make good. I guarantee it.'

"'You can't trust these riff-raff dagos; they have extremely sticky fingers; they don't know English. And most of all, they're dirty—so dirty.'

"'Well, just because you've come from an immaculate environment, A.G., doesn't say anything about you as a person. One might say that you've turned out to be good, in spite of your affluence. Now, we have before us an eminently qualified boy, who has learned what he knows the hard way, through sweat and pain. He is a boy who is old, far beyond his young years, because he didn't have all those little goodies that *you* were blessed with. He's dirty, you say. Yes, he's dirty; he's dirty with all the filth that society's dumped on him—he breathes in the refuse that the factories excrete daily and comes back for more. He's the backbone that has made people like you rich and influential. And now I'm asking you to repay some in kind to a representative of those to whom you owe everything. And what is your response? You spit in his face and call him *dirty!* Well, Mr. Spoon, if that's the fast and loose game you want to engage in, then it seems that I, also, must try my hand at it. Rules can be twisted to make little men like Paul seem dirty, but they can also be twisted in other ways, too. And I'll get to doing some of my own twisting. Good-day, Mr. Spoon.'

"And with that, Rico stormed out of the office leaving Mr. A.G. Spoon sitting at his large mahogany desk, staring at the door that was still open.

"All during the day, Paul thought about what he should put into the letter so that his application might be more attractive. When you consider this process, he thought, I really haven't done very much. I haven't accomplished anything in particular and I don't know anything special. As he continued thinking, he became sad. That night, he made several attempts at writing the letter and finally gave up and threw his letters into the wastebasket. It's no use, he thought, I'll never make it. I'll never be a success.

"A few days later, A.G. Spoon got a call from the president of the university. 'Did you receive a letter from an applicant named *Paul* for admission?'

"'I'm not sure, sir,' said A.G., who was quite surprised about being called by the president. 'I get so many letters.'

"'Stop beating around the bush Spoon, did you get the letter or not?'

"'Ah, seems to me that I may have gotten some sort of letter. (Paul's mother had taken the best version of the letter out of the wastebasket and sent it for him.) But the letter didn't have the standard application attached to it so I naturally ah, ah—'

"'You naturally did what?'

"'Well, nothing.'

"'You mean to say that you did *nothing*?'

"'Well, yes sir.'

"'*Well* you listen to me. You find that application and you go see that boy personally before some other law school gets him.'

"'But sir, he's just a little dago tramp.'

"'Tramp! Tramp! Did you say *tramp*?'

"'Well, ah, ah—'

"'Tramp—well I'll tramp you. What's your expense account, Spoon?'

"'Seven thousand dollars a year, sir.'

"'Well, it's now a thousand, and it won't go any higher until you find out where your brains went off to; it seems that they must be on vacation. A tramp indeed. Now you go and find that boy immediately and give him any financial aid you have to. Just get me that boy!'

"'Yes sir, right away sir.'

"A.G. Spoon put down the phone and thought a moment about what it would be like with only a thousand-dollar expense account, seeing as he had seven thousand dollars of fixed expenses. He shook his head and muttered to himself, 'tramp, tramp, tramp . . . .'

"When Paul got home, he found Mr. Spoon waiting for him to give him the good news.

"'I've come to tell you that your application to the law school has been accepted.'

"Paul's mother ran to Paul and gave him a hug, but Paul was suddenly very calm. He had imagined this moment many times before, and almost always he had been happy almost beyond words, but now that it was *really* happening to him, all he could think about was: who was to look after the family?

"'Thank you very much Mr. Spoon, but I'm afraid I can't accept because my family wouldn't have adequate means to get by.'

"'A very delicate matter,' said Mr. Spoon putting on his gloves. 'A very delicate matter indeed; however, let me suggest that maybe I could arrange for you to be housed near the campus and that way your mother would have one less mouth to feed. We could provide you with meals, lodging, and even a little pocket money. Well?'

"Paul looked at Mr. Spoon straight in the eye and said immediately, 'I'm afraid that would be impossible. My mother can't make enough to feed and clothe all of my brothers and sisters—much less pay the rent. I'm sorry, but I can't leave them.'

"Mr. Spoon was fidgeting. His fat little hands were ever so busy squeezing an imaginary ball that was in the palm of his hands. 'Ah, ah,' he began, as beads of sweat began forming on his brow, 'well, well, ah.'

"He took out his handkerchief and quickly mopped his damp brow with his stubby fingers, which were working furiously. Only a thousand dollar expense account, he repeated to himself. This'll cost at least two thousand a year, in itself—even if I cut back to the minimum. Oh dear! Oh dear!

"'Are you quite certain that—' Mr. Spoon began. He didn't want to have to make the kind of deal that Paul needed; however, he knew that his job was in the balance.

"'I'm sorry Mr. Spoon,' said Paul.

"Paul moved to get Mr. Spoon's coat.

"'Wait,' said Mr. Spoon. 'I just remembered that there is one possibility that we haven't explored as yet. There's an old house that the college owns and is never used by the University. Do you think you could fix it up?'

"'For all of us?' asked Paul.

"Mr. Spoon's hands tightened on that imaginary ball and barely managed, 'Yes, of course, all of you.'

"'And allowances for all of us?'

"A.G. wiped his brow very quickly with short, circular motions. 'Ah, well, I suppose we can work something out.'

"Paul turned to his mother and asked, 'What do you think?'

"'Paul,' she began, then she ran to hug her son as the tears choked her words.

"'Well, mister,' Paul began, his voice thick and heavy, 'guess you've got yourself a student.' He extended his hand, but Mr. Spoon had already turned around as if he were in a hurry to get out of the old tenement apartment. As he opened the door he turned and almost as an afterthought said, 'I'll have a truck by around the first of the week to move your things. You'll report to my office as soon as you're moved in, concerning your class schedule.' These last words were delivered as he shut the door, trying to touch the knob as lightly as possible.

"After that, Paul went to law school, graduated, and became a big success. He became very rich. He never forgot his mysterious friend who seemed to foretell his good fortune and was so kind to him. All through his life, Paul would remember his humble beginnings and always look for ways to help others just as he had been helped. He married and had many children. He lived to be an old man."

"Was Paul ever President?" I asked.

"Certainly, he was," my father would say. "He was one of the most beloved of all American Presidents. He was even greater than Washington or Lincoln."

My head would then be peaceful as I thought about the beauty of my future greatness.

YOU BIG LUNKHEAD; GET THE SMELLING SALTS!

After three months he decided that a building wouldn't be right because a person didn't have a clear enough escape route. But a grassy knoll. Yes, no one would suspect a shot coming from a grassy spot behind a half-wall. He felt a sense of happiness rise within him as he considered his evolving plan.

"LET'S GET HIM TO LIE DOWN ON A BED—NO, NOT IN THAT ROOM, HIS FATHER'S IN THERE, USE YOUR HEAD."

"The first thing you have to remember is that you hold the ball firmly in the palm of your hand and control it with your fingers. Like this—see?"

I took the ball and held it the way Father showed me. "Like this?"

"That's fine. Now throw me one," said Father.

I took the ball and leaned back with my arm as I had seen Rollo and Richard do many times. Then I hurled the ball with all my might, except the ball went sideways along the ground. I felt like crying.

"LISTEN, JACKIE, I'VE HAD ABOUT ALL I'M GOING TO TAKE FROM YOU. NOW *YOU* LISTEN, DAMN IT. I CAN TAKE CARE OF THE BOY. YOU'RE UNDER QUITE A STRAIN, AND I UNDERSTAND THAT. BUT I WON'T LET YOU TAKE THAT OUT ON ME. I HAVE FEELINGS, TOO, YOU KNOW. IT'S BEEN HARD ON ALL OF US. SO NOW LET'S SETTLE DOWN. IT'S TIME WE SETTLED DOWN."

I felt uneasy about being carried. It was my first attempt at playing wall ball at school, it seemed that everyone on the dance floor knew that it was my first dance. It was like they knew everything. Their looks said, "What are you doing here? Who said you could come?" and 'what are you doing with Virginia?' 'Don't you know that she's too good-looking to go out with you? You're just a creep. You've never even been to a dance." But I allowed Uncle Adam to continue even though I was awake. I wondered whether he knew that I was awake. I kept my eyes shut so that he wouldn't know. Somehow things seemed different, but I didn't know exactly how or why.

A strange man stopped Uncle Adam and asked him what was wrong with me.

"It's nothing," said Uncle Adam. "He just had a bad fall."

"A bad fall, eh?" I felt the stranger's hands feeling my head. "Yes, there is a little lump back there. Is he conscious?"

"Yes, the excitement was too much for him, so I'm going to lay him down."

"Lay him down, lay him down, yes, that sounds like a good idea. Lay him down, yes, of course. Well, I'm sorry I couldn't have been more help. Tell your sister that I'm terribly sorry about her loss."

"I will," replied Uncle Adam. "Thank you for trying, Doctor. I know you did what you could."

"The police will be here shortly, routine, you know, but necessary—quite necessary, you know. Well, good-bye."

HE WAS ALWAYS CONCERNED ABOUT BEING SO THIN AND *SHORT,* HIS FATHER HAD SUCH A GOOD BUILD. BUT HIS SON, RICO, WAS SHORT AND ONLY MODERATELY MUSCULAR—THOUGH HE WAS A GOOD FIGHTER. HE OFTEN GOT INTO FIGHTS AT SCHOOL

I sat in my room, staring at the green walls, when an overwhelming sadness came over me. What was I to do? I walked next door to see if Frank or Ed were in, but they were gone. So, I went down the hall knocking on doors, but everyone was either gone or busy. Then I remembered Albert. I didn't really like Albert. He was so scrawny (so much like a woman). Nobody liked Albert, but I really didn't feel like being alone, so I knocked on his door.

He was studying, but I decided to stay anyway. A room with someone in it is better than an empty room even if it was with Albert. I felt calmer as I watched Albert studying: his beady little bug eyes stood out from his head as if someone had begun pulling them out of their sockets but stopped halfway through the process. He was intent on the open book in front of him. Albert had a single room (probably because nobody could stand to room with him). Some people said he was a queer, but I didn't think so— even though he did look like a woman with gentle features and light brown hair.

"Do you have a test soon?" I asked.

"No, just keeping up."

"That's very admirable," I said. Albert looked at me and tilted his head.

"Yeah," he said bringing his head aright.

"I'm finished with my work for the day," I said, rocking back on my heels.

"Oh really, how did you manage that?" Albert now had a scowl on his face.

"Oh, it's not too hard. You can do anything if you really want to."

Albert, tilted his head again and pursed his lips, "I don't know about that. Maybe some people can, but I can never begin studying until late afternoon—sometimes early evening."

Then, Albert began picking his nose. I suddenly felt nauseous.

Then he stopped and wiped his hand on a handkerchief from his back pocket. I felt better, but I sensed that Albert was distressed. He looked down at his shiny gold colored slippers, "Sometimes, I wonder. I do what I can, but shit gets in my way." Albert was shaking his head and staring at his slippers. "It's not so easy, Rico."

"What?" I said. "If you really wanted to finish your work, you could."

"No way. I'm just too tired. I don't get started until late afternoon. There's so much to do." Albert started biting his lower lip.

"If you really wanted to—"

"—Come on."

"—The thing is you don't *really* want to."

He didn't answer. I looked at him biting his lower lip. I didn't want it to begin bleeding.

"Well, what do you want?" I asked.

"I really want to finish my work early."

"I just don't know what kind of ambition that is?"

"It's my ambition. But it's hard to achieve." Albert bit down again on his lower lip.

"Can't you just plan your time?"

"I *do* plan my time."

"Plan extra time," I suggested.

"It's not about *planning.* It's about *execution.*"

"Get out of your rut. Go out on a date."

Albert held himself erect. "Are you kidding?"

"No."

"Dating is a luxury. One does not engage in luxuries until he's done the grit work. That's why I want to finish the grit work early. It's not that easy." Albert held his hands together in his lap. His knuckles were white.

"Do you have a date tonight?" he asked.

"Sure," I replied.

"With whom?"

"A girl named Evelyn who lives over on North Campus."

"Well, that's pretty good, but it wouldn't work for me."

"Why not?"

"Why not?" Albert got up and started pacing, head down, on a short oval path which was around a brown throw rug in the center of his room, "Who are you kidding? Come on." Albert stopped pacing. He lifted his head and looked me in the eye, "Now really, who'd go out with me?"

"There are probably a lot of girls," I replied. I didn't know what to do. *He held the rifle as steady as he could.*

"Don't make fun of who I am."

"I'm not making fun of you," I said. I could sense that he didn't want to talk any more. I felt there was a tension. It was the kind of tension that usually ends up with someone yelling. I didn't want to continue talking, but I didn't have the nerve to walk away.

"Look, I'm only saying this for your own good. I like you, and I don't like seeing you get hurt."

"Thanks, but I don't need your help." Albert got off his oval pacing track and sat down again. He folded his hands and watched himself clenching his hands. Then he looked up again, "Hey Rico, why are you acting like this?"

"I'm not giving you shit, honest. I heard Virginia and Rollo talking about it behind the lockers."

"You must have been mistaken."

"No mistake, honest, it was Rollo and—"

"I told you now, shut up."

"Take it easy."

I was furious. I saw their naked bodies on the sofa. She looked up at me and smiled like there was nothing wrong. My head began spinning.

"Look, are you going to button those?"

"Don't have a cow or nothing. I can understand you being sore, but listen man I'm doing you a favor so don't get so all-hell-fired-up." *She turned around and walked away and suddenly she picked up a stick and came back and swung it blindly at his head several times. She stopped when she made contact and stood poised ready to defend* Bart. Albert went back to work, and I sat there staring at his walls.

LOVE CAN MAKE ALL TYPES GET SMALL AND LOSE THEIR STRUCTURE AND DISCIPLINE

Alone on the weekends! The thought made my body tingle with excitement I imagined all the things that we might do after I went out with her a few times. Well then, I could kiss her and hold her so tightly like Mommy used to do to me when I was—

I longed to turn to her that instant—

"Look out for that car!" Virginia screamed.

I slammed on the brakes. The car skidded. The brakes screeched as the other car veered sharply to his left and just narrowly avoided a collision.

"What's the matter with that dummy?" I yelled to the other driver, who obviously couldn't hear me. "What's he trying to do? Get me killed?"

"He was on a through street, and you *did* have a stop sign," said Virginia.

"There was no stop sign," I replied. My hand was shaking. I looked in the side mirror and caught a glimpse of the red octagon standing quietly on the corner.

THE BALL, INSTEAD OF GOING STRAIGHT AHEAD, WENT SIDEWAYS ALONG THE GROUND. I LOOKED AT THE BALL AND THEN TO MY FATHER, WHO WAS LAUGHING.

Then I left Albert. I didn't say goodbye. I went back to my room. I knew that I couldn't leave my room any more that night or else Albert might see me without a date. I felt I needed

Paul Tillich's "Courage to Be."

One of the basic problems with the book is the failure of the author to really talk about God or religion as it is practiced in real life. For example, he talks a lot about *personal* anxiety, but never really says what he thinks about God and Jesus. I doubt that Tillich is even a Christian. He certainly doesn't speak like most of the priests that I've heard talk in church, like Father Weal.

For example, he never quotes the Bible. Now anyone knows that no priest ever gave a homily without quoting the Bible. Is it possible that Mr. Tillich didn't know the Bible? I wonder. If he did, maybe he could have used it to back up some of his points.

My paper is mainly concerned with the question of God and what He is (or can be thought of as 'to be'). This, as I have indicated, isn't adequately dealt with by Tillich. He seems, in many respects, to have forgotten the fundamental aspect of what God really *is* and how man can come into some kind of meaningful relationship with Him through the body of the congregation. The delineation of the precise nature of God is at best a most troublesome task. Let it suffice to say that I believe that for each person He is different, or can be seen differently (that is to say, He relates to each in different ways). What is important are the parishes of believers. It would be impossible and foolish to try to generalize my impressions and then equate them to universals. However, I can, with some certainty, talk about my own individual impressions and thereby allow any other comparisons that can be made, to be made.

God (to me) can seem as a father of a family. This image comes closest to describing what I think of God. He is a father who stands above men and judges "the quick and the dead." This notion of God as father of a family seems rather reasonable from several aspects. First, it is known that God preceded all, and therefore can be considered as the creator of everything. If God came first and everything followed, then surely God created everything. If my thinking is correct, then this is one indicator that God is indeed a creator and a designer. If this is true, then I see God as a father because, for me, the image of the Father is one through which everything is initiated. After all, in human experience, the male is the cause of the fertilization and is the creator (in sexual reproduction as well as in other cases, like great art), so the image of the Father seems particularly appropriate here.

Secondly, I see God as a Being that judges all men. If we act according to His rules, then we are saved. If we violate His rules, then we are damned. This is an aspect of God as the judicial system of all people in the community. Communities need laws to exist—otherwise there will be anarchy. This is hard and fast. "Those who are not with me are against me." There are not two ways about it. It is an all or nothing proposition.

This raises some very interesting questions from our other reading in Kierkegaard. For example, whether Abraham would have been correct in killing Isaac. God talked to Abraham and wanted to test his faith and see whether he would kill his son just because He told him to; however, in human eyes this would be judged as murder. It seems obvious that if Abraham had killed Isaac, he would be guilty of murder, but would the killing be right? I say, "yes." After all, the law against murder is only a law between men, procured from God via Moses: "Thou shalt not kill." But any law among men is superseded by a command from God. He gave the Law to men in the first place. So, if He thinks the prohibition against murder should be overturned, then it should be. There is no higher authority. God is the ultimate authority. Beyond him there is nothing.

In Him, "Thou shalt have eternal life." What greater proof of "man's love for God" is there than for a father to kill his son? It is the strongest bond in the nuclear family. So, we can see that if Abraham had killed Isaac, then even though he might be judged as a murderer, he still would be saved in heaven, because he followed the command of the Almighty.

But Abraham *didn't* have to kill Isaac— why? Because God, "who can seest into the heart of every man," could tell that Abraham was really going to kill Isaac. Abraham loved God *that much.* He had that much faith in the Almighty. He was willing to sacrifice his son: that for which he had waited so long to have (he was over a hundred years old when Isaac was born) just to please the Lord.

The Lord saw this and had pity on Abraham and sent one of his angels to stop Abraham's blade. This he did because he could tell that Abraham would *really kill* Isaac.

If there had been any doubt in Abraham's heart, then Isaac would have perished, because Abraham's faith would have had to be put to the ultimate test in that reality beyond human understanding and laws. This is the divine realm of Faith that cannot be described except that it is a relationship between Man and God, where Man comes to know God's will and strives to either do it or not. He either passes beyond the realm of the rational and into another sphere, or he falls into the deepest corners of Hell. It is on this battleground where Man either *chooses* to act or he fails to act. And all this is in the context of the community in which the person of faith lives every day.

His choice might not be properly termed a choice at all. In fact, it may be a compulsion of some sort—except that one is, in some sense, totally free. He is free because no longer is he constrained by the pettiness of this world, but is dwelling in the world of Universals and beyond. He enters the realm of a faith that is *terrible*. Man shakes as he comes to know the terrible wrath of the Almighty whose anger sends the weakest souls to Hell and exalts the strong to the eternal bliss of His heavenly kingdom.

God is like a father because He is kind. His gentleness is based on a love that gently soothes, as if to sleep, the restless and troubled soul, "Come all ye who are weary and heavy laden and I will give you rest." This is the prescription for a peaceful community where there is no bullying or rancor.

God stands as the pinnacle of perfection to all. He is that to which we may strive, but never reach. Because those who falsely claim perfection are sent to abide with Satan in the everlasting fire of torment and agony.

God is one who touches all of our lives whether we want Him to or not. He is a terrible, yet loving, father, who can be gentle, but who also can discipline his children. He is perfection, who gave us the rules of life through his Son, who died so that "we may live."

I see God, the Father (my God) as this sort of Power. He is a Power that most of the theologians we have been reading in class seem to either ignore or don't understand. This is because they try to be so smart that they forget the real source of Power: The Lord, and his Son, Jesus Christ.

Rico Patricini, Religion 101 Jan. 13, 1962

Rico, your comments are very interesting; however, I'm not certain as to what this has to say about our reading assignment on Paul Tillich. Kierkegaard was last term. It seems to me that you've missed the whole point of what he was trying to say. To write an entire paper on Tillich, for example and not use the word 'ontology,' seems to be a misnomer of the first degree. You haven't really dealt with any of the real issues of the book concerning the individual in his personal quest for God. You get off-track on the community and parish stuff, and therefore you didn't really fulfill your requirements in the paper as set out in the assignment. (Couldn't you have stuck in at least one "ground of being" somewhere?) It is a rare thing for me to do on such an assignment, but in this case, I believe it is necessary to flunk you. You are a student who shows no real evidence that he has either read the material nor understood what he was supposedly to write on.

I'm sorry, but unless your next paper is better, this grade will stand for the course: F.

After I looked at the toys for a while, I went to see the sporting goods. I always liked to touch the display baseball. It was so new. And I liked to feel the smooth, new baseball bats. I would take one out (it was usually too heavy for me) and swing it around awhile. I'd imagine that I was in a game with Rollo pitching and I was up to bat and it was the bottom of the ninth and there were two outs. We would be behind by two runs and I would get a single to drive in one run and later in the game I'd score the winning run from Richard's hit.

"Daddy?"

"Yes," said Father.

"Doesn't the razor hurt your face?"

"No, it's very sharp and just cuts the whiskers."

"I wish I could shave."

"You will some day Rico. Right now, you're just a little whisker."

"Daddy, I want to shave just like you."

"Not now, little whiskers. Not yet."

The ball rolled sideways along the ground. Father laughed a moment. Then he said, "Hey, what did you do? Remember to hold your fingers tightly around the ball."

I ran and picked up the ball that was lying on the ground next to the swing set.

"Now throw it from there," he said.

I threw the ball so hard that I fell down. When I got up, Father had the ball, and he was smiling. Had I really thrown it that far, or did he go and pick it up? I wasn't sure, but a powerful feeling, like electricity, overcame me so that I couldn't move.

"Now, let's practice catching the ball. You come closer and I'll throw you a few easy ones." Driving isn't so hard, really, once you get the hang of it. It's all in getting over that initial fear that you'll crack up the car at any moment—like the car's controlling you instead of the other

way around. I could hardly wait to get my
driver's license—then I could ask Virginia
out for a date. I could drive her around in
my car, that is, if Uncle Adam would let me
use it. But I didn't see *why* he wouldn't.
After all, I'm a good driver. All it takes is
that

he wants to hard enough

Virginia is such a pretty girl, and her voice
is so clear and mellow. She probably
wouldn't want to go out with me, but if I had
a car to drive

A man can do anything if

*A feeling of elation overcame him as he hid himself in the long,
tall weeds near the white half-wall atop the grassy knoll.*

I was startled by Uncle Adam, "So you're looking at the
baseball bats, eh?"

I didn't say anything.

"Say Rico, about earlier, I mean down on the street. I'm
sorry if I hit you. You know I never intended to hurt you, it's
just that, well, I get mad kind of quickly when I think
someone's just loafing off. Do you know what I mean?"

I didn't say anything, and turned my head away.

"What I mean is, I thought you were getting sassy out
there and I didn't want you causing a scene; besides, you were
sitting there in the snow and you might have caught
pneumonia and died as a result. Now we wouldn't
have wanted that to happen, would we?"

Uncle Adam's voice was so calm, so mock-sincere.

"Look, Rico I was only trying to get you going for your
own good. You know that, don't you? I was only thinking of
you out there."

Michael Boylan   69

I didn't respond.

"Listen Rico," I turned and looked at him again. "Now your mother, she gets worried and sometimes gets very nervous when you make a scene like you did out there tonight. She thinks that I really hurt you. Now you and I know that that just isn't so, don't we? You just like to pretend a little, right? It's a very funny little game and I don't mind it—when we're alone, but you mother doesn't understand about your little games and she thinks that I beat you."

He grabbed a hold of my shoulders with both of his hands. His tone changed, "Now listen little fellow, I don't like your mother thinking that I beat you, do you understand?"

I didn't respond, so Uncle Adam shook me.

"Do you understand, Rico? I don't like your little games."

He was shaking me violently. His hands cut into my shoulders.

"Do you understand, you little brat? I don't like your little shows. And if you keep it up—"

"You're hurting me," I said.

"Shut up," he said and slapped me across the face. "I didn't beat you, you little tramp, but if you pull one of your little stunts again I'll, I'll, k—" Then he let go of me and stepped back, "Well you had just better not, if you know what's good for you." Uncle Adam looked up as the salesman walked over to us. I hurt all over, but was afraid to cry. It was all true what the guys had told me. She was just using me. I didn't know what to do. I felt like I want to k—. But no.

Bill Bonavert. What an absurd name from some nothing little hick town. Why didn't they just tell me. It wasn't fair. It wasn't my fault that those numbskulls— nobody told me about the change. I showed up and nobody was in the room. I just assumed that the test had been cancelled or moved to another day. Who would have thought that now my roommate would find out that I have No Chance? Why did I ever take art history? What I need to do is—

I was upset. I sat in my father's lap for a story: "Rico the Great was confused. In the land there was sickness and sadness. Rico wondered what he could do. So, he went to the priest and asked him. The padre looked sad and shook his head. 'I'm sorry, my son, but this is not the work of God. God only wants good for his children.' Rico the Great was anxious with this response.

"'But Father, what can I do? I can't just let the sadness and sickness continue.'

"The priest slowly shook his head. 'This is a question about the structure of our secular society.'

"Rico the Great turned his head to try and understand what the priest was trying to say.

"'Since the Holy See no longer has secular power because of the rise of Protestantism, secular problems must be met with secular answers.'

"Rico pursed his lips as he tried to understand the priest. 'So, Father, what should I do?'

"'Who rules the secular realm?'

"'Why the King, of course.'

"'And the King is in charge of the secular realm.'

"'Yes.'

"'So, if he isn't doing his job, what should happen to him?'

"Rico the Great took his index finger and ran it across his throat as if he were killing someone.

"The priest smiled."

I looked up at my father to try to fully understand. His expression was inscrutable.

I noticed a car that was parked up the street. It was Bart's car, the lights were off, and it was just sitting there. I wondered if someone stole it. It was just parked it there. I decided to go up and examine it. Then I saw the white wheel covers on the black car. I didn't understand what was taking so long. Mother said she'd be just a minute. I DIDN'T WANT TO REMEMBER. I GOT HOME EARLY. I HAD BEEN PLAYING WAR OVER AT BILLY'S HOUSE WITH TOMMY PERDRE. ANYWAY, TOMMY GOT MAD AND WENT HOME. SO, I LEFT, TOO. PLAYING WALL BALL WITH TWO OTHER PEOPLE ISN'T ANY FUN. WHEN I GOT HOME, I WALKED UPSTAIRS AND HEARD A FUNNY NOISE. IT SOUNDED AS IF THE BED WAS ROCKING NEXT DOOR IN UNCLE ADAM'S ROOM—LIKE SOMEONE WAS JUMPING ON IT OR SOMETHING. I THOUGHT THAT MAYBE DI WAS FOOLING AROUND IN UNCLE ADAM'S ROOM. SO, I WENT TO THE DOOR WITH THE INTENTION OF KICKING HER OUT BECAUSE UNCLE ADAM DIDN'T LIKE PEOPLE HANGING AROUND HIS BEDROOM. IN FACT, IF HE CAUGHT ONE OF US IN HIS BEDROOM, HE WOULD REALLY WALLOP US. ANYWAY, I WENT TO THE DOOR AND WAS FULLY INTENDING ON OPENING IT WHEN I HEARD THE FRONT DOOR SLAM. THEN I HEARD DIANNE SINGING TO HERSELF. SUDDENLY ALL THE NOISE IN THE BEDROOM STOPPED AND I HEARD SOMEONE SPRING UP FROM THE BED. I DECIDED SOMETHING WAS WRONG TO *find something, something that might interest you.* "What do you want?" *he asked his boss in a thick Texas accent.*

"*Nothing. I just found something." His voice was calm.*

"*Listen Patacini, I'm sick of looking at you. Just do your job and make yourself invisible.*"

"What do you want?" I held the paper in my hand. I didn't know why he was being so cruel to me.

"Been snooping around in my things, haven't you?"

I hadn't been snooping. It's just that I left my paper under my dictionary. I had to find it in order to turn it in tomorrow. It had taken me hours in the typing room to finish it.

UNCLE ADAM CAME RUSHING OUT OF THE ROOM.

MY HAND BEGAN TO SHAKE. I WAS NERVOUS. *Could anybody see me behind the half-white wall on the grassy knoll? Governor Connally would be in the car, too. Rico had to wait for the final moment to determine what he would do.*

BUT UNCLE ADAM DIDN'T SEE ME. I HID IN THE BATHROOM. I COULD HEAR HIM RUNNING DOWNSTAIRS. A FEW MINUTES LATER I COULD HEAR HIM TALKING TO DIANNE DOWNSTAIRS. I WAS JUST ABOUT TO LEAVE MY HIDING PLACE WHEN I SAW MY MOTHER EXIT UNCLE ADAM'S BEDROOM. SHE MOVED QUICKLY. SHE WAS—naked both of them lying on the front seat naked I couldn't believe my eyes: first the party and now my own sister I QUICKLY SNUCK INTO UNCLE ADAM'S BEDROOM. I HAD TO SEE WHY THEY HAD BOTH LEFT SO MYSTERIOUSLY. WHAT WAS IN THERE THAT WAS SO SPECIAL? WHY HAD THEY BEEN IN THERE? I KNEW THAT IF I WERE CAUGHT IT WOULD SURE MEAN A WHIPPING. BUT STILL, SOMETHING COMPELLED ME TO GO INSIDE.

BUT THERE WAS NOTHING OUT OF THE ORDINARY EXCEPT A FUNNY SMELL THAT MADE ME SICK TO MY STOMACH. THERE WAS AN APPLE CORE ON THE FLOOR, BUT BESIDES THAT EVERYTHING WAS IN ORDER. THE AMAZEMENT I FELT AT FINDING EVERYTHING NORMAL STARTLED ME SO MUCH THAT I DIDN'T HEAR UNCLE ADAM CLIMBING THE STAIRS UNTIL IT WAS TOO LATE. I TURNED AROUND AND SAW HIM STANDING IN THE DOORWAY.

AS I RESTED ON THE GRASS, I AWAITED THE INEVITABLE BROOM OR SLAP WITH THE OPEN HAND FROM MR. SOUPOSEY. BUT INSTEAD HE ALLOWED ME TO GET UP UNHARMED. I DIDN'T UNDERSTAND. THEN I SAW HIS HAND COME OUT FROM BEHIND HIS BACK. BUT HE DIDN'T HIT ME.

Michael Boylan   73

*"DON'T BE SCARED," SAID MR. SOUPOSEY.   I FROZE
MOMENTARILY LOOKING AT* Uncle Adam.

"Did you win?"

He looked very upset to find me in his room. I was
caught, and I knew it. I resigned myself to the beating that was
to come. He looked AT ME—

*"YOU HAD BETTER GET HOME, SON," SAID MR.
SOUPOSEY.*

*INSTEAD OF RUNNING AT ME AND SLAPPING ME ON
THE SIDE OF THE*
HEAD *(AS HE GENERALLY DID)* Uncle Adam just stood there
looking at me.

"When did you get home?" He asked.

He was still standing there in the doorway, blocking my
route to freedom.

"Just now," I replied.

"It couldn't have been *just now,* because I was
downstairs with your sister, and I would have seen you—"

"I came in the back way."

"Now Rico, you know that you cannot come in the back
way, because the door is broken and will be soon repaired."

"I opened the back window—the one next to the drain
pipe."

He looked at me strangely for a moment.

"I go in there lots of times," I said. My lie which was
designed to make everything go away.

But then, surprisingly, he stopped his harangue. I might
have been mistaken, but I thought I saw a smile forming on his
lips and a light glimmering in his eyes. His sudden act of
acceptance made me afraid.

THEN SUDDENLY HE WALKED INSIDE THE ROOM AND
OPENED ONE OF THE WINDOWS. HE KNELT ON THE BED AND
PULLED UP ONE OF THE SHEETS SO THAT HE COULD SIT
DOWN. HE PICKED UP THE APPLE CORE AND HANDED IT TO
ME.

"WOULD YOU THROW THIS AWAY FOR ME?"

I NODDED MY HEAD, THOUGH I DIDN'T REALLY WANT TO TOUCH THE BROWN, SPOILED REMAINS OF AN APPLE. IT WAS SLIMY AND MADE MY SKIN CRAWL JUST TO HANDLE IT. I QUICKLY TOSSED IT INTO THE WASTEBASKET. THEN HE CHANGED INTO A DIFFERENT CREATURE. HE SMILED, "DID YOU HAVE A GOOD TIME OVER AT BILLY'S TONIGHT?" UNCLE ADAM SEEMED TO SNEER.

"YES."

"WHAT DID YOU DO?"

"OH, WE PLAYED SOME GAMES," I SAID AS I EDGED TOWARDS THE DOOR.

"WELL, THAT'S GOOD. YOU'D BETTER RUN ALONG NOW."

I TURNED TO GO AND WAS HALFWAY OUT OF THE ROOM WHEN HE CALLED TO ME, "OH, RICO?"

I TURNED AROUND.

"WE GOT SOME FRESH APPLES TODAY. WOULD YOU LIKE TO HAVE ONE?"

"NO THANK YOU," I BARELY MANAGED. MY THROAT WAS SUDDENLY VERY DRY.

"WELL, IF YOU DECIDE TO CHANGE YOUR MIND, THERE ARE SOME IN THE KITCHEN."

I DIDN'T ANSWER BUT WALKED SLOWLY OUT OF THE ROOM *it was as if he was watching himself in a movie.* I GOT TO THE BANISTER. I WAS ALL MIXED-UP IN MY THINKING. LUCKILY, I KEPT MY GRIP AND WENT DOWNSTAIRS, TURNED ON THE TELEVISION, AND WATCHED TELEVISION WITH MY LITTLE SISTER. SHE WAS COLD FROM BEING OUTSIDE.

AFTER WE WERE INTO THE THIRD TELEVISION SHOW, SHE ASKED ME, "RICO?"

"HUM?" I REPLIED.

"I'M HUNGRY."

"WANT ME TO GET YOU SOMETHING TO EAT?"

"UNCLE ADAM SAID THERE WERE APPLES IN THE KITCHEN."

"YOU DON'T WANT THOSE APPLES," I SAID.

"WHY? UNCLE ADAM SAID THEY WERE SPECIAL APPLES."

"THEY'RE NO GOOD. THEY HAVE WORMS IN THEM. I JUST WENT TO CHECK."

DIANNE POUTED.

"DO YOU LIKE WORMS?" I ASKED AS I TICKLED HER AS IF MY FINGER WERE A WORM.

DIANNE SQUIRMED AND SHOOK HER HEAD, "ISSHHH."

"ARE YOU SURE?"

SHE BEGAN WIPING HER HAND ON MY LEG AS IF THERE WERE A DEAD WORM ON HER HAND.

"THEN YOU *DO* WANT AN APPLE?"

SHE SHOOK HER HEAD AND THEN she saw me standing outside, watching. I recognized her an instant later. I saw them there on the car seat, naked.

"ARE YOU SURE?"

"I DON'T WANT ANY," SHE SAID AS SHE PUT HER HEAD DOWN ON MY LAP. "I DON'T WANT NO WORMS," SHE SAID AS SHE ADJUSTED HER HEAD TO WATCH T.V.

"WHAT DO YOU WANT TO KNOW ALL THIS FOR?

"I JUST WANT TO KNOW WHERE RICO IS; THAT'S ALL."

"WHY DO YOU HAVE TO KEEP ASKING ALL THOSE QUESTIONS?"

"MRS. PATRICINI, IF YOU REALLY WANT TO FIND YOUR SON YOU SHOULD COOPERATE. WE'RE ONLY TRYING TO HELP."

"BUT WHY DO YOU HAVE TO—"

"—BECAUSE TO FIND YOUR SON, IT'S NECESSARY TO KNOW ALL THE PERTINENT DETAILS."

"BUT JENNY COOPER LOST HER DAUGHTER AND SHE DIDN'T HAVE TO—"

"—I DON'T KNOW THE PARTICULARS ABOUT MRS. COOPER'S CASE, BUT PROBABLY, HER DAUGHTER DIDN'T HAVE A CRIMINAL RECORD."

"WHAT CRIMINAL RECORD? MY RICO DOESN'T HAVE A CRIMINAL RECORD. WHAT ARE YOU TALKING ABOUT? HE'S NEVER— WELL, THERE WAS THAT TIME IN HIGH SCHOOL WHEN HE, AH, GOT INTO SOME TROUBLE. BUT HE'S NEVER BEEN IN JAIL. IS HE WANTED FOR SOMETHING? WHAT ARE YOU TALKING ABOUT? WHAT IS THIS CRIMINAL RECORD?"

"IN DALLAS, MAY OF 1963, I BELIEVE, HE WAS ARRESTED FOR somersaults on the grass

"Yes," said Virginia.

"You liked me for doing somersaults on the grass?"

"Not just for that, silly, I just think it showed what an uninhibited person you are."

"What were you doing around the school last Saturday?"

"I was helping to paint posters for the track meet, silly."

"Pep club?"

"Well, it *wasn't* the letterman's club!" She began to laugh. It was a high girlish sort of laugh that made me feel embarrassed.

"Oh Rico, you're such a *silly* at times. But I like you anyway." She touched my nose as she said that and a strange feeling welled up inside me *as he grabbed his arm.* We were both bouncing around like jumping beans singing and laughing.

"I did it. I did it," Bill kept saying.

"Way to go," I replied.

We kept going around in circles, dancing in ways we made-up on the spot.

Nothing was more natural. We would and just lock arms and swing around.

Michael Boylan   77

"I aced it, Rico!"

"I know, Bill. I know!"

We kept going around and around until we fell onto the floor together. It was the first time that I felt she and I were really together. I mean, we were walking down the hall in school and everybody knew that she was *with me* because she *liked me* and not because we both happened to be going in the same direction down the hall— everybody knew that *she was laughing at me all along just like Rollo had said.*

"YES, BUT HE WAS ACQUITTED FOR THAT. THE WOMAN WITHDREW THE COMPLAINT. THAT'S NOT A CRIMINAL RECORD. THAT'S NOT A RECORD."

She was my girl. As we were walking, I had the urge to reach out for her hand, but I didn't want to seem too obvious. I didn't want it to seem as if I had never held anyone's hand before. If I just grabbed at it, Virginia would know, and perhaps everyone would know: all the guys sitting on the radiators, Rollo and Richard and all the guys would know. And maybe she would take her hand away and not let me hold it. That would be embarrassing. But why should she mind if I held her hand? I could have held a lot of girls' hands before at dances. People hold hands all the time and think nothing of it. What's the big deal?

I'll just reach out for her hand and take it very casually. After all, there's nothing unusual in holding hands. People do it all the time—even with people they don't particularly like. It's no big deal. I moved my hand slowly outward and out to the side so that it touched her hand. As I brushed the back of her hand, I suddenly felt a panic that jumbled all of my thoughts. What am I doing?

Look at you here: you are walking with the best girl in the school and now you're risking it all just to hold her hand!

If you don't watch it, you'll lose her. She may not reciprocate and hold your hand. Not only that, but she may slap you in the face and scream out your shame to everyone

"HE WAS WANTED IN CONNECTION WITH AN ACCUSATION OF RAPE."

Instead of grabbing her hand I lifted my hand quickly to brush my hair back. A sense of humiliation supplanted the panic that had dominated just moments before. Virginia looked at me. I knew that she knew that I wanted to hold her hand but lost the courage.

"Do you have study hall now?" I asked to mask my embarrassment.

"Yes. You know that. Why do you ask?"

Why was *she* asking me those questions? What was she trying to do? Why was she mocking me?

"ARE YOU FROM MISSING PERSONS OR THE POLICE?"

"YOU MIGHT SAY I'M FROM BOTH. YOU SEE, I WORK FOR THE F.B.I."

"WHY ARE YOU ASKING ME ALL OF THESE QUESTIONS?"

"No reason. I thought that maybe you could ask Mr. Snell if you could go outside and sit on the grass with me while I do some sketches for my drawing class."

"Oh, that sounds like fun, let's go." Virginia smiled and bounced in the air.

"You better ask Mr. Snell first," I said.

"Oh, he'll say it's all right."

"I know," I said. "But I'd feel better if it were all on the up and up."

"WELL, I SUPPOSE THAT ANSWERING A FEW QUESTIONS MIGHT NOT HURT."

"Well, all right, but he'll say it's fine, I know he will." She giggled again. "You're a silly boy," Virginia said as she departed for her study hall. Then she said over her shoulder, "I'll meet you outside, sweetie."

Sweetie, sweetie, sweetie: I loved the sound of that word. It seemed so natural. I just stood there and watched her walk away.

What beautiful hips she had, I thought, as we were sitting on the grass. I was sketching her. As I tried to reproduce her, I was almost overcome with the impulse to jump up and grab her. I'd tackle her and rip off those bright green pants crying—

CESTIN, CESTIN—I'VE GOT YOU AGAIN, CESTIN!

"That's really great, Bill."

"Let's celebrate," he said.

"What do you want to do?"

"Let's go to the university tavern," he said.

I frowned. "Is there somewhere else we could go?"

"ARE YOU ALL RIGHT?" ASKED FATHER.

MY NOSE HURT.

"I'M SORRY. MAYBE I THREW THE BALL TOO HARD," SAID FATHER.

"I COULDN'T CATCH IT." I TRIED TO HOLD BACK THE TEARS.

FATHER CAME OVER AND GAVE ME A SLAP ON THE BACK. "THAT'S OKAY, WE'LL START A LITTLE AT A TIME. DON'T WORRY. IF YOU KEEP AT IT, YOU'LL BE A STAR, BECAUSE A MAN CAN BE ANYTHING IF HE STICKS TO IT AND TRIES HARD."

The sketch started to fill out. It was one of my best. I captured everything I found attractive in Virginia.

I PICKED UP THE BALL AND TOSSED IT UNDERHAND TO MY FATHER, WHO WAS STANDING ONLY A FEW FEET AWAY.

"THAT'S GOOD. NOW WHEN YOU CATCH THE BALL, TRY TO USE TWO HANDS. TWO HANDS. ALL THE BIG-LEAGUE STARS USE TWO HANDS."

HE TOSSED THE BALL UNDERHAND TO ME, AND I CAUGHT IT.

I USED TWO HANDS.

"I don't like to drink."

"Don't like to drink? What are you, a queer? Do you have some chick there you don't want me to meet?"

"Oh, c'mon, Bill."

"Where you want to go, eh? To the university tavern and see your little chickadee?"

"Shut up."

"What do you say, Rico. You want to go to the tavern now, eh?"

"I'm out of here," I said. But Bill followed me.

"HEY, RICO, YOU WANT TO PLAY SOME WALL BALL?" BILLY LOOKED EXCITED.

"YOU GOT A BALL?"

"IN MY POCKET," SAID BILLY, TAPPING HIS RUMP.

"SURE, I GUESS SO." WE STARTED TO WALK TOWARD THE GYM WHEN BILLY STOPPED.

"DO YOU WANT TO PLAY FOOTBALL, INSTEAD?" ASKED BILLY.

"NAW. WE DON'T HAVE ENOUGH GUYS. YOU NEED AT LEAST FOUR FOR FOOTBALL. ANYWAY, IT'S KINDA HOT FOR FOOTBALL."

"HOT? MY MOMMY MADE ME WEAR A JACKET TO SCHOOL TODAY. THAT'S NOT HOT."

"YOU HAD TO WEAR A JACKET?" I ASKED. I FELT SUPERIOR TO BILLY FOR AN INSTANT. MY MOTHER NEVER MADE ME WEAR A JACKET, EVER. MY FATHER ALWAYS USED TO SAY, "IT'S BETTER TO BE COLD THAN HOT BECAUSE COLD MAKES YOU WORK."

BILLY HAD TO WEAR A JACKET TO KEEP HIS FAT LITTLE BODY WARM. SOMETIMES I FEEL LIKE GETTING A KNIFE AND CUTTING ALL THE FAT OFF THE TUB SO THAT HE WOULD BE SLENDERER—LIKE ROLLO.

"DOESN'T YOUR MOTHER EVER MAKE *YOU* WEAR A COAT?" ASKED BILLY.

"NAW. I'M TOO BIG FOR THAT. BESIDES, I NEVER GET COLD, ANYWAY."

CESTIN!

"You can be a real ass, you know?" said Bill as he began circling around me.   He had been so friendly when I congratulated him on his "A" grade. But now he was acting so strange. He circled around me. It was creepy.

"I don't think drinking is right at our age," I said. "It *is* against the law."

"Are you putting me on?"

"You can't drink in Washington State until you're twenty-one. Neither you nor I are twenty-one."

"That's a bunch of shit," said Bill.

"Sure, it may be, but it *is* the law."

"I don't give a shit for the law: some old fart making laws about young people he doesn't even know."

"Even if it weren't against the law, I don't believe in drinking."

"Why, you little prick," said Bill, scrunching his face and clenching his hands.

"It's just not right," I repeated.

A strange sensation came over him when he read the newspaper about the Presidential visit. He studied the parade route that they printed in the paper. He decided that he'd walk that part of the route that he knew best.

UNCLE ADAM SMELLED FUNNY. HE HELD A CAN OF BEER IN HIS HAND. HE WANTED ME TO SIT ON HIS LAP, BUT I DIDN'T WANT TO.

A Man can do Anything

"Once upon a time," my father began, 'Rico the Great was riding a horse. This was in the days when cars were just being invented, but since they were more expensive than horses, Rico always rode a horse. *You can never be too frugal.* Well—anyway, at this time the once powerful government was being threatened by an invading force. As Rico was riding, he saw in the distance a small red dot that was growing larger and larger. As the horse and rider approached, Rico saw that it was his good friend Sadju, who was from the Middle East.

"'Rico, Rico,' Sadju began, as he approached, it was obvious that he was quite out of breath. 'Rico!'

"'What is it, Sadju?' Rico replied.

"'A terrible thing has happened.'

"'What's the matter, Sadju?'

"'The country, the Fatherland, it is being invaded by the terrible she-devil from the north.'

"'Are you sure?' asked Rico, who was quite startled by this information.

"'Yes, from the north, with help from her western ally. I only just heard.'

"'But that's impossible. The border is being patrolled constantly. They'd have to know the specific information concerning our patrol system, and that's top secret.'

"'I tell you no lies, Rico. If you want proof, I can show you their camp from the top of Themenie Ridge near the place they call The Skull. You can see their camps.'

"'How many people know about this?'

"'I do not know. I was dispatched by General Edash only just a few minutes ago with the message to you. He said that *you* would know what *he* wanted you to do.'

"'Yes, we'll look at their camp.'

"And so, Rico and Sadju rode off towards the enemy camp. As they rode, Rico made a mental note that Sadju was more nervous than usual.

"'Is everything going all right back home, Sadju?' asked Rico.

"'Back Home? Yes, oh yes—quite well, thank you. Yes, all is fine. What makes you ask?'

"'Oh, nothing, just curious. I haven't seen much of you the past week or so.'

"They rode until they came to the place known as The Skull. It was almost dark and the night began to chill the air.

"'We should put our horses here, so we are not seen,' said Sadju.

"So, they tied up their horses and crept to the top of the rocky ledge, over which they could see the large plain.

"In the twilight, all that could be seen were the dim outlines of rocks and tumbleweeds that dotted the seemingly limitless wasteland of cracked, arid plains, that were bound only by the sunset.

"'I don't see anyone at—' Rico began, when he felt a dull thud of something against his head and his body dropped, unconscious."

He looked up from the empty pews, then began to pray again for Divine revelation. Inside the church, all was quiet.

It was so quiet that Rico hardly seemed to be living at all. The noise from his breath disappeared in the large and empty room that seemed as if it were carved out of stone. He felt he was secluded from everyone and everything. There was no one else in the space. It was as if he were inside a mountain and that the surrounding rock was alive. He became annoyed by his breathing. So much was at stake.

"When Rico the Great came to, he found himself tied up in the camp of his enemies. All of a sudden, the terrible realization came to him that Sadju had betrayed him. A strong feeling welled inside his breast. He struggled momentarily to free himself from his fetters—but to no avail.

"The guard, who had been standing some distance away, noticed that Rico was awake by the sound of his struggling with his bonds. Then the guard called out something to his commanding officer, who immediately got up and walked over to examine his prisoner. The guard followed.

"'This will be a problem,' said the officer to the guard. 'If he continues to struggle, beat him.' Rico stopped struggling.

"'Tell me what you want,' said Rico firmly.

"'I'll tell you (in your own backward tongue), but first I will tell you what will happen to your Fatherland,' he said as he picked up a stick and broke it in two.

"'You don't scare me. There are thousands more where I come from, and you'll have to kill all of them to carry out your evil purposes.'

"The officer took out a knife and slashed Rico's arm so that dark blood began spurting out. 'I'll come back when you're ready to talk,' he said as Rico pressed his arm to his side to stop the bleeding.

"During the next day, Rico was put through all sorts of terrible tortures designed to make him divulge the secrets of the border patrol—but he wouldn't talk.

"Finally, the officer returned with the general, El Cu Mada.

"'They tell me that you are a very difficult prisoner,' said the general.

"'Rico spit in the general's face. Instantly, the general took out his knife and tossed it at Rico's face, but Rico strained and twisted his body so that the knife just missed him, sticking into the post onto which he was tied. The position of the knife made it impossible for Rico to move his head back to a normal position, to avoid being cut by the long, sharp blade.

"'You'll be sorry that you treated me with disrespect,' said the general. 'I'll make you regret this insult.' And with that the general, the officer, and the guard left Rico."

Rico had to get into the pottery room to finish his

"Late that night when the camp was asleep, Rico tried to extricate the knife from its secure position in the post. By straining his head forward, he could barely touch the handle and push it back and forth, unprying it from its secure position in the pole. The knife fell to the ground and Rico picked it up with his feet and slid it back to his hands. When he could grasp the handle, he began sawing at the rope around his wrists. It was a slow process, but finally the bonds snapped. Then he freed his legs. And within moments he slipped unseen into the darkness.

"The next morning, Rico arrived back at the border and got together a patrol to return and kill the wicked Mada, but when they returned, Mada and his band were gone. The tracks pointed toward the border.

"'Do you think he has crossed the border?' asked one of the men.

"'It will be interesting to see if he tried,' said Rico.

"'He's very clever,' said the man.

"'Yes, but not as clever as the patrol. If he crosses, he will be caught,' said Rico. And with that, the patrol rode back to the border."

Rico directed his attention towards the lump of clay on the pottery wheel. It would soon take, shape under his direction. A strange feeling of dread also filled him as he directed his hands toward the shaping of the lump of nothingness that spun before him. It was as if he were about to participate in some holy ritual.

He knelt silently for a time.

As his fingers touched the wet, slippery mass, Rico felt a deep calm. Instantly, his fears and premonitions vanished and he directed his whole sprit onto the wheel and became at one with the clay.

It had been a long time since he had made his first pot. He felt confident in his space. No one would bother him, except old John Pedey. Occasionally, he would come by to chat with his student. At this moment Rico stood alone with the wheel.

He felt that it wasn't becoming as he had wished it would. He had spent forty-five minutes on this pot. Why wasn't it coming-to-be as he had imagined? Then he stopped the wheel. He couldn't take it anymore. He picked up his aborted pot and threw it onto the floor.

The pot collapsed, though the rim was still intact.

"Damn it," said Rico, as he looked at his mess.

I HEARD UNCLE ADAM SCREAMING AT MOTHER, "I LIKE MY TOAST LIGHT BROWN—NOT CHARCOAL BLACK!" I DIDN'T RESPOND. MOTHER DIDN'T EITHER. SHE NEVER DID. SHE JUST WALKED OVER TO UNCLE ADAM AND PICKED UP THE PIECES OF TOAST AND DROPPED THEM ONTO HER OWN PLATE. SHE SPREAD THE BUTTER DELIBERATELY AND THEN ATE THE BURNT BREAD.

I was anxious to get to school so that I could see Virginia before classes started. The weather was getting mild, and I began planning on how I might persuade her to sit with me on the lawn during art class when we were allowed to scatter to do our drawings. She would inspire me. I would draw her portrait. But how could I capture her passionate beauty?

Then Dianne came to the table. She was always the last one up, yet Uncle Adam never scolded her.

I pictured sitting there with her posing for me. She'd be wearing a wide skirt that would serve as a base for the trunk. The wind would gently blow her hair, and on her face a cryptic smile would appear. If I could capture that, I'd be in the Louvre. The sensuality of the picture was sublime.

"How did you sleep, Rico?" asked Mother.

"Fine," I said. But I was still thinking about why Dianne never got scolded by Uncle Adam. He used to hit me. Sometimes he used his hands; sometimes he used his belt like a whip. Why didn't he ever punish her? Maybe girls don't have to be as good as boys.

"Morning Mommy, morning Adam," piped my sister cheerfully as she cozied up to Uncle Adam and gave him a hug. I didn't like the familiar manner in which she addressed Uncle Adam. To me he was always 'sir' or 'Uncle Adam,' but never 'Adam!' She began smiling her sick little smile that made my hands screw my napkin into a tight ball. I couldn't understand why no one but me saw through her little tricks.

"Morning, sweetheart," said my mother, giving Dianne a hug and a kiss. My sister pretended to be so happy. She squeezed Mother so affectionately. I wanted to call an immediate halt to the charade. A drama for my benefit, no doubt. I felt like getting up to leave, but instead I stayed to watch the conclusion of the scene.

"Hello, Rico, aren't you almost late for school?" my mother asked when she finally turned to me. I had half-a-mind to tell her to attend to her own business, and that I could get to school on my own. Then Dianne pointed to the clock.

"Rico's going to be *late!*" Dianne smiled. She had the power. I was nothing. I wanted to hit her, but instead I started laughing. Not a soft chuckle, but a loud, demonic peal as if I couldn't control myself. Then as quickly as it had begun, I stopped so that I wasn't certain whether I had really laughed or whether I had just imagined that I had laughed. I just picked up my napkin, which was tightly rolled into a ball, and dropped it into my milk.

"YES, THERE WAS A HABIT HE USED TO HAVE, AND THAT WAS NOT LISTENING TO PEOPLE. HE WOULD JUST WITHDRAW INTO HIS OWN WORLD AND SOMETIME ACT OUT INAPPROPRIATELY. .

"WHEN WE WERE TALKING TO HIM, HE'D ZONE OUT. THIS USED TO GET ADAM, MY BROTHER, EXTREMELY UPSET. HE COULDN'T ABIDE INSOLENCE. I TRIED TO TELL ADAM THAT RICO WAS A SENSITIVE BOY, BUT HE WOULDN'T LISTEN. HE SAID THAT THE BOY HAD NO RESPECT. AND SOMETIMES I HAD TO AGREE WITH HIM, BECAUSE RICO WOULD ACT SO PECULIAR."

"WHAT DO YOU MEAN *PECULIAR*?" AGENT WALLACE LOOKED UP FROM HIS NOTEPAD OVER HIS BLACK, HORN-RIMMED GLASSES.

"WELL, I DON'T KNOW IF I SHOULD TELL YOU THIS, BUT IT'S ON HIS SCHOOL RECORD ANYWAY, SO YOU COULD PROBABLY FIND OUT ABOUT IT IF YOU WANTED TO. SOMETIMES HE WOULD GO INTO THESE STRANGE MOODS, LIKE HE WAS REACTING TO SOMETHING THAT NONE OF US COULD SEE, AND THEN SOMETIMES HE WOULD COMMENCE A LAUGHING TIRADE. IT WAS THE QUEEREST THING: A LOUD GUFFAW THAT WOULD JUST AS SUDDENLY STOP. IT WAS SCARY, YOU KNOW?"

"AND HOW DID YOUR HUSBAND—EXCUSE ME, I MEAN YOUR BROTHER—"

"THAT'S ALL RIGHT."

"HOW DID YOUR, AH, BROTHER REACT TO THIS BEHAVIOR?"

"HE WAS USUALLY QUITE UNDERSTANDING. ADAM HAD A VERY DIFFICULT CHILDHOOD HIMSELF. HE WAS ALWAYS SHORTER THAN ALL OF HIS FRIENDS, YOU KNOW, AND SO—WELL HE KIND OF KNEW WHAT RICO WAS FEELING SOMETIMES. HE

USED TO SAY THAT IT TAKES PAIN FOR A
FELLA TO SEE THE GUTS OF SOMETHING—YOU
KNOW, HOW IT *REALLY* TICKS."

"Rico," said Uncle Adam.

I looked up.

"Rico, didn't you hear your sister talking to you?"

I looked over at my sister, who was smiling. Then I
looked back to my mother, who had finally sat down to eat her
breakfast. Then I looked at my watch and saw that I only had
ten minutes to get to school before homeroom.

"I got to go. It's late," I said as I stood up.

"Rico," said Uncle Adam.

"What?" I said as I left the room to get my books, which
were in the front room.

"Rico, come back here," said Uncle Adam.

"I'm late. I have to get to school. I'll get in trouble."

"Rico!" he said sternly, but I was already out the door
and into the hall. Uncle Adam flew out of his chair and rushed
after me, grabbing me on the arm and spinning me around.
"Listen, young man, when I ask you to stop, you'll stop."

Then he boxed my ears. They started ringing just like
they always did when he hit me. "Your sister was talking to
you, and you're going to go back into the kitchen and answer
her."

"But I'm late for school."

"You still have five minutes yet," he said looking at his
watch. "Now you go back in there and apologize to your sister."

"What for?" I asked.

He slapped my ears again. "Don't you sass me, you
damn kid. You little spoiled brat. You get in there this instant
or I'll knock your head off."

He lifted his hand and I think that if I hadn't gone back
into the kitchen that he might have *really* knocked my head
off.

"What's the matter? Are you afraid to go
to the party? Are you chicken or something?"

Virginia's face was very serious. I didn't like it. She was becoming Uncle Adam.

"I just don't think it's a very nice party, and a nice girl wouldn't want to go to a party like that."

"I thought you were a man, but now I see you're just a little boy."

"That party's just for hot-rods."

"I don't know *why* you're acting like this. You never used to be a mama's boy. But now you're a sniveling mama's boy."

"Virginia, please."

"Why don't you go back to your mama and her fat lover?"

"Stop it."

"I think you fit in well with those weirdos at your house."

"Stop."

"Rico and his feeble-minded mother who makes it with her own—"

"Now you apologize," said Uncle Adam.

I stood in the kitchen before my ascendant little sister. "What was your question, Di?" I asked. I looked down at the floor.

"I only asked—" she began in soft tones. I didn't look to see the expression on her face.

"Apologize first!" demanded Uncle Adam.

I looked at my mother, but as my eyes met hers, she turned her gaze away. I looked at Dianne and her expressionless face, knowing that underneath it all she was laughing. Laughing uncontrollably.

Only women and children are easily fooled. That is why have men to act as their ministers and rule the country.

I despised the smell of sweet smoke. His breath smelled like he had just taken some cough syrup. He was fast asleep, but I wanted to tell Albert about my fictitious date. Then I picked up a pillow from the couch and started squeezing it together. I grimaced and jumped up in the air, landing on the hardwood floors with a loud thump. Albert woke up.

"I'm sorry," I said as I dropped the pillow.

The words stuck in my throat. Dianne grinned at my pain.

"Louder," said Uncle Adam.

"All right," I replied. I coughed up a burning liquid from my stomach. Then I cleared my mouth with a cough, "Sorry. I'm sorry. I'm sorry. I'm sorry." Each time I tried to say it in a different way—more convincingly perhaps; I don't know. My lips were stretched and my jaw tightened. "I'm—I'm—is that all right?" I asked looking at my Uncle Adam, who was standing to my right with his hands on his hips, his eyebrows furrowed. He was expressionless.

I turned to go.

"Rico," said Uncle Adam sternly.

I stopped but didn't turn around.

"You can go now," he said. "You'd better hurry."

I began walking again and was at the front door when he called out for me again, "Rico!" But this time I didn't stop, but kept walking.

"Rico," he called. "You forgot your coat." I kept walking. "Rico!"

It was eight-o-five and I was still fifteen minutes away. I was in trouble.

SOON I COULD GET THE BALL TO MY FATHER EVERY TIME WITHOUT MAKING HIM MOVE. I HAD IMPROVED QUITE A BIT IN ONLY TWO DAYS. FATHER HAD SUCH A STRONG ARM, AND COULD THROW IT SO MUCH FASTER THAN I COULD, BUT

NOW I COULD CATCH ALL—WELL, ALMOST EVERY ONE OF HIS THROWS.

"NOW YOU HAVE TO TRY GROUNDERS," SAID FATHER.

I WALKED OVER TO HIM. I HAD ONLY TAKEN TWO STEPS WHEN I STOPPED. FATHER'S HEAD WAS DIRECTLY IN FRONT OF THE SUN SO THAT HE WAS BLOCKING THE BRIGHT CENTER WITH HIS HEAD, AND ONLY THE HALO OF ITS OUTER REGIONS WERE VISIBLE. FATHER'S FACE BECAME INVISIBLE IN DARKNESS. I STOPPED MOMENTARILY. I WAS IN AWE OF THE TRANSFIGURATION. IT WAS A WONDERFUL MYSTERY.

A

dark oval   light aura

a halo   that

surrounded   sparkled

and was   infused with

secrecy LOVE AND SALVATION holy

and   meaning

from out of   darkness

illuminating everything

mu

I was nervous the first day that I sat in the ceramics class. I didn't know what to expect. I had always been pretty good at art, but this was for a grade, and I wanted to do well. Secretly I knew that I could—**A Man Can**! I moved my arms slowly, but not without some thought to what I was doing.

"ACCORDING TO THE POLICE REPORT IT WAS FROM BEHIND A WIRE FENCE—A DERELICT TRAIN YARD. LOTS OF BULLETS THERE THAT MATCHED THE GUN ON WHICH RICO'S PRINTS WERE FOUND"

But still the thoughts crept into my head. Without invitation they bored their way into my soul, distracting me from my task. They were intrusions into my consciousness. I wondered if it was my baggy pants that I was wearing that so disrupted my mind. Why couldn't I wear tight fitting stylish clothes that would conform to the contours of my body? Why did Uncle Adam call such attire 'sinful clothes'? What were sinful clothes? How could inanimate cloth *sin*? But he couldn't have been thinking about *that.* He probably was talking about himself, like he always did. He probably meant that when he looked at people wearing tight clothes that he had sinful thoughts. But what did that have to do with me? Was he a homosexual? No. I had evidence to the contrary.

He wanted to act as my father in every way, but he was *not* my father. He polluted everything around him. He was the Devil. He stopped me from wearing fashionable, tight-fitting shirts and pants.

What if I just bought them myself and showed-up fashionably attired? He'd probably punch me down and then strip the clothes off my body. But then what?

"AT TIMES, PERHAPS, BUT GENERALLY EVERYONE ALWAYS GOT ALONG. THERE WERE NO OUT-OF-THE-ORDINARY PRESSURES AT HOME."

"HOW DID HE GET ALONG AT SCHOOL?" ASKED AGENT WALLACE.

"WELL, YOU KNOW, HE WAS SUCH A MOODY BOY THAT HE NEVER HAD TOO MANY FRIENDS OVER. BUT HE USED TO PLAY QUITE

A BIT WHEN HE WAS YOUNGER. THEY USED TO PLAY SOME GAME WITH A TENNIS BALL. THEY'D THROW IT AGAINST A WALL, I THINK. I'M NOT AT ALL CERTAIN OF ALL THE DETAILS. BUT HE PLAYED IT QUITE A LOT. HE HAD QUITE A FEW FRIENDS WHEN HE WAS YOUNGER."

"DID YOU OR YOUR BROTHER EVER ATTEMPT TO HELP HIM SOCIALIZE?"

"WHAT KIND OF QUESTION IS THAT?"

"I WAS ONLY TRYING—"BEGAN AGENT WALLACE, LOOKING DOWN. AS HE DID SO, AGENT FRIEDMAN LOOKED UP FROM HIS NOTEPAD.

"OF COURSE WE DID! WHAT KIND OF PARENTS DO YOU THINK WE WERE, ANYWAY?"

"SORRY, MRS.PATRICINI BUT I'M ONLY—" BEGAN AGENT WALLACE. AGENT FRIEDMAN PURSED HIS LIPS.

"I THINK I'VE HAD ENOUGH OF THESE QUESTIONS."

"VERY WELL, BUT COULD I JUST ASK YOU ONE LAST QUESTION? JUST TO KEEP OUR RECORD STRAIGHT?"

"WHAT IS IT?"

I walked up to the car as Uncle Adam put the newly bought Christmas presents into the trunk, then I got in on the passenger side in the front.

"Rico, why don't you sit in back and let your mother sit in front?"

"Adam, let him sit in front—there's room," my mother said.

"I don't see why he can't sit in back," Uncle Adam replied.

"Don't make such a fuss," said my mother.

"Jackie," he said, lifting up his hands as if he would strangle her.

"Don't try and pull that again," said my mother over the top of the car to Uncle Adam, as I was climbing over the front seat into the back.

"I'm not trying to prove anything. All I did was make a simple suggestion. Now what's there to get all riled about?"

"Oh, that's right; just a simple suggestion, that you make in those sharp commands of yours. It's time you realized that you're not in the army anymore and we're not your old platoon."

"Jackie!"

I laid on the seat. My back itched, and I was tired. THE BALL WAS A LITTLE DEAD, BUT THAT WAS TO MY ADVANTAGE BECAUSE I DIDN'T HAVE AS MUCH POWER AS BILLY, THOUGH I COULD PLACE THE BALL BETTER, SETTLING FOR SINGLES RATHER THAN HOME RUNS. WE WALKED OVER TO THE SCHOOL, WHICH WASN'T FAR AWAY.

"HEY," BILLY BEGAN. "DO YOU WANT TO PICK-UP SOME BUBBLE GUM AFTER THE GAME?"

"I DON'T KNOW," I SAID.

Be Frugal.

"WE MIGHT GET A RICHIE ASHBURN CARD INSIDE," SAID BILLY, WHO LOVED THE BASEBALL CARDS INSIDE THE GUM PACKAGE AS MUCH AS HE LIKED CHEWING THE GUM. "ASHBURN'S PRETTY RARE, YOU KNOW. REMEMBER WHEN HE HIT 18 STRAIGHT FOUL BALLS BEFORE HE GOT THAT HIT AGAINST THE CUBS?"

"I KNOW. BUT I DON'T KNOW IF THAT'S WHAT I REALLY WANT TO DO."

"OH, C'MON RICO."

"IT'S JUST THAT—WELL, MY MOM WANTED ME TO GET HOME EARLY FOR LUNCH TODAY BECAUSE SHE'S GOING TO GET HER HAIR DONE."

"DOESN'T YOUR DAD WORK TODAY?"

"YES, BUT MY UNCLE ADAM IS COMING OVER TO TAKE HER."

"DO YOU HAVE TO STAY IN ALL AFTERNOON?"

"I DON'T KNOW. ALL THAT I DO KNOW IS THAT SHE TOLD ME TO BE IN FOR LUNCH EARLY."

It was easy to buy a rifle in Dallas. Rico thought that with his recent problems—

THE BREEZE COOLED MY FACE AS I TIGHTENED MY ALREADY FIRM GRIP AROUND MY FATHER'S WAIST. SOMEHOW IT SEEMED THAT THE BICYCLE WOULD TIP OVER AT ANY INSTANT. I CAREFULLY TRIED BALANCING MY WEIGHT AND THOUGHT OF HOW I COULD JUMP IF IT TURNED OVER. I COULDN'T THINK OF ANYTHING SINCE the strap across my shoulders limited my mobility. *Instead, he rechecked his grip* and watched all the houses that were passing by. His bus seat was at the window. He looked out. The people and everything else were in some sort of movie to my eyes. It was all scripted by the film director, God.

A h i c k f r o m I d a h o ! I'm r o o m i n g with a
"I don't know what to do," I said to Mother.

"Why don't you find Billy to play with?"

"He's no fun."

"Well, who else can you play with?"

"I don't know."

"How about Richard?"

"He's busy. Besides he doesn't like playing with me anymore."

"Oh, now Rico, I'm sure that's not true. Richard seems like such a nice boy. Why don't you call him up and ask him to play wall ball?"

"Oh Mom, nobody plays *that* anymore. That's just a kid's game."

"Well, you certainly *used to* like it." At times my mother could reach into my soul. She could fathom what I thought without my having to say so. It's just that since his death—

I didn't say anything but sat finishing my milk as the clay spun around its wheel. A strange thrill captured me as I saw the lump of clay begin to take shape *Rico paid the gun dealer the money with a new fifty-dollar bill. The crew-cut, red-faced man behind the counter took the money and handed over the rifle. Rico, waited for his change.*

"Why don't you see what your sister's doing? Maybe you and she could play together."

"Mom!"

"Well, it seems to me that you could do something with your sister. You used to play with her quite a bit. I don't know what's happened to you lately; you're just getting—why not play with your sister?"

"Mom, she's just in grade school."

"You used to be in grade school not too long ago, yourself, young man."

I finished my milk. It was warm and tasted sour.

"WHY DO I HAVE TO GO TO COLLEGE?"

"YOUR FATHER WOULD HAVE WANTED YOU TO TRY IT, RICO. ALL I'M ASKING YOU TO DO IS TRY IT. I'LL PAY YOUR WAY. ALL YOU HAVE TO DO IS STUDY. THAT'S SOME DEAL, I'LL TELL YOU. WHY IF SOMEONE HAD OFFERED A DEAL LIKE THAT TO ME WHEN I WAS YOUR AGE, I WOULD HAVE JUMPED AT THE CHANCE." MOTHER HAD HER GAME FACE ON, WHERE SHE SCRUNCHED UP HER MOUTH SO THAT SHE LOOKED LIKE A PIG.

"BUT I REALLY WOULD LIKE TO TRY ART SCHOOL."

"YOU CAN TAKE ART AT THE UNIVERSITY."

"Why don't you call up Billy and see what he's doing?" Mother had her lips pursed together in her swine mode.

"Naw."

"Why not."

"He's busy."

"How do you know? You can't really say unless you try."

"I think I remember him saying that he would be on a trip today with his mother," I said falsely.

"Well why don't you give him a call. They may have gotten back by now." My mother reached out her hands to me. I came to her and hugged her, but then I pulled away and sat down again.

"I don't know," I said, burying my head in my arms on top of the kitchen table.

I WOULD HAVE JUMPED AT THE CHANCE.

"It doesn't hurt to call, does it?"

JUMPED AT THE JUMP *JUMP JUMP JUMP JUMP JUMP JUMP JUMP*

JUMP

Remember you father
a watch without hands
a future without a past
a cause. without an effect
a-series, b-series
both void

"I don't know."

"Now you get up and give him a call," she said as she took off her white apron with the scalloped border. I heard some yelling outside. I got up and walked over to the phone while my mother cleaned off the table.

A hick from Idaho named Bill

And seyde, "O mercy, God,
lo which a dede!"
Alias, how neigh
we weren bathe dede!"

I picked up the receiver and dialed while Mother put the dishes into the dishwasher.

The time when the tone will strike will be twelve-thirty and twenty seconds.

I heard someone yelling outside—maybe it's Richard chasing after one of Billy's wild throws. "You're getting pretty good," said Father, throwing back the ball to me.

He was right, and I knew it.

TO SEARCH FOR TRUTH IS A FRUITLESS PATH. ONE CANNOT KNOW ABOUT TRUTH THROUGH A SYSTEMATIC SEARCH (AS ARISTOTLE SUGGESTED IN THE READINGS FROM OUR TEXTBOOK). SUCH A CONCEPT IS ABSURD AND CONTRADICTS THE VERY IDEA OF ESSENCE (NOT TO MAKE A BAD PUN) OF KNOWLEDGE.

ARISTOTLE SUGGESTS THAT IN ORDER FOR ONE TO BECOME A VIRTUOUS MAN ONE SHOULD GO AND FIND A RECOGNIZED VIRTUOUS MAN AND IMITATE HIS ACTIONS. HE USES THE LANGUAGE OF FORMING *RIGHT HABITS* AND ACQUIRING THE DESIRE TO DO WHAT IS RIGHT—NOT BECAUSE ONE FORCES ONE'S WILL OUT OF DISCIPLINE ONLY, BUT BECAUSE THAT SORT OF LIFE IS THE HAPPIEST. I SUPPOSE IT IS IMPORTANT TO EMPHASIZE THAT WHAT ARISTOTLE MEANS AS THE JUST LIFE IS ONE THAT REFERS TO A MAN SEEKING EXCELLENCE IN ALL THAT HE DOES: CIVIC ACTIVITY, INDIVIDUAL COURAGE, HONORABLE BEHAVIOR, AND AN ACTIVE PARTICIPATION IN THE AFFAIRS OF THE STATE. ONE BECOMES *JUST* BY PRACTICE. THE *WILL* FOLLOWS SUIT.

ONE CAN ONLY BECOME EXCELLENT BY DEVELOPING AND THEN EXCELLING IN THEORETICAL WISDOM (AS MUCH AS GOD HAS GIVEN HIM) AND BY EXCELLING IN PRACTICAL WISDOM (AS WE'RE ALL GIVEN THE SAME MEASURE OF THIS).

THIS IS BALDERDASH. HOW DO WE KNOW IF WE POSSESS THE SKILLS TO REACH THEORETICAL WISDOM? CANNOT WE BE MISTAKEN? HOW DO WE COME TO KNOW TRUTH, ANYWAY? HOW IS IT POSSIBLE? ARISTOTLE BLATHERS ON ABOUT STARTING FROM LOGICALLY *CERTAIN* BEGINNINGS AND THEN, BY USING PROPER TECHNIQUES, TO CONTINUE. WHENEVER ONE USES LOGICALLY CERTAIN BEGINNINGS AND PROPER TECHNIQUES, HE WILL ACHIEVE TRUTH. BUT DOESN'T EVERYONE FEEL THIS WAY? EVEN IF HE IS A RAVING MANIAC? *Rico positioned himself behind the half-white wall atop the grassy knoll. He set his gun case down.* UNLESS ONE KNOWS THE RULES OF SEEING A REAL TRUTH AND UNLESS THERE IS SOME EXTERIOR SOURCE TO TELL HIM WHETHER HE'S RIGHT OR WRONG, THEN THE POSSIBILITY FOR ERROR IS UNACCEPTABLY HIGH.

ARISTOTLE THOUGHT THAT ALL OF THIS CAN BE TAUGHT. BUT WHO IS THE TEACHER? SOCRATES SAID THAT KNOWLEDGE COULDN'T BE TAUGHT, AND YET HE WAS THE TEACHER. NONE OF THIS MAKES ANY SENSE.

WE CANNOT LEARN FROM OTHERS. WE CAN ONLY TEACH OURSELVES. THAT'S IT. NOT A VERY HAPPY MESSAGE TO OUR GIGANTIC EDUCATIONAL SYSTEM. BUT EXCELLENCE CANNOT BE TAUGHT. YOU HAVE TO FIND YOUR OWN WAY, YOURSELF.

OTHER PEOPLE FOIST THEIR PET PROJECTS AND PERSONAL FETISHES UPON THEIR STUDENTS IN ORDER TO CREATE DICIPLES. AND THIS TO FEED THEIR NEED FOR SELF-IMPORTANCE. ARISTOTLE THOUGHT THAT KNOWLEDGE AND VIRTUE COULD BE TAUGHT, BUT HE'S DEAD WRONG. DESPITE ALL HIS FANCY SYLLOGISMS, HE'S WRONG. THIS IS SHEER VANITY. IT IS A WILD AND CHILDISH ATTEMPT AT IMMORTALITY, NOTHING MORE.

IN ITS PLACE IS *NOTHINGNESS* (**mu**): SIMPLE EMPTY NOTHINGNESS. THERE IS NOTHING AND NO MORE. WHEN YOU SEE THE BUDDHA, YOU SHALL KILL THE BUDDHA.

IT IS GOD'S WAY. IT IS DECREED.

RICO PATRICINI

RICO, I MUST CONFESS THAT I'VE NEVER SEEN A MORE POORLY ORGANIZED OR LESS THOUGHT-OUT AND TRITE PAPER IN ALL THE YEARS I'VE BEEN TEACHING COLLEGE. IT'S DIFFICULT FOR ME TO KNOW WHERE TO BEGIN MY CRITICISM OF YOUR PAPER. YOU WEREN'T DRUNK WHEN YOU WROTE THIS, RIGHT? THERE ARE NO CLEAR ARGUMENTS. INDEED, THERE ARE FEW CLEAR SENTENCES AND SEVERAL MISSPELLINGS. THE SHORTNESS OF THE PAPER IS ALSO A MYSTERY TO ME. THIS WAS SUPPOSED TO BE A FIVE PAGE ESSAY. THIS REMINDS ME OF YOUR PREVIOUS PAPER ON TILLICH. THESE ARE NOT THE WAYS YOU WERE TAUGHT TO WRITE ESSAYS IN ENGLISH 101 & 102. GRADE: "**F.**"

I DON'T KNOW WHAT'S BEHIND YOUR RANTS. PERHAPS YOU SHOULD CONSIDER GOING TO THE SCHOOL PSYCHOLOGIST. THIS SEEMS LIKE SOME SORT OF CRY FOR HELP. I WILL WRITE YOU A NOTE IF YOU NEED ONE.

"What are they talking about?" asked Dianne.

"Shhh. I'm trying to hear," I said. Inside the kitchen Mother and Father were talking.

"You have to be more careful about expenses," said Father.

She just sat silently, fooling around with some papers.

"I don't see how you can have overdrawn again. How do you do it?"

"Well, I don't do it on purpose."

"But there's no reason why someone should become overdrawn if she records each check and periodically computes the current balance."

"Sometimes you just can't put all that information down; you're in a hurry—you have to write a check quickly."

"When does that happen?"

"—Well, ah, lots of times."

"Name one."

"Well, in the supermarket, you know I can't make out the check until after they ring up the total and with all those people waiting. You know I can only go on Saturdays when there's always such a big crowd. I can't get the car on any other day. If we got another car—"

"Now, don't start that again." Father was losing it. Both Dianne and I tensed up.

"Why not? Why can't we get another car?"

"Because we can't afford one."

"Can't afford one! We have a fat bank account." I could hear that Mom was stomping around in her shoes on the linoleum kitchen floor.

"Not enough. We don't have enough money. A person just can't go running down their bank account to zero. There are emergencies that can occur. What happens if one of us got sick—one of the children, maybe? What if then, we didn't have enough money to pay their bills, and *they* would be the ones who'd pay the price? Maybe they would die." I didn't like the sound of that.

"But we have enough money to buy six or seven cars if we really wanted to." She stomped twice as if she were in the military. I heard him walking. Then I heard him playing with a pan—probably it was the frying pan.

"We can get another car and still have enough money for emergencies."

"But you never know how much you'll need—I'd hate to have to have Rico go to work to support me if I went to the hospital."

"You're not going to the hospital, you're as healthy as a bull, and you know it."

"But a person needs money for their retirement—"

"Retirement!"

There was a silence as my mother's shoes made a sliding sound on the floor. "You're only thirty-five years old! You're not some old man dying in the charity ward of the hospital. Don't be ridiculous. We have plenty of money."

"But we won't if you continue to overdraw."

"All right! So, I'm overdrawn. I made a mistake."

"But this happens over and over again. This isn't rocket science. Even Rico could balance the checkbook." I cleared my throat, but nobody heard me.

"You treat me like I'm a child, but I'm not a child. I'm your wife, and the mother of your children. How dare you talk to me like this!"

"I earn the money in this family. We make a budget together. You agree on certain figures of expenditure. But then when it comes down to the spending side—"

"Damn the *spending side.* We sometimes *need* things that haven't been already planned out in your *budget process.*" My mother's voice was full of emotion.

Then there was silence for a moment, which was broken by the quavering, but resolute voice of my father, "I will not become poor. Do you understand? I will not allow myself to become poor."

Then there was silence for a moment more that was interrupted by the sound of some pan hitting the floor. Then the other door shut. I peeked inside. Father was kneeling with one knee on the floor. With one hand he was supporting himself, and with the other he was holding the checkbook.

"What happened Rico? What's going on?" my sister asked.

"Nothing," I said.

"But what was all the fuss?"

I said nothing, but took my sister's hand and went outside with her to play.

It was late one night and Virginia and I were just coming back from seeing a movie. It was a very good film.

THE WATCH HAD NO HANDS; TIME HAD MELTED AWAY When we got inside the theatre I looked carefully around to see if any of the other kids from school were there. I asked Virginia whether she wanted some popcorn and *he was the real President and not just the president of the Rotary, like my dad.* I ordered one large box of plain popcorn.

I THOUGHT ABOUT WHAT I'D LEARNED ABOUT IN COLOR THEORY. EACH COLOR WAS SUPPOSED TO RELATE TO THE WORLD IN A SUBSTANTIVE WAY. IT WASN'T MERELY DECORATION OR THE OBJECT OF FANCY. COLORS AFFECTED ONE'S PERCEPTION AND MADE A UNIQUE IMPRESSION UPON THE BRAIN. THIS WAS UNIVERSAL, YET NOT EVERYONE COULD UNDERSTAND IT.

At intermission I looked at Virginia who had my box of popcorn.

"Want some popcorn?" she asked.

"I grabbed the box but it was empty."

Virginia laughed.

"That's a nice sports jacket," said Virginia's father when I took her home. He invited us in and got us some chocolate cake and milk. "Tell me about the movie," he said. We all sat together in the kitchen.

I was comfortable with Virginia's father.

"It was a war movie," I began.

Virginia's father had fought in World War II in Europe. My father missed service. "Which war?"

"Napoleon," I replied.

Virginia's father leaned back and smiled. He was drinking coffee from a large mug. The man was taller than my father and much heavier. He had a broad, drooping moustache that accentuated his smile.

"It was the war against Russia," put Virginia.

Virginia's father took another swig of coffee and then put down his mug. "Big mistake that was. Hitler did the same thing. So happy he did, the son-of-a-bitch. I think if he'd read history, he'd have never done it. He'd probably have won the war, and I'd be dead—and there would be no pretty Virginia to go out to the movies with you." Virginia's father slapped me on the back. I liked it. I smiled.

I wished there were a way that I could join Virginia's family. It was so nice.

When I left, I imagined Virginia's mother coming out to have a talk with her daughter.

"Why are you dating that guy?" I fancied Virginia's mother saying.

"What do you mean, Mother?" I imagined Virginia was getting another snack in the kitchen. She opened the freezer door and took out some maple nut ice cream.

"Why, he seems so immature. Does he even shave?"

"I'm sure he shaves, though I've never asked him. Rico is an artist. His thoughts are very elevated."

"An artist, eh? Unless he gets skills for a day job, his artistry and a nickel will buy him a cup of coffee."

I imagined the mother stopping her daughter from putting the ice cream away. She wanted some for herself.

Virginia's father shook my hand when I came to pick-up his daughter for another date. My muscles tightened as I looked at the father's expensive suit that had been handmade to fit his body. I was wearing an inexpensive sports coat that my mother had bought for me. The sleeves were too short, and my wrists (and the entire cuff) were uncovered. Virginia's father shook my hand and smiled a condescending smile.

TRAMP TRAMP TRAMP

Suddenly there was no doubt as he realized that someone else was shooting, too. Was this, also, to be denied him?

A Man Can be Anything

Or nothing. *Rico didn't hesitate. He fired a shot at Kennedy.*

Our Father, who art in heaven . . .

Rico saw through his scope that Kennedy had slumped forward. It was time to escape.

HE HAD DONE IT! BILLY HAD FINALLY LOST A GAME! THE FIRST TIME.

A man can be anything

Or nothing
            and with God's help you'll get
                                    Our Father
who art in heaven

DID BILLY LET ME WIN THE GAME?

White wheel covers; it was a strange car—kind of like a boxed rectangle and all black except for I was hungry. It was as if I were watching myself in a movie. R o l l o w a s r i g h t. THE WATCH HAS NO HANDS; TIME HAD MELTED AWAY

"You know how to pick 'em, Rex," the Rotary vice-president said to my father, the president. The v-p sported a crew-cut that stood through thick gel like light-brown spikes atop his head.

My dad broke forth a broad smile and simultaneously put his hand on my head, "Yes, he's quite a boy. Quite a boy."

"Someday he's going to grow up and be President," said crew cut.

"Yeah, and not just of the rotary," returned Father.

I was so afraid of spilling anything upon the white tablecloth that was spread out in front of me. I reached for the water and drank. Then Father passed me the bread, saying, "Eat the bread before you drink the water."

IN REMEMBERANCE OF ME AND BE THANKFUL, AMEN.

I didn't notice that Virginia was ready to leave. She just stood looking at her father.

He was a brutal man. You could tell by looking at his large hands and black sport coat.

Black never occurs naturally in the world

I could take it when Adam hit me. But I hated it when he hit my mother (his sister) when she acted contrary to his wishes.

For the Lord your God is a jealous God

I felt for a moment as if I could confront him but then I backed down. He was stronger than I was and if I failed, then all would be lost

"Uncle Adam, I don't think this is fair," I said.

"What are you talking about *fair*?"

"I want to go to seminary."

Uncle Adam took a swing at me, but I ducked under his roundhouse hook. He had an angry look. I'd seen that look before. I had to stand up. "But Uncle Adam—"

"Listen to me, you para-normal little creep. I agreed to pay for you to go to U-W for four years, but that's the end of it. I'm not going to waste another dime on you."

"But Uncle Adam—"

"Shut up!"

"I have a calling. I know it. I'm not like anything else. I must serve God."

"Serve yourself with your *own* money, creep. Get away from me before I get really angry." He talked in his controlled voice that meant he really wanted to kill me.

"It would be a *loan*. I'd pay you back."

Uncle Adam showed his teeth to me like a rabid dog. I knew it was time to retreat.

The power and the glory forever

Forever gone.

TIME HAD MELTED AWAY
She had to give me a tug on my arm to stir me from my fixed gaze at the lights that were dazzling as we drove home that night. When I pulled up into her driveway I turned and looked at her a moment. I wanted to grab her and kiss her passionately. I wanted to tell her all about my feelings, and how I had longed for her for such a long time. I wanted to tell her how I needed her to be with me always and always.

In the movie, about halfway through, I took her hand and held it. I no longer looked at the form, line, or colors but only at her body. She made no attempt to take her hand back or reproach me for being forward, but instead she sat compliantly: head forward, eyes fixed on the screen. But as the illusions danced, I became calm as our fixed postures seemed to cement us into a statue. I was entranced.

the mesmerizing light

it was false

it   was   taking

Virginia

from me

I touched her hair with my free hand and stroked her ear tenderly. She slowly turned her head away from the screen. But then she snapped back again, and we were statues once more.

After the movie she took her hand away and shot straight up in order to exit. I followed suit.

"Did you like the movie?" I asked as we made our way out of the long line of movie seats.

"Yes," she said, turning back to me. She reached out her hand to me and I took it as we exited the row together.

Everything seemed somehow natural, familiar. It just happened. I didn't have to devise anything on the spot. I knew that I had to make it look smooth (as if I had done this kind of thing many times before and was quite experienced at it). I didn't want to appear awkward. That would give myself away. Then she would know I was inexperienced. Then she might guess that hers was the first girl's hand that I had ever held. Then she might laugh at me.

"Now you have to kiss me," said Dianne.

"Kiss you! I don't want to kiss you," I said.

"Daddies always kiss their mommies." We had been playing house. It was her favorite game.

"This is stupid. I quit. I'm not playing this dumb game. Who ever heard of boys playing house!"

Then she began crying. Uncle Adam came out of *his* house. I knew that I was lost because whenever Dianne started bawling, then Uncle Adam assumed I'd done something wrong. He'd do anything for the little girl who was bawling.

"What seems to be the problem?" asked Uncle Adam. He just stood there with his hands on his hips, elbows stretched out. I knew he wanted to beat me.

"Rico won't play house with me," she said through her tears.

Dianne's tears were like the bathroom faucet that could be turned on and off with the flick of the hand. She framed it beautifully.

"Why won't you play with your sister, Rico?"

"She wants me to kiss her. And I don't want to. And anyway, house isn't a game for boys. It's for little girls. None of her friends play house anymore. I don't see why she has to."

"That's not so!" she screamed. I knew what was to follow, even without a script. I knew her wiles and those phony expressions of hers. Yes, I was well acquainted with them. "Lots of my friends play—"

Even before she was finished, Uncle Adam, seemingly without even listening to her defense (most likely he knew it by heart also) said, "Now, now, there's no need for such a fuss, is there?" He looked at both of us.

"But Rico—"

"—What do you mean? I—"

"Both of you! Be *quiet.*"

Dianne looked at me and a small little smile stretched across her lips, meaning, 'I gotcha now, you little s.o.b.' Her malicious grin formed in disguise as a sweet smile. Uncle Adam could see that she was smiling at me and that I wasn't smiling back, but he didn't understand her smile.

This was more false evidence that she was filing up against me. How clever she thinks she is! How exceedingly repulsive.

"Now, I don't know who started this fuss. It looks as if Rico doesn't want to kiss you. Now Rico, you know that there is nothing wrong about kissing your sister. It's the most natural thing in the world. I don't like that you've acted as if it were something dirty, because it isn't. Kissing one's sister is *not* dirty. Do you understand that?"

I didn't understand why he was bothering to give me a speech. I knew as well as he did what he was going to say. Why couldn't we leave it at that? Why the formalities? Why the tirade?

"Yes, sir," I said.

"Now I want you to give your sister a kiss."

I glared at him for a moment. Never did I dream that he would coerce me to actually kiss that creature who pretended to be my sister. This wasn't in the script. He was *ad-libbing*, and I didn't approve. I had half a mind to call over the director to change the script, but he was out to lunch.

Uncle Adam was infringing on my rights as an actor in his play. I didn't approve. But I knew he had the power. I kissed my sister on the lips. Then I turned and walked away.

"Wait a minute, Rico," called my Uncle Adam.

"Now Dianne, you know that your brother is older than you?"

She didn't say anything. This was also a surprise. I couldn't believe my ears.

"Dianne? I'm talking to you."

"Yes," she said in that falsetto voice of hers that was three-quarters breath.

"Now, it's very nice of Rico to take time out from his day to play with you."

She looked at him with a blank expression. Her smile was gone.

"Now, when someone takes time off to play with someone else, it is *not* nice for her to be so demanding, is it?"

She was silent.

"Do you understand what I'm saying? When your brother plays with you, it isn't because he *has* to—he does it out of the goodness of his heart, because he loves his sister and wants to make her happy. But when you complain because he doesn't want to play exactly according to *your* rules, you are being unfair. Do you see that? When you ask your brother to play, he should be able to make up some of the rules. You can't have everything your way. Do you understand?"

She was silent.

"Do you understand?" he repeated, grabbing her arm. She began to cry.

"Now don't you try and pull that on me, young lady. I know better than that. Now you apologize to your brother for being such a naughty sister."

She just sobbed.

"You apologize, young lady, or I'll tan your hide right here in the yard. I'll tan your bare bottom."

Then she stopped crying momentarily and looked at me. "Sorry," she said.

"And what are you sorry for?" asked Uncle Adam.

"Sorry for being naughty."

CESTIN!

It was a powerful feeling to drive on the freeway. I pushed the accelerator to the floor and got the car up to eighty before slowing down to the seventy-miles-per-hour speed limit.

I imagined myself to be a champion race car driver driving on the most difficult of all race courses in the world. BASE HIT!

So lik a man of armes and a knyght
He was to seen, fulfilled of neigh prowess
For both he hadde a body and a myght
To don that thing, as well as hardynesse

A blue car in front of me slowed down. It would be a difficult maneuver, but I successfully pulled it off— or at least I thought that I did when I moved to grab her arm, as I pulled the car over. I slipped and almost got into an accident before I stopped the car on the shoulder of the road. She was turned toward me. The car was parked, and I kissed her. It was my first time. I held her body, which was vibrant. My lips rubbed against hers.

Even the clock with the melted face, that told the *real* time, continued to tick. The hands hadn't been pulled off the watch yet. Though it was distorted, it continued to record everything.

Then I woke up. It seemed as if I must have been dreaming, but no I had *actually* kissed her. Virginia. She was mine because I had kissed her.

He pulled up his sleeve so that he could see his watch. It was a cheap watch, but it continued ticking—just like the commercial: it takes a licking and keeps on ticking.

"Which one do you want?" asked Bill.

"What are you talking about?" We were downstairs in the dorm lobby near to where the desk attendant sat.

"I like the red-head, but if you want her, I'll settle for the brunette."

We lived in a single-sex dormitory: boys only. Girls were allowed in the lobby to ask the desk attendant to ring one of the rooms. The summoned boy would then come down to the desk and disappear into the night with his date.

"You mean you want me to take one of those girls?"

"Sure, Rico."

"But how—"

"I've got it covered. Let's go upstairs." We walked over to the elevator.

Soon, the car reached maximum speed.

When the elevator reached our floor. I turned around to Bill and said that I thought we should "think about it."

"What's there to think about? I've got two girls around security and they are sitting tight in our room. We're in for a great night."

I stood there right outside the elevator holding my Coca-Cola in my left hand.

Bill walked forward to me. He had an angry look on his face. "Now listen, there are two girls in our room and I can't take care of both of them, so what am I to do with them?"

"That's your problem," I said, as I started for the stairwell to escape.

"Wait a second," said Bill.

I turned around, "You sneaked them in here. Now you handle it." Then I opened the stairwell door and was gone.

GO TO SEMINARY! WHY YOU COULDN'T EVEN

Then the redheaded girl came down after me and stopped me before I'd gotten to the ground floor. "Are you mad at us?" she said in a stilted voice.

I stopped where I was. I turned and saw a good-looking girl who seemed concerned. Suddenly, I felt like a heel. Why was I ruining the party? Why did I always ruin the party? She reached out for my hand. I let her grab it, and she led me up again to my floor.

"Do what?" said Dianne as she looked up. She gave me that innocent look of hers and she smiled. That smile could hide anything, so that you'd never

"IMAGINE HIM. DOING SOMETHING LIKE THAT."

"TELL ME ABOUT THAT NIGHT," INQUIRED FBI DETECTIVE FREIDMAN.

"WELL THERE'S NOT MUCH TO TELL, REALLY."

I went to the prom with Virginia. It was one of those fancy dance nights. "WELL THERE'S REALLY NOT MUCH TO TELL. I MEAN, YOU KNOW, IT WAS ONE OF THOSE. FANCY DANCE NIGHTS:
PROM— PARTY DRESSES, LITTLE GET-TOGETHERS AFTERWARDS."

"YES, GO ON." AGENT FRIEDMAN PURSED HIS LIPS AS HE LICKED HIS PENCIL, WHICH WAS GETTING DOWN TO THE NIB.

"WELL DIANNE, MY DAUGHTER, WAS DATING THIS FINE FOOTBALL PLAYER IN RICO'S CLASS NAMED BART. HE WAS FAIRLY NEW AROUND HERE. I GUESS HE CAME IN ABOUT THE MIDDLE OF HIS SOPHOMORE OR JUNIOR YEAR, I'M NOT SURE. I THINK IT WAS HIS SOPHOMORE YEAR, BUT I COULD BE WRONG, LET'S SEE, AH—"

"—LET'S JUST SAY IT WAS HIS SOPHOMORE YEAR FOR NOW, OKAY?" AGENT WALLACE TOOK OVER AND MADE SOME MORE NOTES OF HIS OWN.

"HE SAID— WELL, I FORGET. BUT BART WAS A BIG BOY, AND HE PLAYED FOOTBALL. HE WAS VERY POPULAR. HE HUNG AROUND WITH ROLLO, RICHARD, AND BILLY. YOU KNOW, ALL OF THE BIG WHEELS. CATCH MY DRIFT?"

"YES, GO ON."

"WELL, BART WAS VERY POPULAR. SUCH A STRONG BOY HE WAS, AND GOOD LOOKING, TOO. MY, BUT HE HAD PRETTY BLONDE HAIR— SO NICE AND SHORT: CLEAN-CUT, YOU KNOW. HE HAD AN ATHLETE'S CLOSE HAIRCUT. MY DIANNE SAID IT SHONE LIKE GOLD. 'LIKE GOLD!' THAT'S WHAT SHE USED TO SAY. AND HOW IT *DID* SPARKLE IN THE SUN. HE WAS SUCH A STRONG BOY. YES, WE WERE MIGHTY PROUD WHEN HE ASKED HER OUT.

"SHE WAS JUST A FRESHMAN AND HE WAS A SENIOR, AND SO YOU CAN SEE HOW IMPORTANT IT WAS FOR HER TO DATE A SENIOR, SO THAT SHE COULD MAKE IT TO THE SENIOR PROM."

"SO, THEY BEGAN DATING?"

"*DID THEY* BEGIN DATING! THEY TOOK TO IT AS IF THERE WEREN'T ANYTHING ELSE IN THE WORLD EXCEPT THE TWO OF THEM. MY, MY, I WOULD SAY TO MYSELF; WHAT I WOULD HAVE GIVEN TO HAVE DATED A SENIOR WHEN I WAS A FRESHMAN IN HIGH SCHOOL—AND NOT ONLY ANY SENIOR, BUT A FOOTBALL LETTERMAN! MY, MY, I USED TO SAY."

"YOU WERE TALKING ABOUT THAT NIGHT, WITH RICO?" ASKED AGENT FRIEDMAN.

"YES, I'M GETTING TO THAT. WELL, BART WAS, IN A CERTAIN WAY, KIND OF SHY. I MEAN, IT WAS POSSIBLE THAT HE MIGHT HAVE NOT EVEN THOUGHT ABOUT GOING TO THE PROM, BECAUSE HE DIDN'T HAVE ENOUGH NERVE TO ASK HER—YOU KNOW HOW GUYS CAN BE SOMETIMES? THEY DON'T KNOW WHAT IT REALLY TAKES TO MAKE A GIRL FEEL WANTED. WHY I REMEMBER THE GUY I WAS DATING WHEN I WAS A SENIOR IN HIGH SCHOOL. HE WAS SO SLOW THAT THE SEASONS COULD CHANGE BEFORE HE HEARD ABOUT A DANCE OR A PARTY THAT WAS GOING ON. WELL, I WASN'T GOING TO LET THAT HAPPEN TO MY DIANNE—NOT THAT I DIDN'T GET TO GO PLACES WHEN I WAS IN HIGH SCHOOL OR DATE IMPORTANT BOYS. I WAS PRETTY GOOD IN MY TIME. DON'T LET MY CURLERS FOOL YOU. I CAN STILL—

"BUT ANYWAY, I WAS TALKING TO DIANNE ABOUT BOYS, AND TELLING HER ABOUT HOW TO HANDLE THAT AND MAKE THEM DO WHATEVER YOU WANT THEM TO. YOU KNOW, MEN LIKE TO THINK THAT THEY

ARE THE MASTERS OF THEIR HOUSES (AND THE UNIVERSE), BUT DON'T LET THAT FOOL YOU. THE WOMEN ARE THE REAL MASTERS BECAUSE THEY LET THE MEN THINK THAT THEY HAVE SOME POWER WHEN, IN REALITY, WOMEN HOLD ALL THE REAL POWER.

"A WOMAN CAN MAKE A MAN DO EXACTLY WHAT SHE WANTS HIM TO, YOU KNOW?"

"YES, I SUPPOSE SO, BUT COULD WE GET BACK TO THAT NIGHT WITH RICO?" AGENT WALLACE TOOK SEVERAL NOTES BEFORE HE LIFTED HIS HEAD TO SIGNAL TO JOCASTA THAT SHE SHOULD CONTINUE.

"OH, YEAH. WELL I TALKED TO MY DIANNE ON JUST HOW TO GET HIM TO ASK HER TO THE PROM. YOU KNOW IF WOMEN WAITED FOR MEN TO MAKE UP THEIR OWN MINDS ABOUT EVERYTHING, WHY MOST WOMEN WOULD BE OLD MAIDS BEFORE THEY EVEN GOT PROPOSED TO.

"HA, HA! WELL, I TALKED TO MY DIANNE AND TOLD HER EXACTLY HOW TO GET BART TO TAKE HER TO THE PROM, AND NOT ONLY THAT BUT TO GET TAKEN TO THE RESTAURANT OF HER CHOICE AND TO GET AN ORCHID CORSAGE!

"YOU KNOW, A LOT OF GUYS TRY AND PASS OFF GARDENIAS OR CARNATIONS OR SOMETHING, YOU KNOW?"

"YES, BUT SUPPOSE WE—"AGENT FRIEDMAN PUT IN FINALLY.

"NO SIR, SHE WAS GOING TO GET THE VERY BEST, AND I WAS GOING TO SEE TO IT. WHY, I REMEMBER MY WEDDING—WHAT I WOULD HAVE GIVEN FOR A MOTHER WHO

COULD HAVE IMPARTED SOME OF THESE POLITICAL FACTS OF LIFE TO ME.

"BUT ANYWAY, SHE GOT HIM TO ASK HER TO THE PROM AND EVERYTHING ELSE SHE WANTED. I WASN'T MARRIED FOR SEVEN YEARS FOR NOTHING! (NOT TO MENTION—AH, RAISING A FAMILY), BUT YOU KNOW I WAS HAPPY TO SEE THEM TWO GOING TO THE PROM TOGETHER.

"WHY, BART COULD HAVE HAD HIMSELF THE PICK OF ALL THE SENIOR WOMEN HE WANTED BUT HE CHOSE FRESHMAN DIANNE. SOMETIMES I WONDERED WHY HE PICKED HER. BUT I WAS SO HAPPY FOR HER GOING WITH A GUY WHO COULD HAVE HAD ANYONE— ANY BEAUTY HE WANTED, BUT INSTEAD HE PICKED MY DIANNE.

"SHE WAS MY LITTLE GIRL. AND I TOLD HER THAT, TOO. YES, I DID, I TOLD HER WHAT I THOUGHT that you're dirty, dirty, dirty. Now you get upstairs and take a bath!" Mother said to my sister. Then she turned to me, "And as for you, young man," she tilted her head. "Pull up your pants!"

I obeyed.

"Now, how old are you?" she asked.

"Six," I said.

"Now, that means you're a big boy," she continued. Her voice was stern. I didn't look at her face, but at the hem of her blue dress. I somehow felt confused.

"Now what were you doing?"

I didn't answer, because it seemed to me that it was obvious what had happened, and I didn't know why her voice was so loud. She talked so sharply.

For a moment I saw yellow dots in front of my eyes. "BUT WHAT WERE THEY DOING?" ASKED UNCLE ADAM.

"WHO? WHAT DO YOU MEAN?" REPLIED JOCASTA (WHO WENT BY 'JACKIE').

"I MEAN, RICO AND HIS DATE." THIS TIME IT WAS AGENT FRIEDMAN WHO ASKED THE QUESTION.

"RICO ON A DATE. YOU KNOW, THAT WAS STRANGE ENOUGH. HE KNEW A GOOD GIRL NAMED VIRGINIA. SHE WAS A NICE GIRL. CAME FROM A FINE FAMILY. HER FATHER WAS A BANKER, A VERY RESPECTED MAN." THE BROTHER AND SISTER SAT DOWN IN THE KITCHEN. ADAM POURED THEM EACH A BOURBON. THE FBI AGENTS DID NOT PARTAKE.

"WELL, ANYWAY, RICO, YOU KNOW I ALWAYS SUSPECTED THAT HE HAD A WILD SIDE "we were just looking," I said. EVER SINCE HE WAS SMALL, HE WAS VERY QUIET, BUT HE HAD A WILD SIDE THERE WAS NO DENYING THAT *Behind the half-wall would be perfect*

"Dianne said she had a hurt," I said.

"Don't you lie to me, young man," said Uncle Adam.

I looked up at her face, which was red.

"You dirty little boy. You dirty little boy."

I looked inside and there on the front seat they were intertwined naked two nuns all in black walking down the street.

"Daddy, who are those ladies? Why are they dressed in black?"

"They're called nuns. You've seen them in church before." The nuns continued to walk past the *Book Depository Building* down Elm street.

"What's a-nun?"

"That's a holy lady who has given her life to the Church."

"Are they Catholics?"

"Yes, they're Catholics, just like us."

"Why are they dressed in black?"

"Because it's a symbolic color. It makes their clothes seem more common, plainer. It's a sign of their vow of poverty."

ANYWAY, I CAN'T REMEMBER ALL THE DETAILS, BUT IT WAS BASICALLY LIKE THIS: HE TOOK THIS NICE GIRL TO SOME WILD PARTY AFTER THE SENIOR PROM THAT WAS RAIDED BY THE POLICE.

"Daddy?"

"Why doesn't Mommy like to go to church?"

"She does. Why do you say that?"

"Well, she doesn't go with us very often."

"That's because she's a Protestant."

"Does that mean she's not a Christian?"

"No, it simply means that she has different beliefs than we do."

"I don't understand."

I was just outside the family room when my father left.

"She asked me to look at her hurt and so I did, and then she asked me if I had a hurt there. I said I didn't so I was showing her."

"You little liar," said my mother, and with that she began to dust the dining room table furiously.

"What's your major?" I asked the red-haired girl.

"None, yet. I'm just a sophomore. I don't have to declare until the end of the year." We had returned to the room.

Then Bill came in. He had two Cokes, one for each of the girls. He handed the first one to the red-haired girl and then sat next to the brunette and gave her the second bottle.

"So, you're a sophomore? I'm just a freshman," I said to the redhead.

"I know. Bill filled us in beforehand."

This made me feel uncomfortable. *She* knew more about *me* than I knew about *her*. "So, you probably know, my name is Rico."

"I do. But you don't know my name. It's Cindy."

"Where are you from?"

"Eugene."

"Oregon?"

"Is there another?"

"I don't know. Geography was never my strong suit."

Cindy laughed.

"But don't they have a state university in Eugene?"

"They *do,* but I wanted to get the hell out of Dodge."

"Dodge? I thought you said—"

"Just an expression, silly." Cindy gave me a faux punch in the arm. I grabbed her shoulders in return. We looked at each other for a moment then I came back to the room where I had left Virginia, and then I found her sitting on Rollo's lap with her arms around his neck then I suggested that we go for a walk. Cindy agreed, and we left Bill with his brunette. There was loud music. Elvis Presley was singing, and we could all imagine him wiggling his hips. Maybe that was why Virginia was being so affectionate to Rollo? I walked up to Virginia and asked her if she wanted to go home. She sneered and told me to take a hike.

"But I brought you to the party. Your parents will expect me to bring you home."

Virginia passionately kissed Rollo. Then she turned her head back to me and said, "Rollo will take me home, won't you Rollo?"

Rollo just kissed Virginia as his response. I didn't know what to do. I left the room to think about it.

I didn't think I could really draw Virginia. I was too close to her. But I had to try. Rollo had been drinking, like most of the people at the party. I don't know why Virginia told me come to this party. I was very uncomfortable. Should I drive to her home and tell her dad what had happened? Would he wallop me like Uncle Adam did sometimes? I'd probably never be allowed to see Virginia again.

"WAS HE EVER CAUGHT?"

"NO, HE WAS ABLE TO ESCAPE JUST BEFORE THE POLICE RAIDED THE PARTY. HE HAD A SIXTH SENSE FOR STAYING OUT OF TROUBLE."

"Well, I guess you would tell what you were doing anyhow. I'll go upstairs and see what your sister has to say. As for you, young man, you go upstairs to your room and wait for me. There may be some punishment here. And I think you know who will get it." Uncle Adam made me walk in front of him up the stairs.

Cindy and I walked over to the student union and got ice cream cones. (She took *strawberry*, of course.) We took them outside where they had tables that sported umbrellas that were bent to the side. In Seattle you had to be prepared for the rain.

Cindy asked me what major I was pursuing. I said 'religious studies.'

"That seems like a funny major," she replied. She licked the top of her cone.

We were silent.

Then she asked me, "What do you do with religious studies? Become a priest or something?"

I nodded. "I don't know. Maybe I will? I don't know."

"WELL VIRGINIA, BLESS HER, CALLED HER PARENTS AND TOLD THEM ALL ABOUT IT. HOW RICO THREATENED TO LEAVE HER AT

THE PROM SITE UNLESS SHE WOULD GO TO THIS PARTY."

"WAS THERE ANY OTHER CORROBORATION?" ASKED AGENT FRIEDMAN. AGENT WALLACE LOOKED UP, TOO.

"WHAT DO YOU MEAN?"

"YOU KNOW, OTHER TESTIMONY FROM SOMEONE ELSE?"

"NO, WHY SHOULD THERE BE? VIRGINIA'S A GOOD GIRL. WHY WOULDN'T SHE TELL THE TRUTH?"

"WHAT DID RICO SAY?"

"HE SAID THAT VIRGINIA WANTED TO GO TO THE
PARTY AND THAT HE WANTED TO LEAVE AND SHE WOULDN'T DO IT! CAN YOU BELIEVE THAT LIAR?"

My mother was dusting furiously. Her face had a determined look to it. "Mommy?" I asked her.

Then Mother bared her teeth at me like a lioness. "Get out of my way, Rico. I've got to clean this place up. It's filthy in here."

I went to my room to await Father coming home.

"You really want to be a priest?" Cindy had just taken a large bite of her ice cream cone and had just gotten over a brain freeze.

"I don't know for sure. Hey, I'm only eighteen. What do I know?" Then I took a lick of my vanilla ice cream. "I also like art a lot."

Cindy smiled. She reached out her hand to me. "So that's why you are so different than Bill. I don't mind at all. So many guys, you know, are only after *one* thing."

I lifted up my shoulders. "I'm not crazy. I'm just not into the American 'boy ideal.' I'm going my own way."

Cindy reached out for my hand and squeezed it. "That's just fine, Rico. Why don't we go to the Showboat tonight? They're doing a version of some philosophy play. I think it's called 'Exit.'"

"'No Exit'?"

"Sounds as good as any. Let's go."

So, we went to the little theater space at UW that was actually on a paddle boat moored on cement. Small space. Big on experimentalism. I liked it.

So, we got upstairs to Dianne's room. When Uncle Adam opened the door, Dianne was playing with her dolls. When she saw me behind Uncle Adam she started bawling. Uncle Adam ran to her and sat next to her on the bed and put his arm around her. "What's the matter, darling?"

Dianne put her head into his chest and hugged him. Uncle Adam waited until she had finished and then when her grip lessened, he asked, "What has Rico done to you?"

Dianne looked up with a plaintive expression. "He wouldn't play house with me."

"He wouldn't play house?"

"No. He wouldn't kiss me."

"He wouldn't kiss you?"

"Yes, on the lips, like you do to Mommy."

Uncle Adam stood up and walked over to me and wacked me with his open hand on my face with such force that I fell down and felt my head ringing. Then he left the room.

It took me a while to get up. But by that time Dianne had already left the room.

"SO, YOU SAY THAT THERE WAS NO OTHER TESTIMONY?" AGENT FRIEDMAN

LOOKED UP OVER HIS BLACK, HORN-RIMMED GLASSES.

"NO. WHY SHOULD THERE BE? YOU HAD THE WORD OF MY PERVERT BOY, RICO, AGAINST A POPULAR GIRL. WHO WOULD YOU BELIEVE?"

"I'M JUST TRYING TO ASCERTAIN THE TRUTH OF WHAT REALLY HAPPENED. WE'RE TAUGHT IN THE BUREAU TO KEEP AN OPEN MIND," SAID AGENT FRIEDMAN. AGENT WALLACE NODDED, THEN ADDED, "WAS THERE A LOCAL POLICE INVESTIGATION?"

"WELL, IT'S NONE OF YOUR BUSINESS. DO YOU UNDERSTAND?"

"SORRY, I DIDN'T MEAN TO BE INSULTING, I ONLY WANTED TO—" AGENT WALLACE TOOK OFF HIS GLASSES.

"TO CALL ME A LIAR AND A BAD MOTHER!"

"MRS.PATRICINI, PLEASE."

"NO, I DON'T HAVE ANY MORE TIME TO TALK NOW. I HAVE TO CLEAN UP THE HOUSE. IT'S DIRTY— VERY DIRTY."

"I'M SORRY IF WE'VE INCONVENIENCED YOU. IF THERE'S ANYTHING ELSE YOU WANT TO TELL US, JUST GIVE ME A CALL. HERE'S MY CARD," SAID AGENT WALLACE. THEN, AGENTS FRIEDMAN AND WALLACE EXITED.

All day I waited for my father. I had unlocked the front door so that it might be easier for him to come in. Mother was in one of her rages again. Dianne and I were supposed to be in our rooms as punishment, but I'm not really sure what we are being punished for. My best guess is that we should have been doing the housework so that she wouldn't have to. Mother always complained that our house was filthy.

CESTIN! I GOT YOU! CESTIN!

Just what it is to be a man

Every moment, the weight of the rifle seemed to increase. Her skin felt smooth. *He reached his left hand to stroke the black barrel of the rifle.*
Her white skin was so soft. My mind went blank. It was as if it moved to a pre-conscious scream.
AND THEN THE WHEEL WAS TURNING AT TOP SPEED. THE ARTIFACT WAS TAKING SHAPE with the blue habits of the two nuns. They shaped his vision. The clay was yielding to his will.

> **That every wight that wente by the weye.**
> **Hadde of hym routhe, and that they seyen shoulde,**
> **"I am right sory Troilus wol deye."**
> **And thus he drof a day yet forth or tweye,**
> **As ye have herd; swich lif right gan he Lede,**
> **As he that stood between hope and drede.**

"What's the difference between Mommy and us?" I asked Father.

"There's no large difference really," said Father. "It's just different ways of worshipping God."

"Is Uncle Adam Catholic?"

"No, he's Protestant, too."

"Is it better to be Catholic or Protestant?"

"Different people think different things. I think it's better to be Catholic. That's the original form of Christianity."

We were walking home from wall ball. I had done really well, and Father had acknowledged it. "Why did they change things? You always said that when they changed the pitch-rules in baseball to disallow the underhand fast-pitch that baseball became worse. Did Protestantism make Christianity worse?"

My Father took out the gum in his mouth and threw it into a drain on the side of the street. "No, sport: not *worse*, just *different*. Your mother and Uncle Adam have their ideas and we have ours. It's okay to be different."

He said it, but I didn't believe him.

Then I told Uncle Adam that I had gotten hurt in the game we had been playing.

"What sort of game were you playing?"

"Doctor."

"Doctor?

"Yes, you go to the doctor and the doctor examines you for disease."

"What *sort* of examination?" asked Uncle Adam.

"Dianne sets the rules. First, you take off your clothes and then the doctor touches you, pokes you, or grabs you. That's how I got hurt. She grabbed my hot dog and pulled it hard. It hurt. It made me cry."

Then Uncle Adam hit me hard to the side of my face. I fell to the floor and I couldn't see anything for a spell. Then I saw him standing over me.

"But *she's* the one crying now."

"I can't say anything about that." Then he hit me again. I fell asleep. When I woke up, no one was around. I didn't feel confident in trying to stand up so I crawled to my bedroom.

" It was by a baseball," I told my father.

"When did you get hurt?"

"Couple days ago. I tried to play baseball; but Father, I don't know how to catch or throw." *His arm began to shiver as if something*

"Big boys don't let women see them with their pants down. That goes both ways. That's a rule in the world. Now, you're my big boy, aren't you?" My father's voice was gentle.

I nodded.

"And you want to grow up to become President? Don't you?"

I nodded.

"Then don't look at your sister's injury, but ask your mother to look at it, all right?"

I nodded. "Yes, Daddy. I will obey."

Then Cindy reached over and kissed me. I tasted the strawberry ice cream from her tongue.

"Let him talk, Rex," said another man across the table. "He's got a right to be proud. After all, isn't that the Rotary way?"

"No," I said when Cindy began stroking my chest. "Not here. Let's go somewhere with fewer people."

"Okay," she said.

We went over to a stone bench that was just inside the penumbra of shadow.

"You're beautiful, Cindy," I said.

And then Cindy kissed me again.

"It's not every young lad that has a father whose business career has shot up as fast as yours has, Rex."

My father grinned. He didn't like calling attention to himself, but he was the president.

Two black nuns with big hats that had white inside.

The President was *a nun dressed in black.*

"I like your kisses, Cindy," I said with as much passion as I could muster. "I'm feeling overwhelmed. Let's take a walk and talk about 'No Exit.' I really liked your suggestion. You know, at one time I thought

I'd go into philosophy, but the professors didn't like my papers."

"Yeah, I've had that happen in English. You know, in my family only my mother went to college. She was an English major, so I was supposed to be, too. But none of the teachers could understand me. They just put me into a box—especially the t.a.s."

"Yeah, I know. Those teacher's assistants don't give a rat's ass about us. It's all about their free tuition and living allowance."

"Yeah. Let's take a walk and talk about the play," said Cindy.

"Okay. I'd like that."

The only life worth attaining is the one of power and glory

"What are you, some kind of nut?" asked Lita. She was sitting on the bed looking down at Rico mumbling on the floor. Rico was on his back with his arms outstretched.

"What's all this about, Power? You're not into S&M are you?"

Then Rico opened his eyes and sat up. "I don't know your problem. I paid you, didn't I?"

"You paid for sex, not a psychological evaluation."

"DID RICO EVER SEE A MENTAL HEALTH SPECIALIST?" ASKED AGENT WALLACE, THE FORENSIC PSYCHOLOGIST.

"NO. HE WAS OKAY WHEN HE COULD STAY WITHIN HIS ROUTINE. HE LIKED HIS ROUTINE. BUT WHEN HE GOT OUT OF IT, THAT'S WHEN TROUBLE BEGAN."

"BESIDES THE INCIDENT IN HIGH SCHOOL, AFTER THE DANCE, WAS THERE

EVER ANY OTHER TROUBLE HE GOT INTO WHEN HE WENT *OUTSIDE THE ROUTINE?*"

JACKIE PATRICINI WAS SILENT AS SHE SCREWED UP HER FACE. SHE STOOD UP AND GOT ANOTHER CUP OF COFFEE AND RETURNED TO THE OAK KITCHEN TABLE.

"WELL, THERE WAS ONE INCIDENT THAT FRANKLY I DIDN'T UNDERSTAND AND PERHAPS I DIDN'T HANDLE VERY WELL." JACKIE RUBBED VARIOUS INDENTATIONS IN THE TABLE TOP SURFACE: ARTIFACTS OF TIMES PAST. "YOU KNOW THAT RICO STOPPED LIVING HERE WITH ADAM AND ME WHEN HE STARTED SEEING A CHEAP HUSSEY. 'CINDY' WAS HER NAME, I THINK." JACKIE STOPPED RUBBING AND COVERED THE TABLE IMPERFECTIONS WITH HER LEFT HAND.

"WHY DO YOU CALL CINDY A 'HUSSEY'?"AGENT WALLACE TIPPED HIS HEAD TO THE SIDE SLIGHTLY.

"WELL, SHE WORE HEAVY MAKE-UP AND SHE WAS ALL OVER RICO."

"HOW DID RICO RESPOND?"AGENT WALLACE RIGHTED HIS HEAD.

"RICO WAS IN OUTER SPACE. I DON'T KNOW WHETHER HE'S A QUEER, BUT HE SEEMED NOT TO NOTICE." JOCASTA CROSSED HER ARMS TIGHT AGAINST HER BODY.

"WAS CINDY A STUDENT AT THE UNIVERSITY OF WASHINGTON?"

JACKIE FROWNED. THEN SHE RELUCTANTLY NODDED HER HEAD.

Cestin! Cestin! Cestin!

Above him were dark colors: the shadows from outside projected by the night lights. "Get up, Rico," said Lita. But Rico remained prone with his arms outstretched, mesmerized by the shadows.

BEING AND BECOMING

I WAS THE HOME TEAM AND BILLY WAS THE VISITING TEAM. HE WAS UP FIRST. THE FIRST HIT WAS A SINGLE THAT FELL IN FRONT OF ME, JUST OUT OF REACH. THEN HE TRIED A SACRIFICE BUNT, BUT BECAUSE I WAS IN MY USUAL, CLOSE POSITION, I WAS ABLE TO BEAT THE "THREE SECOND COUNT" AND COULD CHOOSE WHICH PLAYER WAS OUT—OBVIOUSLY, I CHOSE THE RUNNER ON SECOND. AFTER A MEDIUM DEEP FLY TO CENTER WHICH I WAS ABLE TO BACK UP ON, THE SIDE WAS RETIRED. WOULD THIS BE THE FIRST TIME THAT I WAS TO BEAT BILLY?

It was six o'clock. Rico walked out of the papermill where he worked. It was a boring job, but it was easy, repetitive work. He had to: 1. Tend the machines that cut, then ream, and slot paper roll cores according to the specifications of the work order, 2. Start the machine and cut the core to its proper length using a circular saw, 3. Feed the core into the slotting machine to cut slots in the core ends, 4. Insert metal caps on the core ends using a hammer, 5. Inspect the end product for errors such as defective metal caps, 6. Attach the identification tag and carry the job to the pallets for delivery.

Rico didn't own a car so he waited patiently for the bus. He generally waited twenty minutes (the so-called maximum time between busses). The bus ride itself was also twenty minutes.

When he arrived at his stop, Rico popped into a Greek Restaurant for some takeout. He had three orders that he generally favored. Tonight, it was moussaka. Rico lived in a three-flat apartment building with two apartments on each story. Across from Rico on his level was a Cuban couple. They had left Cuba when Castro came into power. They were also very angry at President Kennedy for the Bay of Pigs failed invasion to recover their homeland.

The wife, Maria, was very pretty. Her husband, Juan, was a bit of a hot head. Rico had little to do with either of them except occasionally. Rico lived alone. His was a one-room studio. Rico slept on a mattress on the floor.

Rico had an old television with tall rabbit ear antennas. When Rico wasn't working or being with Lita, he was watching television. Rico's mother had told him that television rotted the brain, but Rico didn't care. He especially liked "I Love Lucy."

"Hey, Billy," I called. Billy turned his head, but didn't say anything.

I ran up to him.

"You going home?" I asked.

"Yes," he said.

"How do you like Mr. Grabener's class?"

"It's okay." Billy wasn't in a good mood.

"They say he's a real crab; is that true?"

"He's kind of grumpy sometimes," he said, digging his hands into his jean pockets.

"Are you turning out for Little League?" I asked.

"Heck no," Billy said as if it was the stupidest question in the world. "Besides, I'm too old. I'll be thirteen next week." We walked a few steps more when Billy returned, "Why? Are you?"

"I don't know, I was thinking about it."

"I guess Little League is all right when you're younger, but I don't know, I guess I'll turn out for the school team and then do some Pony League in the summer." We walked to Billy's block. "Well—" he began.

I tried to beat him to the punch. "Say, do you want to come over tonight?"

"Can't, I'm going to the lanes with Rollo."

"How about Saturday? Can you do something during the day?" I asked.

"Ah, tomorrow I promised to help my dad paint the garage," he said, walking away.

"It's going to be too wet tomorrow to do any painting," I said, as the forecast was for rain.

"Well, if it is, I'll probably drop by. I'll see you later," he said, skipping across his lawn.

"How did it go with Cindy last night?"

Bill had put up the sign last night when I returned to the room that signaled that I should not come in so I went to the sixth-floor lounge that had some fairly comfortable sofas. I got up early and had breakfast by myself and now I thought I should get back and do some homework.

"Did you *make it?*" asked Bill.

"What do you mean?"

"You know what I mean, you faggot." Bill sneered at me.

"That's not very nice."

Bill laughed and started down the hall to see Albert, who was probably studying— as usual. As Bill sauntered away, I thought I heard him say again, "Faggot!"

One day, Billy challenged Richard to a game of wall ball and beat him. It was the biggest event of the week for both of us. A lot of kids had been watching, too. And being sixth graders and all (the biggest kids in the school) it attracted some attention. Rollo had been sick, so Richard wanted to play Jake Murdock, but Jake was playing basketball. Ed and Jack were playing a match of their own, so that left nobody for Richard to play, but not wishing to yield his wall space to some fifth grader, he decided to take on the first guy he could grab, and that was Billy.

At first the game was a slaughter in Richard's favor, with Billy being kind of nervous and all, but I stayed and rooted for Billy (though most of the other kids were for the more popular Richard). In the bottom of the sixth, Billy scored five runs to tie Richard. But Richard was, as always when he was in situations like these, cool and fully confident of winning (in fact, I don't think he ever entertained the possibility of any other result, even down to the final out).

The seventh was a scoreless inning, so in the eighth, Richard hit a high fly right into the sun (the kind he's famous for) and Billy looked as if he was out-matched.

"No trouble!" I yelled. "You've got it—just a little deeper."

And Billy backed up a little and made the catch right on the homerun line. It was a big out. Richard was unable to score the rest of the inning and in the bottom of the inning Billy scored three runs to go ahead 10-7.

Then Richard got up and started a low one, but Billy got it. He was going to make it! He was going to beat one of the best boys in the school at wall ball.

"Give it a little tug!" yelled Father.

I pulled on the string, but nothing happened.

"More," he said.

I jerked on the line and the kite began to rise into the air—soaring so fast that I could barely get the string out for it fast enough.

"Now tug her easy, back and forth. Easy—back and forth."

I did just what he said and the kite retained its altitude. Father came over and put his hand on my head and mussed my hair. I looked up at him. His head was black as he eclipsed the sun.

"You've got quite a grin on there, little whiskers," he said.

"Look how high it is, Daddy!"

"Yep, you did a real fine job there getting that kite up there, and all by yourself, too. No help from me. Lots of other guys have their dads get their kites up in the air, but I'm glad that we did it this way."

He put his hand on my shoulder. "Just keep the kite-tail down, little whiskers, and you'll have no problem."

I walked up to Billy. "Great game!"

Billy smiled at me. I knew that *he* knew that I was on his side.

I went to help my little sister with her homework, even without being asked by my mother.

Dianne wasn't a very good student in arithmetic and frequently came home with problems that she couldn't answer. I didn't like to help her and always got mad at her when she brought a problem to Uncle Adam, who always said, "Go to your mother." She, in turn, sent Di to *me*. And so, it was a vicious cycle.

"I'm in here," I called.

"Where are you?" she replied.

"I'm in the front room," I said.

She came in with her arithmetic book under her arm. She had a frantic look on her face. Upon seeing me on the sofa, she became energized and hopped over the coffee table and onto the sofa— passing me the book in mid-air without letting a single paper fly out as was usually the result of her aerial antics. I placed the olive-colored book in front of me and began flipping pages, trying to find where the assignment was by finding where the added leaves stopped.

Dianne could see my quandary and so she shouted out: "Page 112."

"Long division?" I queried in a matter-of-fact manner that was aimed at settling little whistle britches down so that I might begin this noxious task.

"Now, which ones did you have trouble on?" I asked.

"All of them."

"Have you tried any yet?"

"Sure, I tried all of them in school."

I pursed my lips. "I think you were more interested in talking with Jenny Murdock than with starting these problems," I said upon lifting out a blank page, beautifully headed with her name and today's date and class, but absent of all other pencil marks except a rose that was drawn in the lower right hand corner.

She looked at me and smiled sheepishly.

"Okay, now let's start."

She bent over and picked up her pencil, "I can't write with this pencil. It's too dull."

"Get to work," I said. "You can sharpen it later; it's fine for now."

She bent down. I set up the problem and she was doing fine until she made a multiplication error. However, I didn't say anything until after the problem was completed.

"Say, why don't you check that last problem?"

"Oh, it's all right," she said. She looked up at me and scrunched up her face and widened her mouth to its full extension.

"I've got a hunch it isn't," I replied. I tried to look neutral so as not to encourage her facial counter attack.

"What do you want to bet?"

"I don't want to bet you anything, and you don't have to check it at all if you don't want to. If you get it wrong tomorrow and get a lower grade because of it, don't say I didn't warn you."

She began setting up the next problem, then stopped and checked the previous problem.

"Behind you, Billy," I called.

He turned quickly to his left and lunged towards the ball. He made the fingertip catch. He was still in the game. Dianne found her error when her answer didn't check out, then he grabbed it and the ball game was over. Billy had beaten Richard! It was the upset of the century!

"Way to go," I said, running up to congratulate him.

"Let's celebrate," said William. "Let's go to the university tavern," he said.

I didn't reply.

"What's the matter, Patricini? Don't you want to celebrate with me?"

"I'm fine with that, but I don't want to go drinking. Can't we do something else?"

"What's the matter?"

"I just don't think that that's a party that a nice girl would go to," I replied to Virginia.

"What's up? Do you have some little chick there? Someone who you don't want me to meet? Think I'll take her from you, eh?"

I didn't reply.

"So that's it, isn't it? Rico has something on-the-side and he wants her all for himself. Now that's not a very nice attitude for your college roommate, is it?"

Cestin!

I took out Father's watch. I timed Dianne as she went through her problems. I didn't tell her what to do, but I told her when she made mistakes.

When he saw the published route of the parade in the paper, Rico carefully clipped it out and put it into the bag he had designated for this sort of information.

"I just don't understand why we have to go drinking. Can't we celebrate in some other fashion?" People were circling around Billy.

"You did it!" I cried. I don't know whether he heard me. But everyone knew that Richard was one of the best at wall ball. And now Billy had turned the upset. I was so happy for him.

It was time to clean house. Mother had dictated it. Circular dusting motions to clean up the house. Yes, it was time to clean house.

"You did it!" I said, running to congratulate Billy when the initial group had dissipated.

"Thanks," he replied. Though I'm not certain whether he knew that he was responding to me or to all the other twenty or so kids who had been crowding around him. Then I saw Ed and Mike coming up from the parking lot.

"I thought you might lose it there in the ninth," I began. "Did you hear me call out to you?"

"Yes," Billy said vacantly. Then he turned and made eye contact with me. He smiled. "Yeah, thanks," he said again in the same tone.

"Let's go eat our lunch," I suggested, putting my arm around his shoulders to lead him away from all of the other kids who were bothering him. Then he saw Mike and Ed. He broke free of my arm and ran up to Mike and Ed, who were among the best Little Leaguers—making the all-star traveling team. Generally, they didn't talk much to the rest of us, keeping pretty much to themselves. I was surprised that Billy would dare to run towards them! Those guys who were never approachable.

"You've got a good mind, Dianne," I said after she had finished her problems. "When I was your age, it used to take me a lot longer to do my problems. You did a real good job tonight."

"Do you want something to eat?" she asked me.

"Sure," I said. "What's out there?"

"There's some cookies."

"That'll be fine."

So, Dianne left, scooting into the kitchen.

"I won!" yelled Billy.

Mike looked at Ed and grinned a half-grin and said in a sarcastic tone, "Who'd you beat? Little Patricini?"

They both chuckled at my name.

"No, he beat Richard," said another boy.

"You beat Richard?" asked Ed, stopping a moment.

"Yeah, by three runs."

"That's fabulous," said Mike in the same sarcastic tone. "What was the matter with Richard? Was he sick?" Then Mike looked at Ed and they began laughing hard. I walked up to Billy, but he didn't want to talk. Billy ran away to the other side of the playground.

I stood alone at the top of the stairs. Father's room was open, but I didn't dare go inside. I thought that I was confused, but I really knew—it's just that I couldn't admit the reality of what had happened.

The pottery wheel kept spinning. It was the way that clay took its shape. Without the artist, it would be nothing: formless. Rico took his responsibility seriously. Everything depended upon the milk pitcher glistening with water beside the white glazed pots.

I waited twenty minutes for Dianne to bring me the cookies. Then the old man came into the pottery studio. He didn't look like any of Rico's other teachers. He was like no one Rico had ever known.

"Are you done?"

"You tell me, sir. I'm happy with it, but I'm no proper judge."

The old man picked up the shaped clay and examined it. "This is a very good start. I will show you how to fix it. After I do this, I want you to tell me what I've just done."

"Yes sir," replied Rico.

The old man smiled and winked at Rico.

"Why don't you stop moping?" said Mother.

"I don't know what to do."

"Why don't you go see Billy?"

"It's raining."

"You could take an umbrella."

"Only girls use umbrellas."

"Well, take a hat then. Do something. It doesn't hurt to get a little wet."

"I don't know."

"You've been moping around all morning. That's not healthy for a young man."

"Yes, I know."

"If you don't want to take my suggestion to play with your friends, maybe you'd like to do some work around the house?"

"I don't want to do any work," I said.

"Well, make up your mind: either go find a friend to play with or work around the house. I need the bathroom floors scrubbed."

"Not now."

"What did you say?" replied Mother, raising her voice. She stood before me with her broom in hand (brush side up). It was her sword with which she was to slay me.

"Nothing, I just said I'll go over to Billy's."

"That's better," she said as she put down the sword.

I marched out with my hands in my pocket and my gaze directed on the cement blocks of the sidewalk. Then I was interrupted.

"Hey, Rico." I was surprised to hear Rollo's voice while I was walking to the pottery studio. I hoped that I would get there on time.

"Hey, Rico. I want to talk to you."

I was behind schedule. I didn't want to be late for class.

I stopped and looked over to Rollo. "What do you want?"

"It's about Virginia," he said. I knew that I wouldn't like this.

I was a little frightened about my first day in seventh grade. I had heard so many stories about rough initiations to Junior High that I was constantly on my guard— lest someone make me push a penny around the school with my nose, or lick the edge of a toilet seat, or clean the steps of the school with a toothbrush. Billy and I sat together on the bus.

"What homeroom do you have to go to?" asked Billy.

"104, I think," I said, though he knew perfectly well what homeroom I had to go to since we'd told each other this information many times before. But somehow, as we were riding the bus a strange premonition arose that caused me to wonder whether he had left the safety of the rifle on. So quickly I searched my

pocket to procure the dilapidated piece of paper that told me where I was to go when I arrived at school.

"Do you remember where my room is?" I asked Billy. "I don't know, I think it's towards the lake, but I could be wrong. I never really went in the building itself—just in the gym to watch my brother play." I knew that Billy didn't know any more than I did, but it made me feel better all the same to think that I had some directions, even though they were probably bogus ones.

"What room do you have to go to?" I asked.

Billy reached into his shirt pocket, but he couldn't find his slip. Then he tried his pants and then his jacket pockets, but he couldn't find his slip. "I can't find it!" he said to me carefully, keeping his voice down. "What am I going to do?"

"Well, do you remember which room it was?"

"I think it was 214—but maybe it was 241, or 142 or—I don't know. I can't remember what it is."

Just as we were considering this new turnabout, the school bus arrived at its destination.

"What am I going to do?" he asked again, gripping my arm with a new desperateness.

"Let's just go inside and maybe someone can help us."

"But I don't know what might happen. If—" Then the motorcade made the turn and he saw President Kennedy. He knew that this was the moment.

"Let's go boys," said the bus driver.

I noticed that we were the last ones on the bus. "C'mon," I said.

"I don't want to. You go ahead. I want to stay here," said Billy.

"C'mon," I said pulling him down the aisle.

When we got out of the bus and started walking, a paper fell to the ground.

"My slip!" cried Billy.

Sure enough, it was his slip that had apparently been placed inside his coat one of the times he had been looking at it. He had no time to check the safety. Now was the moment.

Outside everything seemed quiet. Only the sound of the rain could be detected. But even the misty drizzle reverberated like some distant echo dans le grand vide

IT WAS 11:00.

Class had started. I was going to be late.

Now Father was throwing me grounders. "Just keep your head down and don't quit on them until you feel the ball in the pocket of your glove."

I tried to follow my father's words in my mind as he tossed me a high chopper. I grabbed the ball and tossed it to Father. It seemed hard to believe that only a week before I had hardly been able to throw the ball straight.

A man can do anything he wants to if he works hard to achieve it.

I wanted to be able to play baseball more than anything else in the world. So, I practiced against our garage door after school so that I could learn how to field grounders and fly balls. I was beginning to get some zing on the ball so that it made a noise when he caught it.

I thought about Big Leaguers and how they played baseball all day, every day. How I envied their lot.

Then Father threw a hard grounder to my left. I dove and missed.

"Nice try. Let's do it again, Rico," said Father as I chased the ball. I was mad at missing it. There was no reason to have missed the ball.

"I should have had it," I yelled.

"Well," he said as I threw the ball back. "If you want a better shot at it next time, try anticipating where the ball is going to go, and as soon as you see me let the ball go, move immediately as fast as you can to make the play."

I watched my father intently. He was looking to his left and so I started to my left—then I stopped when I saw that he had thrown the ball to my right. I tried to change directions, but it was too late. The ball trickled past me. My father had tricked me.

"How long?"

"It'll only be for a of couple days."

"But I don't want to stay with a sitter for a couple of days," I said.

"Well, you're only twelve years old. We can't very well have *you* take care of the house, can we?" said Mother.

"This is *his* idea, isn't it?"

"If you're referring to your uncle, I would prefer that you call him Uncle Adam. You should show some respect."

"Well, was it?"

"Was what?"

"Adam? Uncle Adam? Was he responsible for all of this?"

"Now listen, young man, this is none of your affair. Uncle Adam and I have to go out of town to take care of some unfinished business and we'll be back as soon as possible, probably in a couple of days."

"I don't like it; I don't want you to go."

"Now, I wish you wouldn't be like this, Rico. You're only making things more difficult."

"But I don't understand why—"

"Some things you don't have to understand, honey. There are some things that you have to learn to accept. That's part of living."

I walked over to Billy's house and sat down on the lawn of the neighbors. The house was blue. It had just been painted, but it appeared to be finished. I had no idea when they had started painting, since I hadn't been around this part of the neighborhood for a while. Then I heard the front door open, and I scampered behind a bush. Billy and Rollo came out and were laughing and joking. They turned down the street and I watched them until I couldn't see their yellow raincoats any longer.

I suddenly became aware that I was sitting in the mud, but strangely it didn't bother me. Instead, I felt at home in the slimy, warm, wet earth that seemed to surround and hold me fast. *Then a beetle walked across his shoe. The black ridges were precise and natural. Was this natural? What he was about to do? There would be no turning back.*

I brought my finished sculpture to my teacher.

"That's very good, Rico."

"I couldn't believe what he was saying."

"I think you've created a highly original artifact, quite good."

I smiled and looked up into his face.

"You've used hard, firm natural lines. They seem to somehow belong to your work."

I was caught between thinking and feeling. I didn't know how to react to this.

Listen my son and understand just what it is to be be be Become

his white robe that I had despised when I first saw it at mass. I had thought that it made the priest look like a lady. But now the vestment seemed as elegant as any form of clothing. I longed to be dressed like that. "The body of Christ." He was the only one who could say that. Those were the words used to deliver Communion. He could have helpers with the chalice in a two-element service, but only the priest could return the Host.

"Have you planned your classes next term?" My advisor asked me. I shook my head.

"Well, I think you should take classes in drawing and ceramics. You know, you have the potential to be prominent in ceramics. You could get an M.F.A. if you continue to improve like this. It would be a sin not to develop your gift."

I smiled. There was an awkward silence. I realized that I was supposed to say something. But I didn't know what to say. I wasn't used to praise.

"I like art very much, sir," I blurted out. I didn't plan it. I just talked. I wished I had planned it. Maybe I had made a mistake.

"That's good, Rico," began my teacher with a smile.

"I like a student like you: eager and willing to work. Why, you know a lot of kids take art classes and think it's just an easy path." Then he put his right hand through his long, black, greying, straight hair as if it were a comb. "I'm glad you are such a serious student, Rico. You are destined for something *big*. I know it."

I knew I had no real artistic talent. It was all a fraud. I didn't know what he saw in the clay—if he saw anything. It was probably some fluke. I walked back to my sculpture.

"Thank you," I said a little louder than I had managed before. I held the pot in my right hand and walked formally back to my table. What a stupid effort I had made. This was supposed to be about something important. But instead it was a bunch of crap, and I knew it.

When I got out of school, I ran home. I had just learned the rules for wall ball. I couldn't wait to get a chance to try out the new game against my garage door. I ran inside and didn't even shut the door.

"Rico?" my mother called, but I didn't reply. How could I? I had to find that tennis ball and get outside to try the new game.

"Rico? Is that you, dear?"

I looked everywhere. I couldn't find the tennis ball. Where was it? I looked under the bed and on the floor in the closet where I usually kept it, but it was gone.

"Mom!" I yelled.

"Rico? Come downstairs, and shut the front door."

"I can't Mom. I've got to find a tennis ball."

"Come down here and close this door first."

"I will in a second, but first, where is my tennis ball?"

"Rico!"

"I know I put it under the bed."

"Rico, come down and shut the door, and then I'll help you find your tennis ball."

I ran down the steps two at a time and shut the door with a flick of the wrist. The door slammed.

"Rico!" began her reprimand, but I was already halfway up the stairs again.

"C'mon Mom, you said you'd help me find my ball."

"You shouldn't slam the door Rico; you weren't brought up in a barn."

I was already back in my room and searching under the bed again. I had looked everywhere, but couldn't find the ball. Then I sat down on the bed, and when Mother came in, she was wearing her white apron. She stopped in the doorway and put her hands on her hips, creating triangles with her elbows extended. "Now, where do you keep your ball?"

"There or there," I said, pointing to the bed and the closet.

"You keep a tennis ball in your bed?" My mother scratched her head.

"No, under it. I usually toss it in the room and it rolls under the bed or bounces off the wall and into the closet."

"Now you know that's no place for our things, is it?"

I didn't like the tone of her voice. I wasn't interested in a lecture. I just wanted my tennis ball. But I knew that if I argued with her, we would be talking about it all afternoon, and so I said, "No."

"If you're not going to take care of your things, I'm not going to come up here and find things for you. Next time you'll have to sort out your mess for yourself."

"Yes, Mother," I said. I could tell that she was about through because her head was turning around as she was trying to spot it for a quick victory.

"I couldn't find it anywhere," I said.

"When did you have it last?" she asked as she started looking on the top shelf of my closet.

"I didn't put it there," I said.

"Well, it doesn't hurt to look, does it?"

"But I never put my projects on the top shelf; just on the floor—in the lowest cubby." I sat and watched him move about the room in his white apron. Uncle Adam had always said that men who wore aprons were sissys but Mr. Patterson didn't seem like a sissy. His large hands were rough and not at all like a woman's.

"Well, maybe I can see something you can't," said my mother.

"But I hate the sitter."

"Now I think you're being a bit hard on old Mrs. Adder."

"She's a witch."

"Rico!"

"I'm telling you the truth; she's an old witch."

"What a thing to say."

"She's a witch, and I hate her."

"Now, that'll be enough of that kind of talk," she said as she grabbed me by the arm and tried to shake me.

I looked up into his eyes, though he was shaking me, and talking sharply. I could detect a fear in Uncle Adam's eyes, a fear that gave me control over him. My body became limp. He let go, and I dropped to the floor.

"Now you tell your Mother that everything's all right between us. Do you hear?"

I didn't respond. He grabbed me again, and this time lifted me off the floor high into the air. I felt the package slip out of my hands; it was Uncle Adam's Christmas present that had fallen on the floor.

"But Mom, you should see the things that she does after she takes out those little brown bottles and puts stuff into her nose."

"What's wrong with that?" my mother began. "Haven't you taken nose drops?" she said as she straightened my covers.

"But these bottles are not nose drops." I said.

"How do you know?" asked my mother. I cleared my throat, but my mother wouldn't let me respond. "Now Rico," she began again as she straightened my bed covers so that I would go quietly to sleep. "You've just been fancying again. You know how you do."

"No, Mother, they're not nose drops."

"Some people take nose drops in different ways."

"But, Mom—"

"No more tonight, Rico."

"But I know. They are not nose drops, Mom."

"I know dear," she said laying me down again.

"I know because I opened up one of the little bottles once and inside was this white powder." This made my mother start.

"Now Rico, don't make stories," she said, frowning.

"I swear mom. I found her magic powder."

"There's no such thing as magic, Rico."

"Yes, there is," I said, trying to make her understand.

"Now Rico, I've told you before, there's no such thing as ghosts and goblins and witches."

"Then what about church?"

"What about it, dear?"

"In church they talk about the Holy Ghost."

"That's different. Besides, you're not a Catholic anymore. You don't believe in that."

"Why aren't I a Catholic?"

"Because you're a Congregationalist now."

"Is Uncle Adam a Congregationalist?"

"Yes, dear."

"Was he always a Congregationalist?"

"Yes, dear."

"Then why doesn't he go with us to church?"

"Ah, well, he has, ah, work to do sometimes. Your Uncle Adam is a very busy man. Besides he— ah—it's time you went to sleep young man," she said hurriedly. "No more questions now."

"Mom?"

"Rico, it's time to go to sleep."

I knew she wanted me to be quiet, but one question was tossing me about. I just had to ask it. I waited until Mother was almost out of the room, "Mom, if that white powder isn't magic powder, then what is it?"

"It's probably nose drops, dear,"

"Then why does she only take it when I go to the bathroom?"

"Some people are private that way Rico," she said from the doorway. "Now you go to sleep now or the Sandman won't give you happy dreams." I didn't know why she gave me the Sandman-bit. I knew that there wasn't a Sandman, but sometimes she treated me just like a little kid. She treated my sister better than me. Dianne was treated more like an adult.

"YES, HE WAS ALWAYS A VERY HAPPY BOY. BUT HE HAD AN OVERACTIVE IMAGINATION."

"HOW DO YOU MEAN?" ASKED AGENT WALLACE AS HE LOOKED UP FROM HIS NOTES.

"WELL, HE USED TO DREAM UP STORIES OF WITCHES AND BOOGEY MEN AND THINK THAT REAL PEOPLE WERE THE MONSTERS— NOT JUST ANY PEOPLE, MIND YOU, BUT MY FRIENDS! FOR RICO EVERYONE HAD AN IMAGINARY SIDE TO THEM."

Then she walked over to my desk. I quickly intercepted her. "The ball is not in my drawers," I said.

"How do you know? Have you looked?"

"Yes," I said. I lied.

"Well, if you don't mind, I think I'll have a look for myself." She started to move past me.

"But wait a second. What would a tennis ball be doing in my drawers?"

"Young man, do you have any objection to my looking in your drawers?"

"I don't know. I guess not. It's just that you said that my drawers were private."

"When did I say that?"

"To Uncle Adam. He was going through your drawers and you got mad at him."

"When did you hear that?"

"I don't know. Maybe last week I—"

"What have you been doing, you little sneak?" She grabbed me hard by the shoulder.

"Nothing," I said in a little voice, altered by my pain.

"Nothing! It sounds to me like you've been up to quite a bit," she said, letting go of me and walking over to my closet. "You've no business listening to other people's conversations, do you hear?" she told me in a strained voice.

"But I—"

"What else did you hear, you little spy?" She pulled me down onto my bed and sat next to me. There was fire in her eyes.

"Nothing, I—" I folded my hands together just like I used to in church.

"You know, in the Soviet Union they torture little spies. Did you know that?"

I shook my head.

"Now get out of my way," she said as she pushed me down on my bed.

"You should have nothing to worry about unless you have something to hide."

"You have a little chick there? Someone who you don't want me to meet, eh? That's why you don't want to go to the bar with me."

I bounced up from the bed and followed her as she made toward my dresser. She was determined and opened the first drawer. She pulled out some pictures that I had been coloring recently. She gave a look, shook her head and threw them away in the waste basket.

"This desk needs cleaning out. You still have some pictures here from when you used to play with crayons," she said.

"Uncle Adam?"

"What?" he said, frowning at me. He didn't like being talked to when he came home from his work. I sat down on the foot stool adjacent to his puffy, black leather chair.

"Is there any nose drops that comes in powders?"

"Humph," he intoned as he cleared his throat. Then he fixed eyes down on me, "Nose drops are liquid."

"But can't they come in powder, too?"

"Of course not. Who told you that, one of your friends at school?" Uncle Adam smiled at my terrible ignorance.

"I don't know," I said.

Uncle Adam then put the afternoon newspaper onto his lap and said, "You know, you can't always trust what your friends tell you. No sir, I'll tell you sometimes they can take someone who's shy like you and make him the brunt of a lot of cruel jokes—just because you're shy." He looked at me as if I was supposed to respond in some way. I looked down into my lap and then back at his face.

"No, Rico, boys can be cruel. They can give you misinformation about things, like your nose drop thing—and heck, a youngin' like you can't be expected to know all about everything, can you?" He smiled and looked at me again, but didn't wait for a response.

"Today, it'll be nose drops being powder, and tomorrow it'll be pepper in your lunch, or giving you a wormy apple to gift to the teacher. Some boys will do anything to make you look like a fool or get you in trouble." Then Uncle Adam leaned forward and put his hand gently on my shoulder. "But you know what the best thing to do is?"

I shook my head.

"Just ignore them. Pretend that you don't even care about what they've done to you, as if it didn't make a bit of difference one way or the other. You see, the game for them is to get you mad or to provide them with some free entertainment. So, if you foil their gag, you've won and they won't bother you anymore."

Then I looked up to Uncle Adam. I was beginning to trust him.

"When someone does something to hurt you, just ignore it—even if you feel like busting inside. Force yourself to seem completely unaffected. It's the only way to stop them. It's the only way to win."

I nodded, and Uncle Adam took out his pipe, stuffed it with tobacco, pushed the tobacco down with his index finger, and then lit it.

He spread out his newspaper in front of him and began reading. After a minute or so I asked, "Uncle Adam?" He put his paper down immediately and answered in the warmest of his various voices, "What is it Rico?"

"What is it that some people put in their noses and go like this," I put my thumb up to my nose and inhaled sharply a few times.

"Like this?" he said imitating me.

"Yes," I said.

"That's how people take snuff," he said. "Where did you see that? On television?"

"Ah, yeah. It was on a movie."

Uncle Adam lifted his newspaper again.

"Uncle Adam?"

"Hum?" he said without lowering his newspaper.

"Is there something dirty in taking snuff?"

"That depends on how you mean. You grandfather used to take snuff, but that was in the olden days. It was never considered real polite, but it was more accepted than say, chewing tobacco was."

"How about for women? Was it dirty for them?"

"Oh yes, a woman would never take snuff in the presence of a man, though many women used to take snuff on the sly, you know. But none, save the most liberal, would ever consider either taking it or talking about it in the company of a man."

He lowered his newspaper and looked at me for a moment. Then he re-lit his pipe. I waited until he turned the page a couple of times before I asked him, "What color is snuff?"

"It's just like tobacco. It's brown," he replied without losing his place in the article he was reading.

"Oh," I said softly. I liked it when Uncle Adam was in a quiet mood. I used to hold my father's watch to my ear to listen to the ticking: so exact, so regular.

As I was sitting there, I realized that I was seeing things that I had never noticed before. A greenish brown that wasn't to be feared, but to be encompassed within. Ladybugs, that were at first invisible because of their protective coloring. They walked about on the undersides of the shrubs, their tiny reddish bodies moving at a different speed than the beetles— so much more deliberate.

Ambuscading. Behind the white, half-wall on the grassy knoll, he waited, hoping that he was no more visible than an innocuous lady bug—but he was far from innocuous.

All of the sounds and ambient commotion which he normally would have classified as background noise now stood out sharply in relief. Everything in nature was waiting for something to happen.

Then Mother pulled out the tennis ball from the third drawer of my dresser. "I told you I would find it," she said, holding high her accomplishment.

An ant had made its way onto his shoe. Rico looked down and saw it, but he didn't want to bother himself about getting rid of it.

"What's it doing there?" I asked.

She didn't say anything, but simply turned and started to leave. "I never put tennis balls in my drawer. How did it get there?"

As I said this she stopped and turned, facing me (she was now in my doorway). "Are you accusing me of something?"

"No. I just wanted to know how my tennis ball got in my drawer; that's all. Maybe Dianne put it there. . . ."

"Listen, young man, it just so happens that your room is a mess. You never keep it cleaned-up. And I will not have your room a mess. If you want to know where your things are, just keep your room clean and you'll have no trouble."

"But if you'd just tell me you want my room clean at a particular time, then I'd clean it. You see, it never seems dirty to me."

"It's like a pig sty in here. Look at that sock on the floor. And how about your desk? Can you see how the papers are all cluttered?" This was one argument I wasn't going to win. "Okay, I'll clean up my room, but please let me do it and don't—"

"Listen young man," THEN I recovered and dove to my right and caught the ball. Following my momentum, I rolled over and made the throw to Father.

"Good play," said Father. He had a big smile on his face. His black moustache made his grin even more pronounced. "You're very quick, just like a good infielder. My guess is that they'll put you at second base."

"Second base?" I asked.

Several of the boys were snickering. I ran out to my position.

"Rollo, you go to shortstop, and Richard, you pitch, and Frank, you take first."

We all ran out to our positions. The coach hit us grounders. The default was to throw to first and then the first-baseman would peg back to the catcher who would toss the ball underhand to the coach for another hit.

"Now into home," yelled the coach as he hit a grounder to Sam at third.

Sam performed perfectly. Everyone could hear the snap of the ball hitting the catcher's mitt. It was a bullet.

I would be next, I knew it. I leaned forward to the balls of my feet and dangled my arms loosely. "Stay cool," I said to myself

A man can do anything

The ball was hit. It was a hard grounder to my right that just seemed to hug the ground without bouncing. I moved to my right, but I didn't move quick enough to get in front of the ball so I could stick my glove out and make a stab at it. The ball hit my glove, but then it popped into the air. I rushed to get my bare hand on the ball, but it fell from my hand. I picked it up and threw to the plate. My throw was too high and almost went over the backstop. I was a failure. I had thrown the ball so hard that I fell to the ground.

I got up and resumed my position.

"Let's try it again, and this time peg it into the plate."

He hit me another one that was a high chopper that could be easily fielded. I took the ball and threw hard into the plate but again it was well over the catcher's head.

"Okay, let's get those throws down there at second," the coach yelled.

"One more time," he said as he sent a fast grounder skimming my way. I got in front of the ball and went down to one knee to block the ball, picked it up, and made an accurate, but not hard, throw to the plate.

"Okay second, fine, but charge those grounders next time. A fast runner will beat those out on you."

I went back to my position and gripped my knees tightly with my hands.

"Who's that over there?" asked a child. I didn't turn because the President was in sight.

"Let's look alive out there at second."

"What?" I replied.

"I said, Patricini."

"Okay," I said.

"Let's be awake or I'll get someone else out there."

"I don't drink," I said.

"What's the matter with you, are you a queer?"

"I just don't drink, that's all. Isn't there another way we can celebrate your achievement?"

I sat in my father's lap and put down my empty milk glass. I looked up at my father and reached for his moustache, but my arms were too short.

"Daddy, help me," I said.

"You'll be all right," he said, holding my hand, I loved the hand which held me. It was strong, gentle—not at all harsh. It comforted me.

"I feel like I'm going to die," I said.

"Don't worry, you'll be all right," he said. Then I opened my eyes and stared at the white sheets that surrounded him in the box he was lying in. I shouted into the church. It wasn't fair. My father

I WAS SURROUNDED BY A BROWNISH GREEN

I felt as if I was going to vomit, but I suppressed the urge. Then Father finished his milk and lifted the glass to the light so he could observe the white film of the remainder of milk slide down the sides of the glass. It was the remainder of the day. All that was left was to go to bed *and watch the ant change direction as it made its deliberate way off his shoe and back into the dirt.*

"Isn't it time we went?" I asked.

"I'll be ready in a minute," said Father.

"But you told me to get a move on you because Father Weal doesn't want it to last all afternoon."

"Okay, little whiskers, I'll be down in two shakes." I could hardly wait for Father to come down because I was going to play soldiers with David, a kid who lived a long way away from my house and whom I only saw when Father went to the church work events. He was a tall boy with straight golden hair that flopped casually around, instead of being closely cropped as most of my friends' hair was cut. THE EDGES WERE TRIMMED IN A LIGHT BLUE

"Daddy?" I called again.

"Coming," he said, as I heard his door slam. Father came down the stairs very quickly, taking two stairs at a time. I didn't understand why he was moving so quickly, when he usually walked so slowly.

"Let's go," he said tersely.

I followed outside and reached up for his hand. "Daddy?" I said, trying to understand.

He stopped, sighed, and said in his slow soothing voice, "You're right, little whiskers—we're going to church now to labor for the Lord." He squeezed my hand, then lifted me up to his shoulder. "You're a blessing, young man," he said as we walked to the car. "You're a blessing."

How natural the word sounded on my tongue, 'Virginia.'

I don't know how long I sat in the garden. I was immersed in the rich black soil that sustained the moss and beetles as well as the large bushes. I was almost hypnotized each time that I went into the sanctuary. It was so large and filled with so much open space. Sure, there were lots of things inside—like the statues and the candles, and the pews. I was particularly taken by the large area in front with the high altar and its two big candles. A detail I paid attention to was the little candle inside its red glass home, hung by a chain from the ceiling. When the candle was lit, Jesus was present inside the church.

But what attracted my attention the most was the ceiling itself. It made me feel insignificant and small at first, but then there was a transformation. I felt that I was a part of this story. It was almost as if I had become one of the statues—a part of the sanctuary. I was changed as I waited in vast singular silence, thinking about The Father.

But then I returned to the garden where I could become the bug and moss at the same time. There were no other children there today so I decided to help with the work.

Then there was some commotion as the sexton was straightening things. He saw me sitting in the mud, trying to imitate what the adults were doing, "Hey there. Are you okay?"

"My dad's in at Confession. And then he's coming out to help."

Then I heard a voice of someone my age. "It's just Patricini, playing in the mud." The voice was Rollo's. He had a sneer on his face.

From a different direction I heard, "Rico, what are you doing?" The voice was Billy's. I didn't respond.

"What a retard, playing by himself in the mud," Rollo's voice was getting closer.

"C'mon Rico, get up out of there." Billy started running to me. My eyes felt full and heavy.

"Rico," I felt an adult hand on my shoulder.

I LIKED TO WATCH THE LARGE SNOWFLAKES FALLING, CAREFREE FROM THE SKY. THEY JUST FLOATED BACK AND FORTH, SLOWLY DRIFTING like my father's fingers gently coaxing me to sleep.

I LOOKED UP, AND THERE HE WAS, BRINGING HIS ARM OUT FROM BEHIND HIS BACK TO HIT ME AS HE HAD SO MANY TIMES BEFORE. UNCLE ADAM SEEMED TO DERIVE ENERGY AND HAPPINESS FROM BEATING ME.

"Hey Rico, get up." There was a tugging on me from Billy.

"What's the matter with him? Is he sick?" asked the Sexton.

"C'mon Rico, stop playing and get up," said Billy.

In the background Rollo was creating insults against me in a song that he chose to dance to.

"I'VE GOTTA PAINT THE GARAGE."

"IT'S GOING TO BE TOO WET TOMORROW TO DO ANY PAINTING."

TOO WET

TOO WET

TOO WET

TOO WET

TOO WET

"C'mon Rico, you're soaking wet. Get inside and change your clothes."

I got up.

"You sure have queer buddies," said Rollo to Billy.

"You want to come and call your mom?" asked Billy.

I didn't reply.

"Rico?"

"No, it's too wet," I said. "She'd only say that she *told me so.*" I heard Rollo talk to Billy as I turned and walked away. "He certainly is a dumbo."

Billy didn't respond.

"You say he's your buddy?"

"Well, I never did," Billy began.

"Ah c'mon, you used to play together a lot, didn't you?"

"When we were kids. Not anymore."

"But if you used to play together a lot you must still be good buddies."

"Listen, Rollo, we hardly ever talk to each other anymore."

Then the church bell struck two, and I began running.

The baseball game was supposed to start. I felt excited about my first game. My left sock began to slip, so I stopped and pulled it up so that it was all right.

ON THE TABLE WAS A HALF-FINISHED MANUSCRIPT.

DEAR FATHER WEAL,

YOU PROBABLY DON'T REMEMBER ME, BUT I USED TO GO TO YOUR CHURCH WHEN I WAS YOUNG. MY FATHER WAS REX PATRICINI, WHO USED TO COME REGULARLY TO MASS AND HE HELPED OUT WITH THE GARDEN AND SUCH. I USED TO COME UNTIL MY FATHER DIED.THEN MY MOTHER, A PROTESTANT, MADE ME GO TO ANOTHER CHURCH. I DIDN'T LIKE IT. I ALWAYS WANTED TO BE A CATHOLIC. BUT KIDS DON'T HAVE MUCH SAY IN THESE AFFAIRS.

I AM WRITING YOU ABOUT A MATTER I FIND VERY DISTURBING, AND WHICH I HAVE BEEN UNABLE TO RECEIVE ANY APPROPRIATE ANSWERS ABOUT. MY QUESTIONS REVOLVE AROUND AN IDEA THAT HAS TAKEN HOLD OF ME. I DON'T KNOW HOW TO PUT THIS. I'D RATHER BE IN THE CONFESSIONAL RIGHT NOW LOOKING AT A BROWN, PLASTIC MESH SCREEN.

I HAVE NO CONTROL OVER THIS. I'M A COLLEGE-EDUCATED PERSON WHO TRIED PHILOSOPHY AND FAILED. THEN I TRIED THEOLOGY AND FAILED. IT WAS ONLY IN ART AND CERAMICS THAT I FOUND FULFILLMENT. IT IS A CONCRETE PATH TO PEACE.

BEFORE LONG I HAVE AN IMPORTANT DECISION TO MAKE AND I WANT *YOUR INPUT*. I FEEL AS IF I AM ABRAHAM. I HAVE NO SON, ISSAC OR ISHMAEL, TO SACRIFICE TO THE LORD. INSTEAD, *I AM THE SON, AND I MUST SACRIFICE MY FATHER.*

"Under these circumstances, I have a duty against which my habits, even more the pride of my instincts, revolt at bottom—namely, to say: Hear me! For I am such and such a person. Above all, do not mistake me for someone else."

I know that it has been said that God, the Father, is a terrible God in the sense that it refers to the terror one is to feel for the Old Testament Master-of-the-Universe. This point has been made time and time again, despite the cries of Rintrah in the wilderness. And what of the barren heath? And what of the French Revolution?

My friend (as I hope, in all due respect, I may address you, for aren't we all one in the brotherhood of Christ), these fragments are not entirely unrelated! Indeed, there is a radical marriage of these two opposites! Or so it was termed by another prophet many years ago. . . .

Maybe I'm mad! But if I am, it is the kind of madness that sees everyone else as mad, too. Maybe *madness* is a part of what it means to live in this world? I long for the restraints of a strait jacket, but it isn't *me* who needs one, but rather the sick world. The world is sick and dying from spiritual deprivation.

**A Man can be anything he wants to be
If he only sets his mind to it
And he wants it hard enough**

Inside   the   mind   is   living   tissue transcending time: a broken, bent watch that reveals a struggle for money, for food, for calm, for peace, for serenity in a noiseless room. It's all a pantomime of eternity chaos, ANANKE.

"Don't worry, Rico, don't worry."

"But I feel like I'm going to die."

"You're not going to die, Rico."

"But Daddy, it hurts so much."

"That's all right son, things will work themselves out, wait and see." I have to admit that I didn't believe my father when he told me this. I thought that he was probably just protecting me from the awful truth. His hand was large and gentle. I could feel the furry hair on the back of his hand on my arm. Then a sharp pain shot through my throat, making my body shiver. I was confused for a moment; I no longer remembered that I was lying in a hospital bed, but for that moment I felt as if I were isolated in a fit of agony and despair as I arched my back and flopped in the air. I felt like a fish that was just being taken out of water, struggling in my new and painful environment. The hospital walls were again closing around me. I couldn't swallow. The doctors had taken something away from me: my tonsils.

It was the first time I had ever worn a formal coat before. I didn't want to wear one, but my mother insisted. I appealed to my Uncle Adam and though he agreed with me that it was silly and a waste of money, I was still looking at myself in the mirror with a rented tux.

In all honesty, I have to admit that I didn't look bad. In fact, I thought I looked a bit dashing with the cummerbund pulled tightly around my waist.

I wondered whether I looked just a little like a young Clark Gable. I knew that it was stupid to imagine such things, but still I could see myself in a sparkling casino with Virginia on my arm and behaving with a suave, casual ease that made everyone in the casino look up and wonder enviously to themselves.

"Your table is ready, Mr. Gable."

"Yes, thank you. Shall we go, Virginia?"

"Anything you say, honey," she said, looking up at my face in deep admiration.

"After you, my darling."

As President I knew that everyone would imitate my dashing style. At first, I hadn't liked the idea of a blue tuxedo. I mean, everyone would be wearing black and I would be sitting there with a stupid blue tux. People would whisper:

"What is he doing in a blue tux?"

"*Blue!* Whatever gave him the idea that he could wear blue?"

"Everyone looks so handsome tonight in their beautiful and, smart *black* tuxes, except for that freak over there who thinks he can get by with a *blue* tux. How utterly ridiculous!"

Yet when I saw myself in the mirror, standing as that dashing President, Clark Gable, I felt tall. Everything about me suggested that I was that celebrity man. It all seemed so natural. Yes, it was natural to the last detail. I was glad that Uncle Adam had insisted over my protestations that I rent a tux: a blue tux.

> So lik a man of armes and a knyght
> He was to seen, fulfilled of heigh prowesse;
> For bothe he hadde a body and a myght
> To don that thing, as wel as hardynesse;
> And ek to seen hym in his gere hym dresse,
> So fressh, so yong, so weldy semed he.
> It was an heven upon hym for to see.

Then the bullet fired. There was nothing magical about it. Just pulling up weeds one by one as we were cleaning our souls, as Father Weal liked to put it.

Then Rico sat down and wrote his father a letter. Rex had been dead for many years, but Rico thought it was the appropriate thing to do. "And Father, the reason I'm writing to you is perhaps that I have no one else to write to anymore. I have no connection. I thought that I could solve it all with one action, but it has failed. I failed. I don't even know whether I accomplished my purpose." There was another shot! I may have failed. I may have missed entirely! I probably did. This thought torments me continually, giving me no peace. I have tried suicide, but I don't have the nerve. My arm would fail at the critical moment. Once this option is taken away from a man, what choice is there left to him? How is he to define himself? Am I a louse or a Man?

"Father, you are the only one I have to turn to. . . ."

"But I never liked pulling weeds. I always preferred playing soldiers. When I played soldiers, I could lose myself inside my vision of grandeur. Beautiful potency, like the President, who, arrayed in his golden cape, presided benevolently in his glory over every matter of state, because it was his office and his charge" and so I took Virginia's hand and placed it on my arm and left her parents' home. She was beautiful in her white dress with green brocade. I was proud that only the senior girls were allowed to come to the prom in white, and this made her appearance intimately special for me.

"I tell you she's taking you for a sucker," said Rollo as we were walking to the toilet.

"And I'm telling you to buzz off," I replied.

"Listen, I'm only saying this for your own good," said Rollo as we headed for our urinals.

But Rollo wouldn't stop. He kept on it, even as he did his business. "On one level I get a kick out of seeing a guy like you (who always plays it straight) get hurt."

"Well, thanks for your interest," I said as I walked over to wash my hands.

But Rollo grabbed my shoulder with his unwashed hand. "Listen, I know how you must feel."

"No, you don't. There isn't anybody who knows how I feel."

"Look, she's playing you for a joke. She has a bet with some of the guys. I heard her talking about it."

I started to walk away again.

"It's Billy. She's got some scheme with Billy concerning some party after the dance."

I turned around but he grabbed me again. I held my clenched fist to Rollo's face.

"What the hell are you doing?"

"I don't like you to talk that way about—"

Then I stopped.

"Listen, what's the matter with you?"

I didn't answer, but loosened my fist and returned to my routine.

As I walked away, Rollo again said, "Remember, I warned you."

Before I returned to Virginia, I took a moment and opened my father's pocket watch. I wanted to be sure of what was in my power: where I was and *when* I was there.

Driving home from the department store, everyone was quiet. Uncle Adam wasn't saying anything to anyone and nobody was talking to him. From the backseat I could only see part of his face, which appeared blue to me as a result of the funny outside light. It was still snowing. But now the flakes seemed to propel themselves downward, instead of the slow, floating descent I had noticed earlier. Now, they were all rushing, speeding to the ground—yet still

I came upon a single snowflake, slowly meandering through the chilly stream of air. Even though I could no longer see it from the back seat of the car, I still sensed it. Yes, I experienced it almost in a stronger way than I had when I first watched it fall. It was there—yes, there was no fine intricate pattern that I could recognize, but still at that moment, I seemed to know (to apprehend) the snowflake in a way that I couldn't possibly have done at first. It was now fully real.

I suppose my father first began talking about the Presidency when I was three or so. It was my first clear recollection of him. My memory goes like this: we were in the yard and there were some loud sounds. Then I remember being picked up and thrust into the air while my father was yelling something. I can't remember all of it, but what I can remember was the word, 'President,' repeated over and over YES, HIS FATHER WAS FIERCELY PROUD OF THE BOY. WHY, I REMEMBER WHEN HE WAS LITTLE, RICO WAS SUCH A CUTE LITTLE BOY. HE LOOKED SO, HOW DO YOU SAY, LIKE A LITTLE KING?

"REGAL?" ASKED AGENT WALLACE.

"YES, THAT'S IT. REGAL. HE LOOKED REGAL ALL RIGHT. I EVEN BOUGHT HIM A PAIR OF PURPLE AND BLUE PAJAMAS ONCE. WE USED TO CALL IT HIS ROYAL COSTUME. YES INDEED, WHEN WE HAD COMPANY SOMETIMES REX WOULD PICK UP THE BOY AND GIVE HIM A RIDE THROUGH THE AIR, MAKING SOME GRAND PRONOUNCEMENT OR SOMETHING.

"OH, HE WAS FUNNY, MY REX. YES, HE SURE DID KNOW HOW TO MAKE PEOPLE

LAUGH. HE WAS SUCH A TALKER, YOU KNOW, ALWAYS HAVING THE RIGHT LINE AT THE RIGHT MOMENT, SO THAT EVERYBODY WAS KINDA RELIEVED OF THE TENSION.

"WHY, I REMEMBER ONCE WHEN WE WERE HAVING A PARTY. IT WAS A POKER NIGHT. WE WERE PLAYING POKER WITH TWO OTHER COUPLES. HOW I *CAN REMEMBER* THAT NIGHT. IT SEEMS LIKE—LIKE, WELL YOU KNOW, LIKE JUST A COUPLE DAYS AGO."

"YES, THE PAST DOES HAVE A WAY OF GETTING AWAY FROM ONE," REPLIED THE FBI PSYCHOLOGIST WALLACE AS HE TOOK OFF HIS BLACK HORN-RIMMED GLASSES AND CLEANED THE LENSES ON HIS TIE.

"WELL, LEN BRASHER GOT INTO AN ARGUMENT WITH ONE OF THE MEN. I THINK IT WAS RICK PAINTER, BUT IT COULD HAVE BEEN SEAN NOEL, HE FILLED-IN SOMETIMES WHEN WE WERE MISSING THE OPTIMUM NUMBER FOR THE POKER PARTIES.

"WELL, YOU KNOW HOW POKER ARGUMENTS CAN BE—WHY, THEY CAN JUST BREAK-UP THE ENTIRE EVENING. GOODNESS KNOWS IT'S HARD ENOUGH TO KEEP A POKER GROUP TOGETHER, BUT WHEN THERE GETS TO BE ANTAGONISM, THEN IT'S ALL OVER. YOU MIGHT AS WELL GIVE IT UP RIGHT THEN AND THERE."

"YES, THAT'S PROBABLY TRUE. BUT WHAT HAPPENED THEN?"

"SO, LEN MAKES THIS BIG TO DO ABOUT RICK OR SEAN OR SOMEBODY. NOW THAT I THINK OF IT, I DO THINK IT WAS SEAN. BUT ANYWAY, RIGHT AT THE CRITICAL MOMENT, MY HUSBAND RUNS AWAY FROM THE TABLE

AND DISAPPEARS, RIGHT? NOBODY KNOWS WHERE HE WENT, EXCEPT THAT MAYBE HE HAD TO GO TO THE JOHN REAL QUICK. YOU KNOW WHAT I MEAN? SO, ALL OF A SUDDEN HE'S BACK AND HE'S CARRIN' LITTLE RICO OVER HIS HEAD, YELLING, 'HA HA,' HE WAS YELLING, YOU KNOW IT MAKES ME SMILE AT THE, 'HA. HA.' I SPLIT MY SIDES JUST TO RECALL IT, 'HA HA,' HE WAS YELLING, 'LONG LIVE THE PRESIDENT, THIS BOY'S THE NEW PRESIDENT OF THESE UNITED STATES. LET HIM SETTLE THE DISPUTE!' AND HE RAN AROUND THE ROOM WITH LITTLE RICO SEVERAL TIMES AND THEN PUT HIM DOWN IN FRONT OF EVERYONE ELSE AT THE POKER TABLE. AND RICO, 'HA HA HA,' HE TURNS TO SEAN AND HE—OH IT WAS SO FUNNY, IT WAS LIKE IT HAD BEEN REHEARSED OR SOMETHING, IT WAS THAT GOOD. RICO TURNED TO SEAN AND LOOKED UP AT SEAN, THEN HE JUMPED INTO SEAN'S LAP AND WET HIS PANTS. IMMEDIATELY, RICO STARTED CRYING. IT WAS SO FUNNY.

"HA HA HA HA, YOU SHOULD HAVE SEEN SEAN JUMP. HE GAVE A YELL THAT YOU COULD HEAR ACROSS THE COUNTY. IT WAS SO FUNNY. THE ARGUMENT ENDED JUST LIKE THAT! OF COURSE, SEAN HAD TO GO TO THE BATHROOM AND WASH HIMSELF THOROUGHLY. HE WAS ALWAYS SENSITIVE ABOUT GERMS. IT WAS SO FUNNY.

"YES, MY REX WAS QUITE A MAN."

"WHAT ABOUT THE BOY?"ASKED AGENT WALLACE, LEANING FORWARD.

"HUH?"

"WHAT HAPPENED TO RICO?"

"WHAT DO YOU MEAN WHAT *HAPPENED* TO RICO?"

"I MEAN, WHAT HAPPENED TO RICO DURING ALL OF THIS?" AGENT WALLACE TOOK OFF HIS GLASSES TO LOOK AT JACKIE.

I was sick. I had never really been very sick before. I wasn't used to it. I felt as if I were going to die. The only thing I remember was his hand. Father stayed with me all through the night, just sitting there. And whenever I woke up, he was right there and would move his hand to stroke my head. When he did this, I would grab it and go back to sleep.

The strength of that hand gave me the power to open the door after I knocked, and walk right in.

"Oh, hello Rico," said Virginia's mother.

"Good evening," I replied, nodding my head. "Is Virginia ready yet?"

"I'll go and see. Why don't you sit yourself down in the front room while I call her?"

I generally hated to go in the front room because that meant that I had to talk with her father, and I hated those little encounters when he would sit there and mock and laugh at me. I would have to sit there because if I did what I thought was appropriate (that is what I wanted to do, namely to hit him in the mouth and then run home), I'd be forbidden from seeing Virginia ever again. I didn't want to risk that.

"Yes, thank you," I replied to Virginia's mother (and for once I really meant it). On this night I didn't mind seeing her father. In fact, I rather looked forward to the encounter. Somehow, something was different. I couldn't really tell exactly what it was. Maybe it was the rented tux or something, but anyhow I felt more confident and full of strength. This was a feeling that I had only known previously in my dreams.

I moved into the courtroom (I mean the front room), and greeted Virginia's father who had extended his hand to me. "How do you do, Rico?" he said.

"Pretty chipper, and yourself?" I ventured, though I had never asked him before how he was. I had simply answered the salutation and seated myself.

"Not bad, thank you," was his reply. He was smiling.

We sat on the brown leather sofa. He was in his white-collar work clothes, but he had taken off the tie. His white shirt was wrinkled. There was a pause and I decided to be the next to talk, "You look like you're getting a tan already," I said, as he did have a slight darkening or maybe it was just a reddening of the skin.

"Thank you," he replied. "I did play a little golf yesterday."

"Yes, it is a pretty nice spring now that the 'monsoon' season is over." I didn't know what I was saying. Usually our conversations were characterized by long embarrassing silences that bothered me to the point of frenzy at times. *I* knew that *he* knew that *I* hated these pauses. Sometimes I could even detect a slight smirk just when I was finding the silence unbearable because *he* knew and *I* knew that *he* knew that I couldn't stand it. But not today. He was wearing a light green sports coat and I was wearing a blazing blue tux that emanated its freshness.

"You have to be careful. Put on the *Sea and Ski* for protection. Because it's sunny days like this that one can become badly burned."

I nodded. "Yes, I suppose that's true."

"Yes, that's true," he replied. "But I think my skin is pretty tough."

I nodded my head, but then leaned forward. "You never can tell, though. I have an uncle who usually gets tanner than an African but when he was out the other day, he got quite a little burn on his nose."

"His nose?" He asked.

"Yes, his nose of all places. He got burned on his nose. It was the oddest thing because he usually never gets burned. Instead, he tans darker than an African."

"Well, that's something all right."

"You might watch out for you own protection. A burn can be very painful," I put in.

He didn't answer but only gave an ironic little chuckle, the kind that he thinks will always bring me to a complete silence, but somehow it didn't seem to bother me.

Instead, I continued, "I noticed that your lawn has quite a lot of thatch on it. Do you plan to rake it?"

"Hadn't really noticed," he replied, trying to make me think he didn't care, but I knew better. I was only getting warmed-up when Virginia came into the room. She was there: bright and full of life.

Virginia stood delicate in every detail. It would have been enough just to sit there and gaze upon her. That would have been enough for a night. There, in front of me, she stood. I approached. I brought out the orchid corsage. Her father jumped out of his chair so *he* could pin it on.

Then we were out the door. She took my arm as I walked her to my uncle's car.

"I guess I'll take Patricini," said the older boy.

I ran over and stood behind him. I was the first-picked for the gym sports team. I had never been picked *first* before. I didn't know what to do except pound my fist into my mitt and start offering advice to my captain as to who to pick next. He picked Johnny Handle.

"Oh, why did you pick *him*?" I asked. "He's no good."

"Aw, shut up," said Richard.

"No," I said.

"You're no better," he said.

"Then why did he pick me first?" I replied.

By now our captain had finished picking our team. "Because the other captain was picking the lousy guys first, so that they wouldn't feel bad. I wanted to follow suit," Richard said.

"Oh, sure," I said.

"That's right," said Richard. "Just ask your captain."

I turned around and asked the captain, "Is that true?"

"Is what true?" he replied.

"Is it true that you were only picking the lousy guys first?"

"No, of course not. You'll play right field. We're up first. You're eighth in the batting order."

When he got home, he put the pitcher on the table. He had made that pitcher when he had gone to college. It was one of his few heirlooms. But over time the pitcher had sustained several surface cracks in the enamel. These had occurred because he had not been careful enough with the basic structure of the artifact. It was flawed from within due to inadequate preparation.

*However, now he looked at the pitcher with admiration. The blackness of its sides exuded to him an otherworldliness. The pitcher was his soul. He would never **be** a president of anything. No, instead he would be the pitcher with the surface cracks that indicated an internal flaw.*

Rico picked up the afternoon newspaper and read about President Kennedy's talk to the Steel Workers' Union in Tampa, Florida on the 18th of November. The President said that everything was moving well for the steelworkers and for the unemployment rate, in general. But things weren't working out for Rico. He had lost his last job. If something didn't come up quickly, he'd be thrown out of his apartment. The general unemployment rate isn't worth much when you are unemployed.

Uncle Adam parked the car in the church parking lot. I got out and opened my mother's door. The Protestant Church reminded me of school. People picked up their Bibles during the sermon as if they were textbooks. I longed for the ceremony of the Catholic Church. I was never much for school, so I got up and sat down on cue, just like saying the Pledge of Allegiance.

"AMEN."

I lifted my head with everybody else and looked into the bulletin to see what was next even though I knew that it would be a song. Uncle Adam had a terrible voice and sang very softly. I hated it when he came to church, but as he wasn't there very often, I felt that I could be a little charitable. We all stood up to sing:

Faith of our fathers, holy faith
We will be true to thee till death.

I wasn't really a good dancer. In fact, I had never been to a dance before the prom so I didn't exactly know what to do. But I had seen tv shows like 'American Bandstand' and had watched the people dancing. It didn't look too difficult but, nevertheless, for the next few weeks, I tuned in on Saturday mornings to the rock-and-roll shows and when no one was watching I would try and dance like they were doing on the television. Now, I hadn't actually asked Virginia yet to the prom, but it didn't hurt to get myself somewhat in the swing of things. In fact, I didn't know how I could expect Virginia to actually go with me if I hadn't really been to a dance before. I mean, what would happen if I went out onto the dance floor and made a fool out of myself? I might start dancing the wrong dance to the music and everyone would kinda look over at me and then one couple would actually stop dancing and bend over to stare at me. And then another couple would do the same. And pretty soon everyone on the dance floor would have stopped dancing and would be staring, pointing, and laughing so hard that they could hardly stand it. I would become a bump in the floor: a defect that everyone would avoid.

The deacon began, "I am obliged to announce the marriage banns of Bart

BLACK ROBES

"Why do I wear blue and Dianne wears pink?"

"Well," began Father, "that's because boys wear blue and girls wear pink. 'Blue' is the color for a man."

"But why does mommy wear green?"

My father scrunched up his face. "I don't know—why don't you ask your mother?"

In front of him was the black pitcher. Rico was still tired from lack of sleep, but the sight of the pitcher made him stop and almost reverently genuflect and stare at it. Part of the newspaper he had been reading had curled up on the table and blocked part of the pitcher's visual presentation. This bothered Rico. Then one of the nuns stopped and asked if anything was wrong. It had been a long time since I'd been in a Catholic Church. I didn't want them to tell me to leave. I so longed to return. I said nothing was wrong and I moved into a pew and picked up a prayer missal. I looked at the high altar and a tall wooden crucifix hanging behind from a chain attached to the ceiling.

One day I asked Di to dance with me so that I could have practice dancing. I couldn't ask Virginia because then she'd know that I couldn't dance. My mother and Uncle Adam were out together so that left Dianne and me alone. She once had said that she was willing to dance with me. She had been to dances before so she knew more about it than I did. Anyway, we were sitting and listening to the boob-tube when I mentioned that the song playing was a real favorite of mine and why didn't we dance to it.

"I don't feel like it," she said.

"Oh c'mon," I said, standing up from the sofa. "It's a real cool song."

"But that's silly; dancing in front of the television? Who does that?"

"All we're doing is dancing to some music." I began some dancing motions.

"Well," she began. "Ok." The song was almost over.

"C'mon," I said. "They're bringing on the Everly Brothers."

My sister slowly got up. She really liked the Everly Brothers. The song began. Dianne cleared her throat and shook her head as if she was awakened from sleep. "Ok."

We started dancing separately. Then I took her hand and put my arm around her waist. Her eyes got bigger, incredulous. I thought she would shout out "Cestin!" Then I stepped on her bare foot with my slipper.

We stopped.

"What are you doing?" I asked.

"What do you mean?" was Dianne's reply.

"You're supposed to follow my lead."

"Well, I would if you didn't change what you're doing all the time."

"The partner has to be flexible. You should move like this." And I showed her.

"C'mon, the record's almost over," Dianne said.

We continued dancing through the next song a little more smoothly, though I could tell that she was a little stiff. It was as if she were watching my feet so that she wouldn't be stepped on again.

The next dance was a slow dance. I was about to say that maybe we'd had enough and that maybe it would be ok to stop when she put her arms around my neck and looked up and smiled. I froze.

She took the lead and brought my arms down and around her waist.

A strange sensation came over me for an instant as I looked into her eyes. "Should I kiss her?" I thought. "I want to, but still, is it the right moment?"

I looked into Virginia's eyes on the dance floor. "No, maybe I'd better wait until later. Yes, there's plenty of time for all of that. Yes, plenty of time." I felt confirmed in my thinking. But yet, what if she's expecting a kiss and I don't give it to her? Then she'll think I'm some kind of social retard, still wet behind the ears. I've got to show her I'm not green. I looked at Virginia; she was facing me.

"It was a nice movie," I commented.

"Yes," she replied, almost blankly.

Then I moved to her. I brought my hand behind *the butt of the gun to place it securely against his shoulder. He sighted into the place where the cars were supposed to arrive. Then the first cars were in sight—and then all of them. Rico held* her tightly as my lips pressed against hers. I felt the tightness of my lips against the softness—almost sponginess of her lips. Then I began to relax my lips, but she simply began caressing my lips lightly with her lips, back and forth so that I grabbed her again tightly and pressed her body against mine.

Virginia's lips, which had been so soft, now took on a new firmness as she pushed lightly upward, coaxing my mouth open ever so gently, so that I might feel the wetness of her tongue carefully outlining those lips, which just moments before had been fully engaged in empty conversation.

"You know, you are very strong," said Di, as she smiled up at me.

I never liked the way she smiled—Why had she played with those pans? It was at that moment that I knew that something must be wrong. I ran upstairs. I opened the door and went inside. My mother looked upset. Mother's eyes were red. She was sitting on my bed.

"You must be tired," I said.

"I'm not tired," she said softly. It was a voice that I had never heard her use. I had never seen my mother cry before. Her eyes were red where they should have been white.

"But your skin is so flushed," I replied.

My mother grimaced, closed her eyes momentarily, and then she put her arms around my neck and moaned.

"I think I want to dance some more," said Dianne. I didn't understand what she was doing. Why was she acting like this? I didn't want to slow dance with her, I didn't understand why Mr. Souposey was so friendly to me when I went home. I cut across his backyard and he didn't even yell like he always used to.

For a moment, Rico froze. I didn't know what to say to her.

"C'mon Rico," Dianne coaxed, but my legs were firmly planted to the floor. Suddenly I got the urge to go to the bathroom, but my mother couldn't let go of me. She was hugging me so tightly and crying.

"I want to sit this one out," I said to Dianne.

"But I really like this one. C'mon, Rico."

"I don't want to," I said, as I tried to pull myself away.

"Rico."

I tried to pull away with no success until I gave one furious attempt to free myself and only succeeded in pulling both my sister and me onto the couch with her on top of me. Her hair was messed up and her skirt was hiked up above her hips.

I felt so confused. Then she grabbed my head so that I was looking right at her. "Kiss me, silly," she said.

I kissed her.

"That's better," she said as she said as she opened my mouth with her lips and began stroking my chest. Then she stopped and slid out of her sweater, which dropped noiselessly to the floor. She continued to undress us until it was over. *When it was over, he wasn't sure what had really happened.*

"Well, you know what you just did?" She gave me that innocent look of hers. Those eyes of hers that could hide anything, no matter what mischief she got into. But I didn't have any time. I had to go to the bathroom! Mother was sobbing. "Your father, my Rex, your father your father..."

"Are you hurt?" asked Mr. Souposey with a smile. I had never seen Mr. Souposey this way

A MAN CAN! A MAN CAN! A MAN CAN DO...

Virginia's lips were so soft and gentle. I began to feel the contours of her lips—that is, the geography of the skin surface and under her tongue, again made everything smooth yet charged with energy.

"C'mon Rico, relax," said Cindy with a faint smile. There was still a little ice cream on the top of her lips.

I felt at ease, but yet when I saw her green sweater on the floor and her taking her pants off. QUITE A POSITION, QUITE A POSITION, QUITE A POSITION, EH?

"Virginia," I said in a thick voice. She continued to kiss me. My neck tingled as her skin rubbed easily against mine.

"Oh Virginia, Oh Virginia, you know I—" I stumbled. "You know I love you, Virginia. Oh, I do. I love you."

Uncle Adam stopped hugging Mommy when he saw me coming out of the bathroom. His breath smelled funny, like he had just taken some cough syrup.

"I want to talk to you about your father, boy."

"Oh, Rico," she said, leaning forward so that her body pushed me down. We slid on the seat so that she came to rest over me and I looked up and *he pulled the trigger.*

"Rico, my boy," she began, but I looked the other way. "Rico, look at me, I have something to tell you."

I didn't want to listen.

"Don't turn your head away," she said. But how could I not? Her sweater was so green. *He told himself he must be calm or the shots would go astray. This was his last moment. There would have to be some purpose to his existence.*

She kissed me and gently played with my shirt. Then she lifted her head slightly and said, "I love you too, Rico. I love you." Then our bodies drew together tightly and I felt a powerful surge of strength within me.

"Rico," he said, as he grabbed my shoulders in his hands and turned me around so that I was facing Mr. Souposey, the man who had kept such a tight control over his grass that we all had to go the long way to school. This was the man who used to slap his own son in the head and scream at him in front of the neighborhood. This same Mr. Souposey was now talking calmly to me, "Rico, you need to go home now. It's about your father. Your father has had a heart attack. Your mother called on the neighborhood phone tree. I just heard." Then he stumbled with his words and stopped. He turned away. "You should go home now."

And then everything was calm. The funeral parlor that Father was taken to was a white building with pillars in front of it. I thought that it reminded me of a postcard that my father had bought me once of the White House: 1600 Pennsylvania Avenue, Washington, D.C. The White House was the home of the President of the United States.

As we were getting ready to go to the funeral, Uncle Adam came into my room with a pair of black pants and a black coat. "I've brought these for you to wear," he said.

"But I don't want to wear those clothes. They're not mine," I said.

"You don't have any black clothes. I rented these at a store. It's proper to wear *black* at a funeral."

"But I want to wear my summer coat, the one Daddy gave me."

"You can't wear light colors at a funeral. It isn't respectful. Now you put these on. I don't want any more discussion about it." Uncle Adam talked as if he were a machine. Then he quickly walked out, shutting the door behind him. I took off my pants and began getting dressed when suddenly I got the urge to look at my old coins. I opened the bottom drawer of my dresser and took out my coin box that I kept hidden there. The key was secretly inside my old stuffed chair.

Inside the box were all the coins that my father had given me, but the coin I liked the most was a shiny new steel penny from 1943, the year I was born. The coin was sealed in a small plastic container so that the air wouldn't tarnish it. There was strength in Lincoln's gray-metallic portrait. I held the coin container tightly so that it began to warm in my hand. I wondered how a man got to be as great a president as Lincoln was.

A MAN CAN BE ANYTHING

I tried to imagine what it would be like to be President and live in the white-pillared house.

The men in the dark coats lifted the box where my father was lying and walked out, carrying it at the level of their waists. Why didn't they hoist it high over their heads?

I felt sad that they would take him from the spotless white funeral parlor where everything was so peaceful to the cemetery. I wondered why we didn't go to our church: *Our Lady of Victory: Roman Catholic Church*? I supposed that was because only Father and I were Catholics. I didn't know about Dianne.

At the cemetery, they lowered him down into the ground with three ropes manned by six strong blank-faced drones— all dressed *appropriately* in black. But none of them knew Father. The head funeral parlor employee was mumbling platitudes. I kept thinking, "why is he there?" He's no priest. He isn't even a nun. I wanted Father properly buried.

The funeral parlor was within sight of the cemetery. This meant that I could count the edges on the pillars in front of the building instead of listening to the mortician guy read his script. Unfortunately, some of the pillars were blocked from my view by some trees in the cemetery.

BLESSED BE THE FRUIT OF THY WOMB, JESUS.
HOLY MARY, MOTHER OF GOD, PRAY FOR US
SINNERS
NOW AND AT THE HOUR OF OUR DEATH

The answer I think is six. I tried my best to estimate the number of pillars.

I looked at the box; it was light mahogany that seemed slightly flawed in several areas. It had a dull finish. My father and I made the box from scratch. It was my most precious possession. Objectively, the box had nothing particular about it that would bring it to my attention except its light-colored wood and the flaws in our construction. These flaws were not clearly visible. The blue handle grips on the side of the box seemed as if they might break under the stress, but they didn't.

"WELL, HIS FATHER DID DIE WHEN HE WAS YOUNG. BUT I DON'T THINK THAT THAT HAD ANY EXTRA-ORDINARY EFFECTS, AS YOU CALL THEM. AFTER ALL, HE DID HAVE HIS UNCLE TO LOOK AFTER HIM—AND HIS UNCLE WAS NO STRANGER IN THE HOUSE."

The cathedral was empty. I couldn't concentrate on my purpose as I looked about me, into the vast empty space. I wondered how many people came into the cathedral during a day. Then, another lady came in and sat near the front of the church. That didn't bother me since it was a big space. I wanted desperately to become lost in the vastness of it all, not to evaporate but to become merely a part of some infinite whole. I was searching for some large community

TO SEARCH FOR PURPOSE IN ORDERED TIME

I felt alone. I wanted/desired something. But nothing happened. The ego was too strong; it could see too much. I was lost, and I needed salvation.

Vainly, I wished for a miracle. Then two sisters passed me and I caught a glimpse of a plain wedding band on their hands.

TO BE MARRIED TO THE SPIRIT; TO BE SUBSUMED UNDER A FINAL CAUSE

The ring was a part of the furniture. It was nothing, in and of itself. It derived its value extrinsically. Like a scene in a movie: everything had its place in order to produce the proper effect. It was like a well-made ceramic pot. The construction had a lot to do with its impact: line, thickness, glaze—they all were important.

Sometimes Rico would sit for hours watching the morning come-to-be. He sat next to his black pitcher. There was no purpose to it all. He was fixated upon becoming; the next stage in the drama of life.

BEAUTY WAS TAKING ITS LAST CHANCE TO EXERCISE ITS POWER OVER ME, TO BLIND ME. . . KASHIWAGI WAS RIGHT WHEN HESAID THAT WHAT CHANGED THE WORLD WAS NOT ACTION BUT KNOWLEDGE.

The Temple of the Golden Pavilion, *was one of the few texts that Rico carried around with him. He now looked at the book that was on the cardboard box that acted as his bedside table. His bed was a simple mattress that he had found on the street and carried to his Dallas abode. He bought his sheets and a mattress pad at the local Goodwill.*

Now he watched a brightly colored beetle mount his bedside table and climb upon the red-colored cover of Mishima's novel. Just before Rico became cognizant of the intruder's presence, he turned his gaze to the book that resonated with his own life. When he noticed the insect, he was not inclined to kill it or shoo it away. Rather, he wanted to be mindful of the other living entity in the room.

"WELL, YOU SEE, IT'S LIKE THIS, MRS. PATRICINI. HE WAS MIXED-UP WITH SOMETHING IN DALLAS, AND THOUGH, LIKE YOU SO APTLY MENTION, HE WASN'T CONVICTED OF ANYTHING, WE HAVE REASON TO BELIEVE THAT HE WAS INVOLVED IN THE RAPE OF A NINETEEN-YEAR-OLD GIRL.

"IT SEEMS THAT HE WAS SEEN ON OR AT THE SCENE OF THE CRIME, BY A WITNESS." THE F.B.I. INTERROGATOR, WALLACE, LIT A CIGARETTE. TODAY, FRIEDMAN, THE TOUGH COP, WASN'T PRESENT.

"IF HE WAS SO GUILTY, THEN WHY DIDN'T THEY CATCH HIM AND TRY HIM IN A COURT OF LAW?"

"WELL, I DON'T HAVE ALL THE PARTICULARS OF *THAT* CASE RIGHT HERE, BUT POLICE HAVE TO BE CAREFUL IN INVESTIGATING CRIMES IN CERTAINS PARTS OF THE CITY—IF YOU KNOW WHAT I MEAN."

"RICO NEVER FIRED A GUN IN HIS LIFE," SAID JACKIE.

"WELL, MA'AM, THEY HAD NO WAY TO KNOW THAT.

"WHAT PROOF DO THEY HAVE THAT IT WAS RICO?"

"THE VICTIM DESCRIBED HIM ACCURATELY AND IDENTIFIED HIM IN A PHOTO DISPLAY. THUS, RICO WAS POSITIVELY IDENTIFIED."

"COULDN'T THERE HAVE BEEN SOME MISTAKE?"

"OF COURSE. NONE OF OUR PROCEDURES ARE COMPLETELY FOOL-PROOF, BUT WE USUALLY CONSIDER THAT POSITIVE IDENTIFICATION BY THE VICTIM CONSTITUTES A VERY STRONG ALLEGATION."

Just moments before the shot, Rico braced himself again. The timing would be critical. The rifle seemed heavy in his hands. Everything should be fine. It was just like the practice sessions he had taken at the abandoned rail yard. He just needed to control his breathing and focus his thoughts. The first cars of the motorcade were in sight. Then he saw the President. BANG. He heard another shot. It was a trigger for him to act immediately.

I was taking out the trash. I saw my father. I went outside so that Uncle Adam or Mom wouldn't see me. I pulled out the paper. It was the obituary of Rex Patricini. They had a picture and four lines: **Rex Patricini was a local businessman and president of the Seattle Rotary Club for the past five years. Patricini is survived by his wife, Jocasta, and his two children, Rico and Dianne. He will be interred at the Johnson Funeral Home on Thursday.**

I would not let *this* be in the trash. I used my hands to rip the obit out of the newspaper—leaving margins at the edges that I'd later trim, eventually putting the article in a sealed plastic holder that I kept with me always.

"It certainly is a nice night," I said.

"Yes," replied Virginia.

"The band is supposed to be quite good."

"That's what I hear." We got into Uncle Adam's car. I drove down the streets that were so familiar to me, following the two intersecting beams of car's headlight that were leading me to my destination.

"Did you hear that Billy was chosen as a graduation speaker?" she asked as we left the neighborhood.

"Oh really?" I replied. I hadn't heard that so I paused and then asked, "Who is the other speaker?"

"I think it's Linda Hoftsmeister," was Virginia's response.

"Oh really? I think she's a creep."

"So do I," said Virginia, as she began preening her hair. "Have you seen the clothes she wears? So out of style! She has no taste in anything. She's such a loser." Virginia paused as we stopped at a red light. Then she said, "You have to admit that she has a brain, but I don't find that really attractive in a woman." Virginia turned her head toward me. "Do you know what I mean? A woman trying to be a man?"

I didn't have a ready response, but then said, "Yeah, what a creep."

"In spades," added Virginia.

Sometimes the men at St. Anne's used to sing when they were pulling weeds. Father would take me there occasionally in the spring for a work day. Father Weal had a beautiful voice. All the parish men and their sons had such a good time when Father Weal would begin a song. And it wasn't always a Christian song, either. Sometimes we would sing the folk songs of Pete Seeger.

Though our group was small, we could produce stirring music together. Whenever the group started singing, we would work even harder. We sang and worked in unison.

Bill and I started walking to the University of Washington bookstore. "What are you taking this term?" I asked Bill.

"Two chem courses and differential calculus."

"Sounds tough," I said.

"Well, the chem labs are a bitch, but lectures are copasetic—besides I know where I can buy the full lecture notes so that I don't even have to show up, if I don't want to."

"No way!" I said.

"Oh, yes. I just have to turn over a 'Ulysses S. Grant' to Alpha-Alpha-Omega and they give me a full set copied by one of those new Xerox machines."

"I've heard about them. There's one in the U-District, right?"

"Yes, I'll take you there sometime. It's an amazing machine."

We walked a little further when I asked, "How did Alpha-Alpha-Omega get these lecture notes?"

"Oh, it's standard fare for all the large lecture courses. They get one of their best to take notes or tape the lecture with a hidden mike. At $50 a pop, if they only sell to 20 out of the 150 in the class, they've made a grand! Not bad, eh?"

"That's sure a lot of money. You could almost pay tuition plus room and board for a year with that kind of dough."

"Yeah. They know how to do it at Alpha-Alpha-Omega. I've got them as my permanent rest stop on the way to medical school."

"Medical school?"

"That's where I'm headed—just like my dad."

I nodded. "Just like my dad," I thought, "And I'd be in the ground: six feet under."

There was a sharp grounder to second that hit a little stone or mound of dirt and bounced up over my glove, but I was square in front of it so that it hit me in the chest and fell down in front of me. I was able to pick it up with my bare hand and throw the runner out at first. The next guy up, Garret Wilson, walked. There was now a runner on first with one out. Then Tommy Smith hit a grounder to short. I went to cover second for the possible double-play. Garret wanted to break-up the double play by running outside the base path (illegal) to tumble me as I was throwing to first. I made the throw two steps over second when Garret undercut me (also illegal). I came down on Garret, with my knee striking his throat. Then there was pandemonium.

Garret was shaken up badly and his mother rushed down to the field and was telling everybody what to do as if she were a chief surgeon in a hospital performing some historic operation or something, but they got him up and into his mother's car.

The other coach went to the umpire and said I should be thrown out of the game. My coach decided to bench me even though Garret broke the rules and I could have been the one hurt by *his* rule-breaking behavior.

I took a seat at the end of our bench. It was the first double play I'd turned since making the Little League team. Because a couple guys hadn't showed up, I was all by myself at the end of the bench.

I had to park at the end of the parking lot—quite away from the door. But there were no mud puddles or anything so I figured it was all right. Virginia and I got to the dance about a half hour after the time that was printed on the tickets as my uncle had suggested, but it seemed as if everyone had already arrived.

THE WHEEL STARTED TO TURN

We went inside and Virginia checked our coats and then took my arm to the entrance to the ballroom. It was kind of hard for me to get extremely enchanted with a 'clubhouse at a golf course' for a dance, but everyone had thought it was a good idea. Uncle Adam really let out a belly laugh when I told him that the dance was to be held at a country club. He made a lot of smart little jokes about renting a caddy or bringing Virginia some golf tees for her corsage, but I had taken it all quite well.

My opinions were formed when we got to the entrance to the ballroom: dim lights, tables with white linen cloth atop, and a large wooden dance floor. The lighting on the floor was accented with pastel gels in some of the ceiling lights. Couples were dancing. Couples were sitting at tables enjoying snacks. It was a mellow atmosphere. I felt relaxed.

Then I was confronted by a tall, old white-haired man in a black tux. He had a very severe look on his face. He reminded me of an FBI man. He wanted to see our tickets. I fumbled for the tickets in my pocket, but they weren't there! I rushed through my mind at where I could have left them. Was it at the restaurant? No, that couldn't be. I would have recognized their presence or absence. Maybe I left them in the car? Maybe they were still at home? I'd have to go out to the car. But what would become of Virginia? What a disaster! Why did this have to happen tonight of all nights? I would have tried my coat pockets, but they were sewn shut.

I turned to go back to the car and ran into Virginia.

"What's the matter?" she asked.

"The tickets. I must have left them in the car."

She put her hand on my shoulder, stopping me.

"Oh, you silly, I've got the tickets. You gave them to me, remember?"

Obviously, I didn't remember. I tried to smile as she handed the tickets to the FBI mannequin.

"All right, let's get 'em," I yelled. The ball was hit sharply to third, I ran over to cover second, but they had the guy on third in a rundown. The pitcher eventually tagged the guy out. There was one out. I started to chatter, "Ok, let's go Rick. Let's go. Put it right in there; you've got it Rick, babe. You've got it big fella, c'mon big boy let's go—"

The ball was hit sharply to my right. We needed a double play so I moved to my right.

ALWAYS KEEP DOWN ON THE BALL SO YOU DON'T MISS IT

The ball took a small hop so that when I got there the ball hit my glove and bounced up in the air just as my knee collapsed. I rolled onto the ground and tried to recover, but it was too late. The first baseman scrambled for the ball to mitigate the disaster: runners on second and third with one out, E-4, the second baseman. That episode might be responsible for us losing the game.

Everyone was excited as we went up to bat in the bottom of the eighth down by a run. Richard led off and struck out, then Arne doubled. There was a pause in the action as the other team changed pitchers. When he was ready the umpire called time and walked over to our coach, asking for a batter.

"Get up there Patricinio; get a little rap," said the coach.

I got up and looked for a bat.

I heard the rest of the guys saying, "Oh no, Rico's up. That looks like out number two."

"Why don't they let Frankie hit?"

"He's no better than Rico."

"And Frankie can't field."

"Did you forget Rico's error?"

The coach let me hit.

The first pitch was a strike. I didn't swing. The pitcher was laughing at me—and why not? My own team gave him the idea that I was a sure out.

The next pitch was so outside that it went wide of the backstop. Arne took third. Then the pitcher threw the next one in the dirt. The smirk was off his face. He was bearing down. I watched the ball leave his hand.

THE POTTERY WHEEL WAS SPINNING FURIOUSLY

"Now, you know I've talked about this with you before," said Father. They were in the kitchen. Dianne and I were supposed to be upstairs in our rooms.

"We cannot afford to continue to be overdrawn on our monthly statements like this." I didn't like these 'bad Jackie' talks, but Di and I were positioned at the top of the stairs so that we could hear every word.

"But you can make it up tomorrow. It's not the end of the month. I had to buy a dress and I figured that you could put the money in before they cashed the check."

"You know that's very poor economy. It isn't sound. Why, if I had abided by those principles in my work, I'd be fired."

"But it was just one dress."

"What was so special about *that* dress? Don't you have enough clothes?"

"But I don't see why—"

"You don't see? We don't have that kind of money to just throw it around."

"It was only twenty dollars."

"And what was the other five dollars for?"

"I wanted to buy a belt to go with it."

"You see? That's just my point: we don't need those things. We have enough. We must make do. It doesn't hurt to be frugal, you know."

"But you make over thirty thousand a year."

"And I wouldn't have a penny of it left if you did what you pleased with it. Besides, you don't know how much I make."

"I have a good idea; Cindy Peterson—"

"Cindy Peterson, bah, what does she know? She's just a bag of hot air."

"She is not."

"She didn't know 'up' from 'down' when she gave you that figure." We could hear pounding of feet on the linoleum kitchen floor. We often heard this pattern as if they were stalking each other.

"Anyway, it doesn't make a difference. What's important is that you stop spending money like we were Rockefellers."

My mother didn't respond right away, but then she said, "Of course not. I know that, but then *you're* not as well dressed as I am either. You just wear your clothes out until they fall apart. You're not fashionable. Well, I care about what people think about me."

"You care more about that than our family's financial situation? Do you want to drive me to the poor farm?"

"Rex, they don't have poor farms anymore."

"No, they might not, but that still doesn't deter the thousands who die every day in gutters and hospitals that smell like gutters. All over spending beyond one's means. It can ruin you. It ruined my brother."

"That's because your brother is an idiot—not like my Adam."

"Screw your Adam."

Then there was another long silence. My mother started to walk out of the kitchen. We could hear by the sounds of her shoes. Then she stopped and said, "Your principles are based upon tight miserliness. Your guidelines are all wrong, and I will not follow them."

"Well, go ahead and do what you want, but just remember who brings in the money around here."

"And what's that supposed to mean?" asked my mother in a different voice than before.

"I'll let you figure that one out."

Then Mother walked upstairs to their bedroom and slammed the door behind her.

I didn't follow her.

I SAT DOWN NEXT TO SOME FRIENDS OF VIRGINIA'S SO THAT SHE WOULD BE COMFORTABLE. I WANTED TO GET UP AND DANCE RIGHT AWAY SO THAT I COULD SEE HOW IT FELT TO HAVE ALL THOSE COLORED LIGHTS TURNING AT ME AS THE MELLOW MUSIC PLAYED ON. INSTEAD, I SAT DOWN AND DIDN'T KNOW EXACTLY WHAT THEY WERE TALKING ABOUT BECAUSE MY INTEREST WAS ELSEWHERE. THERE WAS NOTHING BUT

THE ENCHANTED DANCE FLOOR AND MYSELF.
The next pitch was a ball, putting the count at three and one. I
stepped out of the box and picked up some dirt and rubbed it
between the palms of my hands.

A LIGHT BROWN MAHOGANY TABLE WITH A PITCHER ATOP

"RICO PATRICINI AND VIRGINIA
WITHERSPOON," THE MAN ANNOUNCED. I
FELT EMBARRASSED TO BE CALLED-OUT IN
SUCH A MANNER. THEN, WHEN I LOOKED
OVER AT VIRGINIA, SHE APPARENTLY DIDN'T
SEEM TO MIND AT ALL.

"Hit batsman," yelled the umpire. The pitch had come
in hard and inside. I stepped into it so that I could pull the
ball, but the ball kept coming inside and knocked me in the
head. The next thing I knew I was on the ground, my cloth hat
off my head and in the dirt. I looked up and saw the umpire
standing above me. "Can you hear me, son?" asked the man
in black.

I smiled.

"How many fingers am I holding up?" asked the ump.
There were three. I lifted my arm and showed him three
fingers. Then I saw a shadow come over me. It was the coach.
He had a canteen and gave me a drink of water. I drank the
water and allowed him to get me to my feet.

"Are you well enough to stay in the game?" asked the
coach. I nodded as I allowed him to escort me to first base.

"What are you talking about? Don't be
ridiculous."

Richard and Rollo both told me that she
was planning something like this. But I
didn't want to believe
it. But they just wouldn't believe the coach trusting loser
Rico. It was the bottom of the eighth. The game was on the

line. But now I was on first base. Arne was on third. We were down a run in the bottom of the eighth inning. With one out, I didn't want there to be a double play. My head was ringing. I had to concentrate. The third base coach was giving the signs, but the way my head was, I couldn't follow. I just had to take my lead after the ball left the pitcher's hand. I didn't want a double play. I wanted to do it the right way: I had to get a jump on the ball.

"I don't know what's gotten to you," said Virginia.

"Oh, you don't, do you?" I grabbed her by the sides of her pretty dress and drew her to me. "You've been playing me for a sucker all along, haven't you? Your dumb little puppy, eh? Is that what I am to you?"

"TO COME TO THE TAVERN WHERE YOUR LITTLE BITCH IS? YOU DON'T WANT ME TO MEET HER, DO YOU? AFRAID I'LL TAKE HER AWAY FROM YOU?"

Billy hit the first pitch sharply to left for a single. Arne was off with the crack of the bat. The left fielder was charging fast. He wanted a play at the plate, but he stumbled picking up the ball. However, he had a great arm and threw exactly to the plate. I went to third on the throw. The throw beat Arne, but he ran into the catcher. They both went over as the force of the collision knocked them backwards. The umpire was about to call Arne out, but then the ball started rolling free; the catcher had not maintained control of the ball.

There was confusion. I ran recklessly for home. The pitcher scrambled towards the plate. It was a footrace. The catcher righted himself and searched for the ball. Then he tossed it underhand to the incoming pitcher. I went in head first and beat the tag. We were in the lead.

THE WHEEL STOPPED TURNING. IT WAS THE MOST BEAUTIFUL CERAMIC PIECE I HAD EVER MADE. I KNEW THAT I WOULD COLOR IT BLACK WITH A SEMI-GLOSS FINISH.

Then I felt a pounding in the back of my head. I was slow getting up. But I didn't want to sit on the bench for the beginning of the ninth.

"Shall we dance?" I asked Virginia.

She smiled and got up.

I WATCHED THE SNOWFLAKES FALL SO SLOWLY As I looked up from my place on the ground. I wondered what Mr. Souposey might do to me, and what I would do in response. How could I get away? There seemed to be no way out--so I slapped her arm.

"Why, you little bastard."

"That's not very nice language, Virginia."

"What's gotten into you?"

"You know," I said. "You know very well."

"If you're talking about that stupid dance—"

"I suppose now you're going to tell me that you didn't make any wagers concerning whether you could get me to go to a kegger?"

I TOLD YOU; I DO NOT DRINK: I'M FRUGAL—*though sometimes he left a little Dewar's whiskey in the glass.*

"I don't know what you're talking about," was Virginia's reply.

"Oh, you don't, do you?"

I was face down in the dirt. Then my teammates came over, talking and hollering. I felt an arm lifting me up. I'd just scored the go-ahead run.

"Are you all right, son?" said a voice. "Are you hurt anywhere?"

"No," I said as I was assisted to my feet.

"What do you mean?"

"Rollo told me all about your plan, but I wouldn't believe him. I preferred to believe *you* over *him*. I guess I was mistaken.

Michael Boylan   203

Tonight, you have done everything in your power to persuade me that go to *that very kegger*. Now if that's not proof, I don't know what is."

"Are you sure you're okay? You took quite a slide there; you must be hurt."

"No," I said. "I just want to dance."

"You'll have to excuse us," said Virginia in an apologetic and embarrassed tone. We got up and left the table.

"I don't see why we have to leave so soon," I said. "I want to dance."

Virginia put on her angry face. "These are my friends. I already committed to them. They are my friends, and I'd like to talk with them on the night of my only senior prom."

"You can talk to them later."

"They might not be around later, or they might be otherwise engaged."

"Then don't see them at all."

"I can't see them outside of school. My parents don't like them."

This was my chance. "You never told me about this twist to the evening."

"How could I? My parents —"

"But they're not *my* friends," I returned.

"Well, you could put yourself out for *others* a little, you know."

"Oh, c'mon Virginia. I came to a *dance* not to an *alternate party*. Right now, I want to take you out on the dance floor and show off the moves of the nicest girl at the prom."

"We needs you to cover table three, Rica."

"My name is 'Rico' not 'Rica,'" he replied.

"You want to keep this job, Rica, then get your ass out to table three."

So, we began dancing. I was a bit stiff at first, keeping her a little ways away from me. But as soon as the first song neared completion, I felt an easing of tension. I looked down at Virginia and smiled. Then she hugged me.

"You scored!" yelled Rollo. "Way to go Rico, way to go. This will be it. We'll win this game."

But Billy walked up to WILLIAM BONNAVERT, WHO SAID "LET'S YOU AND I GO TO THE TAVERN EVEN THOUGH THEY—"

"Nice going," said someone else.

Rollo took my arm and helped me up.

"That was really fearless baserunning, son," said the coach. I was being helped over to our bench. I was tired, but I was happy. My head still throbbed.

"Are you okay?" asked Rollo.

"Yeah, I'm fine. I just have a little headache, that's all."

"Well, it's no wonder. First, you get hit in the head by the pitch and

then you slide headfirst into the catcher. That was a gutsy thing to do, but it's the only way you would have scored."

Rollo sat me down on the bench and then put his arm around my shoulders. "Yes, sir, that was some play. You *really* did good out there."

"Thanks," I said.

"Don't thank me. It's *you* who put us ahead." Rollo was all smiles. "If we can only hold that lead in the next inning, we'll be in the playoffs for sure."

We sat on the bench together, and for the first time, I sat near the coach. I looked down at the other end of the bench to the guys who didn't get into the game. They were involved in their own simple pastimes like throwing little stones and seeing who could toss a pebble closest to the fence that separates the bench from the playing field.

This was a big game for the baseball team and these benchwarmers had accepted that the team would lose. At least they wouldn't be a part of it. But contrary to those gloomy assessments, we shut the other team down in the top of the ninth and won the game. We were in the playoffs. And I had something to do with it.

"How are you guys doing?" I asked the bench sitters.

"What's the score?" asked Sam, who everyone called the chocolate banana because of his dark skin and his rather misshapen back.

"The game's over. We won."

Sam nodded and got up to join his father in the wooden bleachers.

I was all alone in the garden with nothing to do except pull weeds. So, I walked over to Father Weal and started picking weeds.

"Rico?" said Father Weal.

"Yes," I replied.

"When you pull weeds, you must pull from the bottom, or else they will grow back very quickly. Let me show you." He grabbed a weed next to the ground and lifted, gently pulling out the roots. "One must go straight to the base and pull easily, and the weed will come readily. But if you try pulling from the top, you will not get the root of the weed, and it will grow back quickly. In order to get the root, one must pull from the base."

I pulled out a weed the way he showed me. It came right out. "You were right," I said. "Thank you, Father."

He smiled and touched my shoulder. We had danced about five dances in a row when Virginia said that she was thirsty and wanted to get something to drink. I wasn't averse to the suggestion, so I told her to find a table and sit down, and I'd get her something.

This time she sat at an empty table and was looking at me as I walked across the room, balancing the glasses.

"I thought you might spill," she said as I set the glasses down.

"Well, it is quite a task there, dodging in and out of traffic with two glasses filled to the brim," I replied, seating myself. "And you didn't help matters any with this corner table."

"But it's so intimate. I thought that's what you wanted?"

"Ah, what devotion she has," I thought to myself. "You've finally recognized my true worth," I mused inwardly as I smiled. Then I spat on the ground. Pulling weeds is such hard work. My back began getting a little sore.

"Hey Rico, how about a little song?" put Father Weal.

"I'd like that," I said.

"There's nothing like a good song to lift your spirits when you feel low and have a lot to do. What shall we sing?"

"I don't know," I said. My mind was blank. I knew, by heart, just about every song that the men used to sing. But right now, my mind was a sieve.

"Do you know 'Oh, you can't get to Heaven'?"

"Yes, I like that," I said.

"Well, I'll sing a verse and we'll sing the refrain together, and then you can sing a verse if you know one."

"All right," I said.

> Verse:
> Oh, you can't get to Heaven
> On roller skates,
> You'll roll right by,
> Those pearly gates.
> [repeat the verse]

Refrain:
Oh, you ain't a going to grieve my Lord no more
[repeat the refrain three times—faster each time]

"Dad, let's go out and have our picture taken in one of those machines."

"What do you mean?" he replied.

"Our pictures. They take your pictures, and it only costs a dollar or something."

BE FRUGAL MY SON

"A dollar, eh?"

"Yes, and you get four pictures, two large and two small."

My father paused. Then he said, "Well, I guess so. Would you like that? So long as they are nice pictures, okay."

"Sure, they're beautiful."

"Yeah, it was beautiful," said Rollo.

"I don't know how you did it, Rico," said Billy as we took the field. We had a one-run lead going into the top of the ninth. The first batter up flied out to center. The next guy up was their big gun. He was one of the best batters in the league: a tall and heavy-set boy. When he connected, the ball often went hundreds of feet away. He swung at the first pitch; it was a high chopper to the right side; the pitcher lunged for it but missed; it was up to me.

CHARGE IT

I charged. The ball was on a high hop. I didn't know whether to take it on that high

hop or wait for it to bounce again. I
hesitated and the second bounce was
funny. The ball hit me in the chin. A pain
shot through my jaw.

FIND THE BALL
YOU CAN STILL GET HIM
GET THE BALL
PICK IT UP AND THROW IT

I looked for the ball, and it was in front
of me. I reached down for the ball and IT
SLIPPED FROM MY HAND, BOUNCING SOFTLY AGAINST THE
WALL. BILLY LUNGED FOR IT, BUT IT FELL IN FOR A HIT. MY
IMAGINARY RUNNER WHO WAS AT THIRD AUTOMATICALLY
SCORED. IT WAS THE FIRST TIME I HAD BEATEN BILLY. WE
NEVER GOT ANY OF THE GOOD WALLS AT SCHOOL, BUT BILLY
WAS ALWAYS SAYING THAT SOMEDAY SOON HE WOULD BE
PLAYING ON THE GOOD WALL IN A BIG MATCH. BUT I DIDN'T
BELIEVE HIM. AFTER ALL, HE WAS ONLY A SECOND GRADER.
BUT HE USED TO SAY, "WAIT AND SEE."

I wristed the ball to the first baseman
to get the slow runner. Two outs. The next
batter swung on the first pitch and hit a
liner to Rollo at shortstop. Rollo lifted his
glove casually and snared it, then pegged it
to first. The game was over.

THE CLAY WAS NOW A SPHERE AS HE PUT HIS HANDS
ON THE TOP TO BEGIN MOLDING THE INSIDES

"Smile," the photographer said. I liked the idea of being
so close to Virginia and having our memory immortalized on
film. She was so soft and sweet smelling. Then I saw my
sister, Di. I said, trying to get her attention,
"Hey Di, I want you here."

Virginia smiled. I smiled. The photographer smiled.
This was a night of smiles. Dianne paid no heed to

me. In school, she pretended that she didn't know me.

"There are sure a lot of people here tonight," I said.

"Quiet, he's going to take another picture. Sit still. I want a framed picture of this. My mother has hers. I want mine," said Virginia.

TALKING TO MISTER SOUPOSEY MADE MY HUNGER RETURN. IN THE DRIVEWAY WAS A BLACK CAR WITH WHITE WHEEL COVERS. I HAD NEVER SEEN A BOXY CAR LIKE THAT BEFORE. STANDING NEXT TO THE BOXY CAR WAS UNCLE ADAM

"Where should we go?" I asked Virginia when we got into the car after the prom.

"I don't know," she replied. "Where do you suggest?"

"We could go to Bridgemans."

"You mean for ice cream?"

"Yes, they have terrific sundaes there."

"I don't know," said Virginia, taking her seat. She looked down to her folded hands and then up to me. "I don't exactly feel in the mood for ice cream, myself. But if that's where your heart is set. Why don't you go by yourself and I'll get a lift to the after-prom party that everyone else is going to."

I didn't like this response. If I let Virginia go off on her own and something happened to her, then I'd be blamed. After all, I took responsibility for her when her father turned her over to me to take her to the prom. I could not show myself to be unworthy of this trust.

"I hear the party is being held in Issaquah," said Virginia. She now leaned forward and stroked my face.

I guess that sealed it. We had to go to the party. I felt very uneasy.

I walked home after the game. Most of the other guys had their parents watching this important game. My mother and Uncle Adam were too busy.

"It's a swell party. Joey Smitherton and most of the kids who live on the eastside are going," said Virginia. "I even have directions written down on a piece of paper. I can be the navigator."

"Really?" I replied.

"Yeah, I thought that it might be fun to go." Virginia smiled.

"I don't think so," was my response.

Virginia changed her expression to a frown, "Why, you're beginning to sound awful silly. There's nothing wrong with the party."

I looked away from Virginia and said, "I just don't think it's a very nice sounding party, and a nice girl wouldn't want to go to a party like that."

"How do you know what kind of a party it is?"

"It doesn't sound too nice, that's all."

"And what does a nice party sound like?" Virginia now had on her game face. She was now determined.

"Listen, why are you so set upon going to this party?" I said as I pulled the car off to the side of the road and parked it on the shoulder.

"All my friends are going to it, and I like to see them and to socialize a little."

"You can do that anytime you want to. Why do you have to do it tonight?" I was now looking directly at her, since we were parked.

"Listen, you can't just simply monopolize me. I'm not your property to do with as you please." Virginia folded her arms in front of her.

"What are you talking about?" I queried while shaking my head.

Virginia lifted her right hand and pointed her index finger at me. "Back at the dance I sat down with a few friends and wanted to talk a little. But *no*, you didn't like that and gave me some big tirade about how a dance was for dancing and that you didn't want to just sit and talk. So, I went along with you. Maybe you didn't want to socialize at the dance. Maybe the dance is a little too formal or something. I don't know. There's no one who knows what goes on inside that pointy head of yours. But if you're going to deny me a little socialization at the dance, then please let me have it at a party afterwards where all my friends will be."

"But it isn't a nice party. They'll be having beer and stuff like that there." I didn't want to go to this party. Why was she doing this to me?

"Well, you don't have to have any beer. You can do what you like and just talk or you can sit in the corner and sulk. I really don't care. What I *do* care about is seeing *my* friends. A girl only has *one* senior prom. I want mine to be just as I please. Is that too much to ask?"

"But drinking alcohol by minors is not legal. I don't want to give my support to an illegal gathering."

"Oh, don't be such a prig," said Virginia to her car door window.

"Who's being a prig? I just don't want to go, that's all."

"I thought you were a man in your own right, but now I see you're just a little boy," chided Virginia, turning her face back toward mine.

"That party is just for the fast group," I said—still shaking my head.

"It's not. Who says it is?"

"I've heard about it."

"From who?"

"I don't want to say."

"Oh, you can't say, can you? Is that because you aren't so sure of your facts anymore, eh?" I didn't respond. Then she said, "Well I planned on going and even told some people that we were going. And they were so sure that you wouldn't go because you were such a twit. But I stuck up for you and said you would. I supported you. I said that you were mature enough to be able to attend a party without necessarily doing everything that some people might be doing. Sure, there's going to beer at the party, but what can you expect from a party on high school prom night where there are no parents?"

I didn't like the sound of this. But what could I do? I was responsible for Virginia. Her father turned her over to me for safekeeping.

"I can see you really don't get this. Don't think about whether or not there will be beer at the party, but instead think about all the fun talk with friends."

"*Your* friends." I was frowning.

"They can be *your* friends, too." She was smiling.

The runner on third raced home and scored easily. The game was now tied, with two out.

"You make me sick," I said.

"What's the matter, little prig?" She was now sneering.

"Boy, was I wrong about you," I said.

"Why, you little bastard," she said, baring her teeth.

"That's not very nice language, Virginia."

"What's gotten into you? Are you deranged?"

"It's all that Patricini's fault. First, he missed that ground ball then, the throw to second; that would have been three outs right there," said Johnny Hansen.

"But how about the plays that you bungled?" asked Arne. "It seems to me that you made just as many mistakes as Rico."

"You mean that throw to the plate? That just hit a stone for a bad hop."

"Yes, and how about that throw to first that scored the tying run?"

"Well, on that throw to the plate, I was going to let the throw come—it was a perfect throw, but that Patricini yells to cut it off so I had to move into position to get the peg and try to make an impossibly fast throw to the plate. I mean, if I could have just been able   to   do   it   my   way—"

"Hey, stop belly-aching down there on the bench," said the coach.

"I don't know what Rollo told you," began Virginia. "He's very full of himself and sometimes exaggerates. If he said *anything* to you about the party, then don't believe him. There was a comical episode when I was walking down the hall with a couple of the jocks and we were talking about the party. They went over-the-top."

There was a silence. Then I asked, "Did you talk about *me* with them?"

"Why would you say that? Did Rollo say that?"

I sighed and looked away.

"Hey, this was only a big game. They were all very full of themselves as you guys often become when you're around a girl. They said you wouldn't go to the party because you were such a prude. But I defended you to them. I proudly said you were my prom date and that you'd take me where I wanted to go."

I looked back to Virginia. "Really?"

"Sure. I even bet them five dollars that you'd take me to the party."

I put the key back into the ignition. We were going to the party.

Rico met Lita at a bar in Dallas. He was sitting at the far end of the bar. There weren't many people sitting at the bar. She decided to move in order to sit next to him. She had dark straight hair that was braided—just like his mother. The woman ordered a beer.

Rico was drinking whiskey. He was on his third one. "Say, what's your name?" asked the woman with a smile.

Rico was unprepared to talk to a woman so brazen. For a moment he was reluctant to reply. Then he said, "Rico. What's your name?"

"Lita," she replied.

Rico nodded. He was never a great one for conversation. He fancied himself to be more of a counter-puncher. She picked up on this and asked, "Do you live around here?"

Rico nodded.

"Oh, really, so do I."

After the ice cream, Cindy and I went back to her off-campus apartment. It was so weird to see an undergraduate so independent. That was because Cindy was a sophomore and also because her father owned the three-flat in which she lived. He was into real estate for a living.

Cindy's place was decorated on the theme of the *Wizard of Oz*. She had an obsession for that movie—especially between the two witches. I was transformed. She had me under her complete control, and I loved it.

When we got to the party it was on the early side since we left the prom before it was over. Still, I had to park two blocks away. I could hear the music when we reached one block away. This made me nervous. What if the police were called? Would I end up in jail? Would that go on my permanent record?

YOU'RE SO DAMNED PARSIMONIOUS

"WHAT HAPPENED EXACTLY?" ASKED AGENT FRIEDMAN. HE HAD A STERN LOOK ON HIS FACE.

"WELL, IT SEEMS THAT THE KIDS HAD THIS DRINKING PARTY OVER IN ISSAQUAH AND SOMEONE CALLED THE POLICE," REPLIED JACKIE.

"WHO SENT IN THE CALL?" RETURNED AGENT FRIEDMAN.

"THEY DON'T KNOW, BUT THEY SAID THAT IT SOUNDED LIKE A YOUNG FEMALE VOICE—A TEENAGER. I'M NOT SURE, HOWEVER, IT'S BEEN SO LONG." JACKIE TOOK OUT A TISSUE FROM HER POCKET AND TOUCHED HER EYES.

"YES, I UNDERSTAND; GO ON."

"WELL, RICO HAD TAKEN HIS GIRL TO THE DANCE AND APPARENTLY, AFTERWARDS, HE FORCED HER TO GO TO THIS PARTY. THIS SHOWED A LACK OF JUDGMENT. HE SHOULD HAVE KNOWN THAT THERE WOULD BE TERRIBLE THINGS GOING ON AT THAT PARTY. THE KIDS WERE DOING 'GOD KNOW WHAT ALL,' BUT THEY WERE DOING IT ALL RIGHT."

"YOU MEAN LIKE NECKING, PETTING, AND THE LIKE?" F.B.I. AGENT FRIEDMAN PUT HIS HAND ON JACKIE'S SHOULDER.

"WELL, I DON'T KNOW EVERYTHING THAT WAS GOING ON, MIND YOU. I'M NOT ONE OF YOUR CURIOUS CITIZENS WHO HAS TO BUTT HER NOSE INTO EVERYTHING. I MEAN, I THINK THAT PEOPLE SHOULD LOOK AFTER THEIR OWN BUSINESS. IF EVERYONE DID THAT, WE'D HAVE FAR FEWER TROUBLES THAN WE HAVE TODAY!" JACKIE RAISED HER GAZE TO THE CEILING.

"YES MA'AM," SAID THE TWO AGENTS IN UNISON.

"YOU'RE DARN TOOTIN' I'M RIGHT," SAID JACKIE, STANDING UP AND WALKING TO THE FAR END OF THE ROOM. THEN SHE PIVOTED BACK AND SAID, "FAR LESS TROUBLES WOULD OCCUR IF WE ONLY LET PEOPLE *BE.*" THESE LAST WORDS WERE SAID WITH ENTHUSIASM AS SHE LIFTED HER ARM

ABOVE HER HEAD AND CLENCHED HER HAND INTO A FIST.

"YES, MA'AM," BEGAN WALLACE, "BUT COULD WE GET BACK TO THE PARTY?"

JACKIE NODDED HER HEAD AND RETURNED TO HER CHAIR, "OH YES, WELL, ANYWAY, I HEARD THAT SOME OF THOSE KIDS WERE DOING THINGS THAT EVEN THE OFFICERS HADN'T EVER SEEN BEFORE."

"YOU MEAN SEXUAL ACTS?" ASKED OFFICER WALLACE.

"THAT'S EXACTLY WHAT I MEAN. THEY WERE A CARRYIN' ON LIKE THERE WAS NO TOMORROW."

"Don't lie to me, young man," said Uncle Adam.

"Dianne said she had a hurt."

"You dirty little boy. You dirty little boy."

"I'VE GOT YOU; I'VE GOT YOU."

ROUND CIRCULAR MOTIONS, CLEANING THE HOUSE OF ALL THE DIRT, ALL THE DIRT, ALL THE DIRT, ALL THE DIRT: CESTIN!

"You little liar," she said.

AN OLD NUN SMILED

"But Dianne said that she—"

Then Uncle Adam hit me with the back of his hand, sending me to the floor where I hit my head hard. I knew I had to run, but I couldn't get up. But when I saw all the beer drinking and sex stuff, I decided it was time for an exit. I went to find Virginia. She was making-out with Rollo. He had unzipped her dress and was taking it off. I had only kissed Virginia a couple of times, but it looked as if she was going *all the way.*

"Virginia!" I called.

She turned her head, sneered, and gave me the finger.

"I'm leaving," I said.

"Get the fuck out of here, then," she said.

I moved past couples in various stages of undress. I couldn't get out of there fast enough. Virginia would have to fend for herself.

"YES, THE POLICE CAME AND RAIDED THE PARTY AND TOOK SOME OF THE KIDS IN THEIR SQUAD CARS. (SOME OF THE GIRLS WHO WERE TAKEN WERE NOT EVEN ALLOWED TO FULLY DRESS THEMSELVES.) BUT IT SERVES THEM RIGHT; KNOW WHAT I MEAN? THOSE KIDS CARRYIN' ON LIKE THAT. BUT ANYWAY, THEY TOOK A LOT OF THEM DOWN TO THE JAIL AND CALLED THEIR PARENTS."

"YOU SAID THEY ONLY TOOK SOME OF THEM DOWN TO THE POLICE STATION?" AGENT FRIEDMAN HAD OUT HIS SMALL NOTEBOOK AND PENCIL. HE PAUSED AS HE JOTTED SOMETHING DOWN.

"WELL SURE, THERE WERE SO MANY OF THEM AND SO FEW POLICEMEN THAT SOME OF THEM WERE BOUND TO ESCAPE."

"BUT COULDN'T THEY HAVE SIMPLY SEALED OFF THE ACCESS ROADS OUT OF THE PARTY?" PUT FRIEDMAN.

"I DON'T KNOW. I'M NOT A POLICEMAN. THAT'S YOUR LINE, NOT MINE."

"YES, OF COURSE," BEGAN AGENT FRIEDMAN AS HE

MADE HIS LAST NOTES, THEN LOOKED UP, "GO ON WITH YOUR STORY."

"WELL, ONE OF THEM THEY CAUGHT WAS VIRGINIA."

"WHO?" ASKED FRIEDMAN.

"THE GIRL RICO WAS TAKING TO THE PROM."

"YES, GO ON."

"WELL, SHE WAS CAUGHT. AND SHE AND SOME OF THE OTHERS IMPLICATED RICO AS ONE OF THE ORGANIZERS OF THE PARTY. AND HIM ESCAPING MADE IT ALL THE WORSE."

"WHAT HAPPENED?"

CIRCULAR MOTIONS, DUSTING

I was so upset that after a half-hour or so, I stopped the car and got out. I was on Cougar Mountain Road, a very remote location. There was hardly any moon visible. It was dark on Cougar Mountain Road.

I saw what I took to be a farmhouse— maybe a half-mile away—with its lights on. I decided to get back in the car and to drive directly home.

"And the King is in charge of the secular realm."

"Yes."

"So, if He isn't doing his job, what should happen to him?"

Rico the Great took his index finger and ran it across his throat as if he were killing someone.

The priest smiled.

"She asked me to look at her hurt and so I did. And then she asked me if I had a hurt there and I said I didn't so I was showing her."

It was a small sequin-studded purse. Rico looked up to Lita and she seemed to be inviting him to follow her home. At least, that's the way Rico interpreted it.

"What's the matter with you, Patricini? Are you asleep or something?" the coach roared. "If you can't stay awake out there, I'll get someone who can."

A MAN CAN DO ANYTHING
BE ANYTHING
IF HE ONLY APPLIES HIMSELF FRUGALLY

"I am not parsimonious! You think that because I like to conserve what I have and only buy the things that I really need," yelled my father.

"Well, I don't think it's right to expect that this family can cut its electric bill by five dollars next month. Do you?" my mother was screaming back at him.

"I mean, all that would be entailed would be monitoring the house temperature and turning off lights when you leave rooms, instead of leaving everything on all of the time," said my father in a calm voice.

"No one leaves lights on all the time, and you know it. Besides, our electric bill isn't that large; we can handle it very well."

"That's what you think, but anyway that's not the point. What I'm trying to impress upon you is that we should not overheat the house and that leaving lights on when no one is using them is simply wasteful. Especially, when you go to the store and leave the lights and heat on when no one is even here. It doesn't pay to be wasteful. Will you agree to that?"

I heard my mother leaving the room. Father followed.

"Will you agree, at the very least, that being wasteful sets a very bad example for our son and daughter?"

CIRCULAR MOTIONS—DUSTING, DUSTING

Every night when Rico would wake up from his nightmares, he would go to the bathroom and shave. Then he would get back into bed to try and recreate his dreams.

TWO BLACK NUNS—NOW ONLY SPECKS

I turned on the AM station and listened to the sort of music that they had played at the prom. I didn't know why Virginia agreed to go with me since she hardly did any dancing and simply talked to her friends and dreamed of the after-prom party. I was simply a prop. I didn't like being a prop.

"Daddy?" I began, "what's the difference between Protestants and Catholics?"

"That's a very difficult question," he said. "As people they are the same. But they hold different beliefs about what it means to be a Christian and how we can come to know and worship the Almighty Father."

"But how are they different?"

"You know the answer to that. You've been taking classes from Father Weal for two years—almost."

"I know all about the catechism stuff like that, but what I really want to know is how are *they* different from *us*?"

"I guess I don't really understand your question. Could you rephrase it, or be more specific?"

Peace will come to every heart,
The love of Jesus shall unite us all,
And we shall be one from the very start,
Harkening to the work of our Masters' call

Father Weal's voice was strong and full as he boomed out each verse telling about personal hardships that were to be overcome by the grace of God.

I once knew a man, in the gutter he lay,
Sleeping from drink, and smelling of dirt,
He had no money, but I lifted his day
By bringing him into the home of the Spirit

I looked up at Father Weal when he was singing, and his head blocked the sun, making it look as if the halo of the sun was around his head.

"You sing a verse Rico," coaxed Father Weal.

"I don't know any," I said. My mind was racing.

"Go ahead, Rico." But the voice was my father's. I knew that I should; so, I started without really knowing what I was saying:

There lived a young man standing alone,
He was helpless in the midst of distress,
I brought him to church to give him a home,
And now he lives in great happiness.

Rico walked along Dealey Plaza. He wanted to get a sense of the territory. He felt a calling, and it would come to fruition here. He wanted to pray, but instead he took the bus to see Lita.

"She asked me to look at her hurt and so I did and then she asked me if I had a hurt there and I said I didn't so I was showing her."

Rico stayed in a flop house for his first week in Dallas. He was practically broke. He had to wait for his first paycheck, which was after the second week. But then he had to find a check-cashing store that charged him 20% to give him his money. Rico vowed to get a bank account when things calmed down. After a month, he was able to rent a studio apartment in a cheap part of town.

The room was in the center of the hall. The landlady took her master key, which she wore around her neck, and opened it up for him. There was no first and last month's rent in this part of town.

"You can put your things down there," she said, pointing to an old purple chair that had part of an old spring sticking out. Rico walked up to the chair and touched the spring: it was slightly rusted and sharp. "Note to self: I'll buy some Duct Tape to repair that so I don't get hurt. The silver tape would be a nice contrast to the fading purple."

"Say, Albert," I said.

Albert grunted. He was reading a magazine with nude male and female pictures.

"Do you want to go to Mass—I mean church tomorrow?"

Albert grunted.

"I say, do you—"

"No. Now be quiet."

I realized that I didn't know what religion Albert believed in.

"Albert?"

Albert looked up. "Get the fuck out of here, Rico. I'm busy."

I got up to go. "I'm going to the 9:30 service at St. Anne's. If you want to come, I'd be happy to go with you."

Albert grunted. I arrived home just after 1 am. Uncle Adam was there to greet me. "Where have you been? The prom got out at 11." He stood in the entryway with his arms folded. The thought of his hitting me flitted through my head.

"We left a little before 11 for an 'after-prom party.'"

"So, how long did it take for you to get there?"

"Around 45 minutes."

"Where was this 'after-Prom Party'?"

"Issaquah," I replied.

"Okay. That brings you to around 11:45?"

"Sure. And then it took around 45 minutes to get home."

"So now you're at 12:30."

"Yes."

"And you walked in here at 1:15 a.m."

"Yeah."

"That means you were *only* at the party for forty-five minutes?"

"Something like that. A little more because we left the dance a little earlier. I'd say an hour would be more accurate."

"Why spend 90 minutes on the road for just an hour at a party?"

"It was Virginia's idea. I didn't want to go there. I was the odd man out, so I left."

"You just left? What about Virginia?"

"She was with her friends. She told me to go away." Uncle Adam shook his head and turned, muttering something about the "younger generation."

"You did yourself proud out there today, Rico," said the coach.

"Thank you, sir."

The coach put his hand on my shoulder. "I know it's been a struggle for you, son. But you have the heart to make it happen, and you made it happen here today. We're in the playoffs. Winning is a team effort, but *you* came through in the end. You played a big part in our win today. I'm proud of you, Rico."

Rollo was right. Virginia was only using me to get to the party. It was a ploy. Her parents saw through the "fast crowd" so she needed someone "safe." That was me. She didn't like me. She just wanted to get drunk and have sex with various guys. I was such a chump.

I might have been okay in Little League, but it never went farther than that. I didn't make the Pony League team, and I didn't make my high school team. My grades in junior high and high school were always passing but were only good ("B to A-" range) in social studies. I had opinions I could express on politics and religion. The rest was very tough. But I still maintained a "B-" overall grade point average.

I didn't dress well. My mother got my clothes second-hand. They were never in fashion. I wore such baggy pants when all the cool guys had tight, tapered pants. Sometimes, I felt as if I were being punished for my father dying. But I didn't kill him. He had a heart attack. Why did I have to pay?

I WAS TAKEN WITH THE CHARACTER MIZOGUCHI IN MY ASIAN PHILOSOPHY CLASS. WE WERE READING YUKIO MISHIMA'S *THE TEMPLE OF THE GOLDEN PAVILION.* MIZOGUCHI WAS A ZEN BUDDHIST NOVICE SEEKING TO BECOME EITHER A BROTHER OR A PRIEST. THIS SEEMED TO FIT WITH MY OWN BACKGROUND. ONE OF THE THINGS THAT I LIKED ABOUT THE ZEN BUDDHISTS WAS THAT THEY REALIZED THAT COMPLEX RELIGIOUS MESSAGES WERE LIKE LITTLE PUZZLES. SO, WHEN FATHER NANSEN KILLS A CAT (THAT BOTH DORMITORIES WANT AS THEIR OWN), THERE IS A DISPUTE CONCERNING THE MEANING OF THE ACT. IN THE END, WHAT IT MEANT TO ME IS ENCAPSULATED IN THE PHRASE, "WHEN YOU MEET THE BUDDHA, YOU MUST KILL THE BUDDHA." THERE IS SOMETHING TRANSCENDENT ABOUT THIS PHRASE.

"So, you really get off on 'The Wizard of Oz.'"

"The way I see it," began Cindy, "It's really about the relationship between the so-called witches. According to the Disney version, they are called: Glinda (the good witch who rules over a peaceful and just kingdom), and Evanora (a witch who is a powerful presence and advisor to the Wizard), and Theodora (a naïve creature who awaits the coming of a new wizard who will bring forth a more perfect order).

"Of course, the real writer of the book, L. Frank Baum, only named one witch by name: Glinda, the good witch of the South. Others are *rumored* to be, but not specified."

I was very taken with this. It was just the sort of thing I would do, were I to become obsessed with a book. I'd try to bring the characters into my very being.

We sat on the bed and Cindy brought out a picture book with pictures of various versions of the witches.

Rico and Lita walked to her apartment. It was a second-floor walk-up. When they got inside, Lita motioned for Rico to sit on the bed. He did so. She sat next to him and kissed him. He was unsure of himself. Then she lifted his hand to place it on her chest. Rico's mind was confused. Then Lita reached down and stroked Rico on the crotch. Rico was in her magical powers.

Cindy knew so much about the witches, and what they meant to her, personally. I was drawn to Cindy. But soon my eyes made contact with her clock. It was after midnight. I had to get up for mass the next morning: it was time to go.

I reached out for Cindy's face. She let me touch her cheek. "I really like your interest in Oz, Cindy. I hope you will invite me back to see some more of your books, but it's getting late for me. I have to get up early tomorrow."

Cindy tilted her head. She had a quizzical expression. "Don't you want to see more now?"

"Sure I do, Cindy. It's just that I'm a very habituated guy. I need so much sleep each night to make it. Otherwise, I'm a wreck."

"Well, okay. I'll let you go now on the condition that you'll come back. I really had a good time tonight."

"So, did I," I said, smiling.

Then Cindy kissed me.

When Rico turned away from Lita, she reached out her hand to him—palm up. Rico was picking up his clothes that he had strewn onto the floor, and getting dressed.

Lita pulled her hand back and then reached it out again. Rico noticed Lita's gesture. He reached out and grabbed her hand. "I had a really good time," he said.

"Five dollars," was Lita's reply.

"Five dollars? You need a loan or something?" Rico's jaw hung open.

"C'mon buster. You got what you came for, now pay up."

Rico finished dressing. "I don't know what you're talking about."

"Bullshit. Of course, you do. I picked you up at the bar and you knew what you were getting yourself into. What do you think? I give it away for free? How would I pay my bills?"

"Who are you?" Rico scratched his head and then zipped up his fly. "I don't pay for sex. I've actually never even had sex before. You are the first."

"Well, then, here's the crash course: when you take down a working girl, there's always a cost. Now pay up."

Rico turned to go. He didn't want to pay for sex.

"If you try to stiff me, I'll file a rape complaint against you. Now, five dollars, buster." Lita was intense.

Rico paused. Then he frowned and exited. When he got outside the apartment, he started into a run. He didn't know where he was going, but he knew that he had to get there fast.

MICHAEL O'MEARA DIDN'T KNOW HOW TO DEAL WITH WOMEN, EITHER. THAT'S WHY I LIKED *THE EXTINCTION OF DESIRE* IN MY ASIAN PHILOSOPHY CLASS. I ALSO IDENTIFIED WITH HIM.

It may have been fortunate that Virginia and I had had that fight. I completely misunderstood what she wanted of me. I was a taxi service to a party and her friends. I was "parent-approved." I was a shield. And as it turned out, I was almost the "fall guy" when I had to go to the principal's office and talk to Officer Guttman. He was a sergeant and was trying to put together what happened at the party. I gave him the scoop, and he seemed to believe me—unlike my mother and Uncle Adam.

Cindy and I met again the next Friday. We went to a movie venue on campus that played old films. We saw the classic 1939 version of "The Wizard of Oz." We went to a little diner afterwards and had a sandwich and some coffee. It was a great venue to talk about the movie. Afterwards, we went back to Cindy's place and looked at another book she had on the classic movie. Cindy had also checked out a copy of the actual movie script from the library and we read some of her favorite scenes together.

I really enjoyed reading parts in a play script. I had never tried out for a school play or anything. And we never did anything like that at home. When you read the lines of another character, then you can become someone else. As a person who really doesn't know himself, this was reassuring in a way. When I left around midnight Cindy held onto my hands at the door. We promised each other to do something every day this week-end. Tomorrow would be the Whidbey Island Ferry and an afternoon hike. Cindy kissed me again and when I got to the end of the hall I looked back and waved at her. She was still watching.

Two days later, there was a knocking on Rico's apartment door just as he had returned from work. It was an Officer Malbane from the Dallas Police. He wanted to talk to Rico concerning the rape complaint made against him by Lita Lore. According to procedure, he had to take Rico to the local station and photograph and fingerprint him before sitting him down in a small room for interrogation. Officer Malbane was middle aged, balding in both the front and back. He had jet black hair and a sallow skin color. His left incisor was golden. He sat in the duct-tape-repaired stuffed chair. Rico thought he looked Polish.

"Now lookee here, Patrocini."

Rico did not correct the officer on the pronunciation of his name. Instead, he just nodded.

Officer Malbane nodded back and smiled. "Don't get me wrong. I have nothing against Dagos like you. My wife has a friend at church who's a Dago. The Dago woman has five kids, but then, your type is always very fertile, right?" The officer smiled at his joke and lifted his hand to make it look like a gun with his index finger being the barrel. He pretended to shoot Rico.

Rico looked straight ahead.

"Now, lookee here, Rico. This Lita Lore, she's a whore. I'm not about to believe a word she says. Probably mad that you didn't tip her enough. Was that it?"

Rico grimaced. Officer Malbane took that to be an affirmative response. The man scratched his stomach on the right side. As he did so, Rico noticed that the man had a large sweat stain under that arm pit.

Michael Boylan 229

"Now, I don't want to make too much of what a common whore says, but she's a feisty one. I suggest you give her the tip she wants and then ask for something extra next time." *Malbane laughed as he got up from his chair. He moved toward the door, then stopped and turned. "We on the same page, compadre?"*

Rico nodded.

"Now, you said the last time we talked," began Officer Guttman, "that you didn't know anything about this party until the night of the prom."

"Yes, sir." I was seated in a flat-back red plastic chair. We were in the conference room right next to the vice-principal's office.

"Now, I've had a chance to interview twenty students who went to the party and thirty more who only went to the prom and not the party."

I nodded.

"It seems that, like most high schools, there is a *fast crowd* and then there is a *normal crowd.*"

"Yes, sir."

"From what I've been able to determine, your Virginia is part of the fast crowd along with about six other students: Rollo, Bart, Billy, Arne, Mary, and Lucy. Would you say that is an accurate description?"

I didn't know what to say, so I paused.

"Rico, I've asked you an important question. Please answer it."

"Yes, sir. You see, I *do* know all of the students that you mention. And they are the popular students. That's for sure. I don't know if that makes them *fast.* I never really understood why Virginia agreed to go to the prom with me. It was Lucy who put the idea into my head. She said that Virginia hadn't been asked and wanted to go.

"I had some money in my bank account from my summer jobs and the occasional work I've done at the movie theater in the concessions. I'm not a regular at the theater, but one of their top subs when someone is sick. That's where I got the money for the prom tickets and the pre-prom dinner at the restaurant."

Guttman nodded.

"I didn't understand what I was getting myself into, going to that party. But I went even though I knew that I was *out of my league.* I mean, Virginia is part of the popular crowd, and I'm just a jerk. I thought when she agreed to go to the prom with me that I'd died and gone to heaven. Then it turned out to be the other place."

Officer Guttman leaned forward and patted me on the shoulder. "This is the last time I'll be talking to you, Rico. You have been obviously abused in this whole thing. I suggest you don't talk to any of the *fast crowd* until we finish our investigation."

"Yes, sir," I replied. Then I got the job. It had been an easier interview than I imagined. But it was for only 10 weeks. I'd be living at no cost in Tacoma where they had some rooms for the temporaries they hired in the summer. It was with a national company. I'd be working with my hands. I liked that. I'd be part of the manufacturing of paper, something Tacoma is known for. And I'd be walking away with over $500! What could be better?

When I finished my pitcher and glazed it, I took it to my dorm room. I showed it to my roommate and to Cindy, who thought it was very beautiful—why, it could have even come from Oz!

Well, I was off the hook with the law. Officer Guttman took care of that. But I was not off the hook with the popular kids at school. We only had three weeks before graduation, but I didn't know whether I would last. I was fearful *because that part of town that Lita lived in was tough. Rico was going to follow Officer Malbane's advice and just pay Lita the five bucks. He came by her apartment around noon on Saturday.*

He could have gotten an overtime day at work if he had chosen to, but he wanted to get this "rape" thing taken care of.

Rico knocked on her door. No answer. Rico knocked again. No answer. Rico knocked a third time and then he heard some footsteps. The door opened an inch until it was stopped by the chain restraint. Lita looked like she had just been awakened.

"What do you want?" barked Lita.

"Your money. I want to pay you your money."

There was a pause. "Okay. Hand it over."

Rico got out his wallet and handed her the bill. She took it and started to shut the door. "Just so you remember. My name is Rico Patricini. I was a client of yours. It was all a big misunderstanding. I'm sorry."

Lita grunted and shut the door.

When she shut the door, I felt devastated. During the last two terms at college Cindy and I had been seeing each other regularly. I thought that when I got back from my summer job, that we'd pick up from where we left off. But when she opened the door, it was as if she had just gotten out of bed even though it was ten o'clock in the morning. That wouldn't have been so bad if I hadn't seen the naked guy behind her in the middle of the room. Obviously, we were through.

It didn't need to be said. But I knew I'd never talk to Virginia again.

"That's just the way it is," said Dianne. "You are a marked man at school. I've got to keep my distance or else I'll *never* be popular. Face it, Rico, you're a loser."

"FACE IT, RICO. THAT PROM THING BROUGHT NOTHING BUT SHAME UPON THIS FAMILY." UNCLE ADAM HAD ON HIS GAME FACE. EVEN THOUGH IT HAD BEEN WELL OVER A YEAR SINCE THE INCIDENT AT THE AFTER-PROM PARTY, IT WAS ALL HE COULD TALK ABOUT.

"BUT THE POLICE—OFFICER GUTTMAN SAID—"

"I DON'T GIVE A RAT'S ASS ABOUT ANY OFFICER GUTTMAN. YOU ARE *HISTORY,* MAN. YOUR SCHOOL STARTS IN TWO WEEKS. WE WILL PAY FOR YOUR FALL TUITION AND ROOM AND BOARD, BUT BEYOND THAT, RICO, YOU ARE ON YOUR OWN. YOU'RE A FINANCIAL BURDEN TO US. AFTER THE FALL TERM, WE'LL PACK UP YOUR THINGS AND PUT THEM INTO A SMALL TRUNK WE BOUGHT FROM SEARS. YOU CAN STORE THEM IN YOUR COLLEGE DORMITORY OR WE'LL TRASH THEM. WE'RE THROUGH WITH YOU, BUSTER."

My summer job at the papermill didn't pay me enough for me to make it through the year. I decided to go to Cindy's place to talk to her about my predicament. But then—

I had only kissed Virginia a couple of times before. I wanted to respect her. So when I saw Rollo unzipping her prom dress— the one she had gotten for *me,* it sent me into outer space. Virginia had gone to the prom with *me—not with him.*

Cindy had told me how much she admired the black pitcher that I created in ceramics class. She had insinuated it into her *Wizard of Oz* worldview. I thought she *liked me.* I mean, every night when I left around midnight, she acted like she wanted me *to stay with her even longer.* But when I saw a naked man in her apartment, I knew it was over between us. She had had sex with him. We never had sex. What was I missing in all of this?

"And the King is in charge of the secular realm."

"Yes."

"So, if He isn't doing his job, what should happen to him?"

Rico the Great took his index finger and ran it across his throat as if he were killing someone.

The priest smiled.

So, what was the point? I stayed in university for the fall term, but then I had to get a job. I contacted my summer employer about my interest in full time employment. I worked in Tacoma a while doing various temporary jobs in the paper fabrication process. Periodically, I stopped in to see if a more permanent role would be opening up. One day I got lucky. The HR guy told me about a job opening in Dallas that had just opened up. My destiny was set.

I looked at my black pitcher and I thought about the Japanese word, *mu*, which means emptiness. It was so important to me to learn about this concept that was central in the books I read for Asian philosophy: *The Temple of the Golden Pavilion* and *The Extinction of Desire*. I suppose that was the goal to which I aspired: **mu.**

I was seven years old when Father gave me a vintage watch that used to belong to *his* father. He was sitting downstairs in his favorite chair when I came in from playing wall ball.

"How did it go?" he asked.

"Pretty good," I replied.

"Play wall ball?"

I nodded.

"Did you win?"

"No," I said.

"Who did you play?"

"Billy," I said.

"He generally beats you, doesn't he?"

"Yes," I said.

"That's really surprising to me, when you have more potential in you than he'll ever have. You know, I think you have the ability to beat him every time. Would you like to do that?" My father leaned forward when he delivered these words.

I nodded.

"Well it's not hard, you know. All you have to do start playing some smart wall ball, you know what I mean?"

I shook my head.

"Sure, you do. Your denial means that just haven't thought over the problem clearly. The key to success is *out-thinking* your opponent. How
do you suppose that I got to where I am today in my job?"

I shrugged my shoulders.

"It was by using my head: my little noggin," he said as he took my hands to hold his head on the sides of his skull. "Sure, there are lots of men with more raw ability than I have, just as I'm sure that there are more boys your age with more raw baseball talent—I mean more *natural* talent than you have. But don't let that deter you. It should spur you on to newer and greater heights. You *can* beat Billy or any of your friends, but first you have to *want* to beat them. If you really want to beat them, then you'll use the appropriate means to do so. Remember, you first have to *want* to win really badly. Then, secondly, you have to apply yourself strategically so that you stress your strong points and play to your opponents' weaknesses." My father picked me up and set me on his lap. "Do you understand?"

I opened my eyes wide, but I didn't move my head.

"Listen, it's like this: a man can do anything, and I mean *anything* he wants to do, if he wants to hard enough and applies himself."

My father then gave me a hug. "Now, take the case with Billy. How did he beat you?"

"He got more runs than I did," I said.

"Yes, of course. That's the surface answer. What I want to know now is *how* he did it. How did he get *hits* against you? How did you try to get *hits* against him? This is important information that will allow you to create a winning strategy."

"He gets mainly home runs, but a few doubles, too," I replied.

"Where do you play?"

"On the side of Billy's house."

"And what's a home run there?"

"Over the rose bushes on the fly."

My father scratched his chin. In the later afternoon that meant it would make a sandpaper kind of sound. "If I remember their yard correctly there are only three rose bushes there and they're over to the side."

"Yes. They act as the marker."

"Then there's nothing between you and Alex Pigstin's lawn except on that one corner?"

I nodded.

"Well, here's one thing you can do: play him behind the home run line and when he tries to give you that long stuff, you can always catch it."

"But then he'll get singles," I said.

"No, he won't. You've got a good throwing arm$_s$ and you can charge the ball and throw it to the wall in three seconds, even from behind the home run line, can't you?"

"I don't know," I said.

"You can, and I'll prove it to you," he said standing up. "Where's your tennis ball?"

"Upstairs in my room," I replied.

"Get it and I'll meet you outside," he said as I raced upstairs after the ball. Outside, father had paced off the driveway and had made two marks with some bar soap on the cement.

"Now, here are the approximate dimensions of Billy's yard on the side of his house where you play. I'm going to give you a grounder at the forward line—the line where you used to stand. Then I'll give you one at the line where I suggested you stand. Let's see what happens."

Then he threw me several grounders of varying difficulty and counted out loud as I threw the tennis ball against the wall. Then he did the same at the farther line, giving me different types of "hits." After we were done, I was convinced that I could field better at the back line than the front.

"You see," my father began, "at the back line it's harder to get balls past you for extra bases. You are also better positioned to stop the home run threat. This is the primary reason you moved back. The only drawback to your position now is that he can drop a bunt on you more easily—but you can stop that by 'faking to charge' several times during the game. Besides, the bunt is a worse percentage 'hit' than a hard shot. If Billy tries a bunt, it's a finesse play. Often, they result in a pop-up. Pop-ups are easy outs."

I nodded and smiled. Father put his arm around me, and walked inside the house with me. We went into the kitchen where we had a couple of lemonades, when suddenly Rollo tipped the ice cream into my lap.

"Rollo, what did you do that for?" I screamed.

"Who moved?" yelled my Father, who had been trying to take our picture.

"Rollo spilled ice cream in my lap on purpose," I cried.

"I did not," he quickly replied.

"You did too."

"Did not!"

"I saw you."

"Oh, yeah?" he challenged.

"Now, boys," said my father.

"Keep it up, Rico, and I'll give you a knuckle sandwich," said Rollo.

"Stop it now, both of you," shouted Father.

We were both silent, not out of fear of what he might do to us, but because we all respected him so much that when he told us to be quiet, we obeyed.

FOR I AM THE LORD, THY GOD.
I AM A JEALOUS GOD,
VISITING INIQUITY UPON
THESE CHILDREN EVEN UNTO THE THIRD

GENERATION
FOR THOSE WHO DO NOT ABIDE BY MY
COMMANDMENTS.

Father Weal's voice rang out loud and clear. There was a
ringing quality to his voice that made some of the things he said
stick in my mind.

THE WHEEL FINALLY BEGAN SLOWING

"Having a plan and a positive attitude makes all the difference,
Rico."

I puckered my lips. I didn't understand the causal matrix behind
this. My father saw that I wasn't on board yet, so he said, "Take your wall
ball game, for example. I'll bet you that the next game you play with Billy
will be a close game—you may win it, you may not (I don't know how
much confidence you've developed yet) but one thing is for sure, that
before the week is out, you'll be beating Billy and beating him regularly."

I started to laugh.

"You'd like that, wouldn't you?" he said, as he tickled me. "You've
got quite a giggle there little whiskers," he said.

THE WHEEL WAS SLOWING DOWN, GRADUALLY GIVING FULL VIEW TO ITS FINISHED PRODUCT

Mother told me that her brother (my uncle) would be
coming to live with us now that my father was dead. This confused
me. I read in Sunday School that:

Matthew 22:24
"Teacher," they said, "Moses declared that if a man
dies without having
children, his brother is to marry the widow and raise up
offspring for him."

Now, my father *did* have children: me and Dianne. And my
father was an only child without a brother. Does this mean

that my mother is required to marry her *own* brother and have children?

This prospect bothered me. I really didn't like Uncle Adam. If he thought that he was going to take the place of my father, then *"I will kill him," said Rico.*

"You know, we got a call from the police about you," said Uncle Adam. I was in the kitchen. I'd just finished one of those Washington State apples they always brag about.

"That's history. It was over before I graduated from high school," I said. "Officer Guttman told me that the other kids' stories weren't consistent. They were playing me for the *fall guy.*"

"Well, apparently everything isn't over. There is an accusation that a rape occurred at the party. The statute of limitations on rape is ten years."

"What does this have to do with me? I was hardly at the party." I finished my apple.

"Or so *you say*," put Uncle Adam.

"You remember when you called me out for leaving so early and not taking Virginia home. I wasn't there long enough to eat a sandwich much less rape someone."

"Humph." Uncle Adam got up to leave. Then I hurled the apple core at his back. It bounced harmlessly down to the floor before it reached him. I was infuriated. Uncle Adam heard the core fall and stopped.

He turned, bent down, and picked it up. Then he walked towards me, the core within his closed fist. When he got over to me, he gave a roundhouse swing at my jaw. I ducked away, falling on the floor. Adam picked up a chair and held it over his head as if to knock me to Kingdom Come.

"Go ahead, Uncle Adam. Kill me."

Adam sneered for an interval, still holding his weapon until he changed his mind and put it down. As he turned to walk away, he said, "Your late father would certainly be ashamed of how you've turned out."

THOU SHALT HAVE NO OTHER GODS BUT ME

When my pitcher came out so wonderfully, I felt that I had achieved something. It was my last term at college since my mother and uncle had decided not to support me anymore. Therefore, this pitcher might be my primary accomplishment in college. Cindy had left me after my summer job. My first year (assigned) roommate would have nothing to do with me for the next year. I successfully petitioned to have a single dorm room for fall term. This was for the best.

I enrolled in the three classes that I thought would help me the most: Ceramics, Asian philosophy, and the History of the Protestant Reformation.

I have come to the conclusion that I have been dedicating myself to the wrong ideals. I have been perverted by false images, and they have blocked the true light of the sun with dark shadows.

I knew that I didn't fit into the regular groove. My community didn't care much about religion. We were in a new era. When I went to college it was 1961, which is a magical year because when you twist that number and turn it upside down, it still reads 1961.

Now, it is the autumn of 1962. In the meantime, John Glenn has been sent into outer space, and he circled the earth. There was a problem with Cuba in which our country's father,

President Kennedy, brought us to the brink of nuclear destruction. Black people are going to college in the South, and most important of all: Seattle hosts the World's Fair with its famous 21st century Space Needle and Monorail. I live in the center of the universe—and yet I cannot stay. My time is temporary.

I am not a part of the Protestant Reformation. I try to seek community, but it is denied me. I have been away from the Church for a long time. I haven't been to mass for four months. I haven't been to confession in a year. It is probably a good thing that my Protestant mother and uncle will now be divorced from my life so that I might start anew.

I CAUGHT THE BALL. IT WAS THE FINAL OUT. I HAD BEATEN BILLY, JUST AS MY FATHER HAD PREDICTED. I c a m e r u n n i n g   h o m e .

When my father got home, he gave me a big hug and then he took me upstairs to his bedroom. He sat me on the bed and went into the closet. When he came back, he was carrying a piece of jewelry. Father sat next to me and showed me what he had been carrying. It was a gold watch.

"It's solid twenty-four karat gold, or so my own father used to tell me. It was the only thing he left me; he didn't have much. He died poor in a hospital, but through it all he never pawned the watch that *his* father got for him when *he* was just a boy of twelve." He turned the watch over in his hands a few times and then picked it up by the chain and let it swing. "Do you want to hold it?" he asked.

"Yes, very much," I said quietly.

ON THE TABLE SAT A BLACK PITCHER

I held it tightly in my hand. It was very heavy, and I was afraid of dropping it--even onto the bed. All over the watch was very intricate metal work showing on its back side a scene where one character was chasing after another with some sort of weapon.

"What's this, Daddy?" I asked, pointing to a weapon.

"I don't know exactly but it looks like a sickle or something, doesn't it? I've always thought this scene was one of those scenes out of Greek mythology or something like that." Father jutted his jaw forward.

"How come?"

"Well, you can sort of tell by the way the entire scene is constructed and by the clothes the people are wearing—or gods or whatever they are."

"Does it still tell time?"

"Well, you know it's funny that you should mention that, because from almost the first day that my father got the watch from his father, almost 70 years ago, it has always kept time only intermittently—that is, sometimes it works perfectly, and sometimes it just stops." Father paused a moment. "Yes, it's a queer thing. A real queer thing."

"Father, maybe that's really the way time is."

Father tilted his head. "What do you mean, little whiskers?"

"What if time weren't so regular as *tick-tock* all the time? What if sometimes it stopped and then started up again in another way."

My father frowned. "I'm not sure what you mean, little whiskers."

Then I laughed and handed him back the watch. But Father wouldn't take it. "No, I want you to have the watch, Rico. This will be the fourth generation of ownership. Maybe you'll give it to your son sometime? That is, unless time stops all together. You know, because Time has melted away." Father chuckled at this last idea.

When Father left the room, I took the watch over to my sock drawer where I kept my valuable possessions. I placed it down right next to my tennis ball that I used for wall ball.

"Thirty-five dollars," said the man behind the counter.

Rico paused. "That seems like a lot of money for a used rifle," replied Rico.

The owner of the store, a short bald middle-aged man with red suspenders holding up his light gray trousers, said, "Take it or leave it. I don't give a damn."

Rico thought it over some more. He fingered the twenty dollars he had in his pocket. He also had a few ones and a new fifty-dollar note. "Okay. I'll take it."

The owner reached out his hand for the money. Rico noticed the man's white short-sleeved shirt covered up a

tattooed picture of a comic book superhero on his upper arm.
That picture made Rico hurry to turn over the money.

The man took the bill and then opened the till. After
looking Rico over one more time, he handed over the weapon
and his change. Rico took it with two hands and felt its
significance via its weight. Then he turned to go.

"Hey, boy. Aren't you forgetting something?" asked the
store owner.

Rico stopped. He was confused.

The owner laughed and opened a door to a glass cabinet
that stood in front of him. "You're going to need some
ammunition for that thar gun unless you intend just to play
with the mechanism."

Rico grimaced and returned to the store owner.

So, I had one more term left at the University of
Washington. Once upon a time, Mother had told me about a
fund that Father had left for my college education. Father had
never gone to college, but he wished he had. Therefore, he
created a special fund for my education. It was in Polaroid
Stock. My father had bought the stock in the 1940s when I was
just a little whisker. It had grown many times its original price.
Back in the day, my father thought I could go to college for
$1,000 for a four-year degree. So, my father bought the stock
for $500. But that turned out to be a bargain. The price went
through the roof. But then so did the cost of college. When I
enrolled at the University of Washington as an "in-state"
resident, I could attend for $1,500 a year so that the total cost
was around $6,000. However, as best as I could estimate from
what Father had said and from what I could glean at the public
library, that initial outlay Polaroid Stock was now worth
$15,000—almost three times the cost of four years of tuition,
including room and board. What were they going to do with
the money my father had put aside for me? But Uncle Adam
said that there was no money for me. What had happened to
all that money?

There was a similar pot for Dianne, who was now a junior in high school and into cheerleading. She was as positively popular as I had been negatively
despised. Dianne was angling for a husband so that she could get married at 18. No college for her.

Besides, her grades were even worse than mine had been.

Then Rico asked Lita, "Will you marry me?"

Lita put her hand on the right spaghetti strap of her white flannel dress with red borders. She breathed deeply twice. "Why?"

"I need you—just you and I want to be the one for you."

Lita got up and walked about her studio apartment. Then she came back to Rico, who was seated on the bed, and stood above him. "I'm not the marrying type. I'm a whore. Nobody marries a whore."

Rico replied without missing a beat, "If you married me, you wouldn't be a whore. I have a steady job at the papermill. I could support us both." Then Rico began breathing quick, shallow breaths. "I'd even have enough to pay for your G.E.D. Then you'd feel better about yourself." Rico stood up and walked to Lita. He put his hands on top of her spaghetti straps and grasped the hemispheres that were her shoulders, "The way I see it, it's like this: both of us are treated like shit in the society. We're both better than that. Why not put it together and try it out? Our community of two might just get us over the hump."

I thought about my father's watch. I imagined giving it to my son. I took my life from my father.

"AND THEN THERE WAS THE TIME THAT RICO THE GREAT HAD JUST WON A JOUSTING CONTEST WITH THE SILVER KNIGHT, WILLIAM (SOMETIMES CALLED 'BILLY'). IT WAS A LONG CONTEST LASTING OVER AN HOUR. IT WENT BACK AND FORTH. RICO HAD LOST TO SIR WILLIAM SEVERAL TIMES IN THE PAST. BUT THIS TIME WAS DIFFERENT. RICO HAD CONSIDERED A NEW STRATEGY. IT WAS BASED UPON

WHAT *HE* WAS GOOD AT. AND WHAT *SIR WILLIAM* WAS GOOD AT. RICO DECIDED NOT TO ENGAGE IN THE LANCING BUT TO TRY TO GET THINGS ON THE GROUND AS SOON AS HE COULD. THIS MIGHT MEAN LANCING SIR WILLIAM'S HORSE TO BRING THINGS TO THE TURF. ON THE GROUND, RICO THE GREAT WAS UNMATCHED.

"AND SO IT WENT. RICO'S LANCE WAS AT THE SHOE OF SIR WILLIAM'S HORSE SO THAT THE HORSE STUMBLED (THOUGH THE HORSE WAS NOT INJURED) AND SIR WILLIAM FELL DOWN. THEN RICO JUMPED OFF HIS MOUNT AND BESTED SIR WILLIAM (THOUGH SPARING HIS LIFE) TO WIN THE GOLDEN GARLAND."

I ran into Cindy on campus. I asked her how she was doing with her new boyfriend.

"His name is Raulf. He's from West Germany. He's a business major."

"Okay," I replied.

Cindy sensed my tension. She reached out for my arm and touched it. "I'm very sorry things didn't work out between you and me." She paused. Then she said, "I actually wanted our relationship to go forward, but I sensed that you were very unsure. It was as if you had been very badly burned before."

I ran into Virginia in the hall on Tuesday after the prom. She didn't want to talk to me, but I grabbed her shoulders so she would have to stop. "Let go of me, you creep," she said.

"Why do you call me that? After all, you went to the prom with me."

"Pooh," was the sound of the air through her mouth.

She tried to spin free of my grasp. But I continued. "You were using me."

"Using you?" Virginia laughed. "No way you can *use* a loser." Then she turned and walked away. I stared at the watch in my hand. I was enraptured by its flat, simple purity, something that I could strive to emulate. It was the only thing in my life that was not bent out of shape. I immediately knew that this watch was meant for me.

"IT TURNS OUT THAT RICO WASN'T INVOLVED IN THAT RAPE THAT I HAD DISCUSSED EARLIER WITH YOU."

"I just want to look at this watch for a few minutes, and then I'll be right down."

"Fine," said Father. "I think there's some bread in the drawer if you want some toast and jelly."

"What kind of jelly?"

"I think we have cherry," he said, knowing that it was my favorite.

"I'll be right down," I said.

"Fine, I'll put the bread in the toaster."

I felt the heavy watch and counted the number of links in the watch chain. They were long links and were designed to fit together so that they would lie flat and not turn themselves over easily. There were nine links in the chain. On the back of the watch were four gods, or whatever they were, and two little nymphs or little kids with wings, who hovered above the four figures.

I always loved Tuesday evenings right after Father's work. He always got home early on Tuesdays. Mom was gone to her exercise class. Di was usually over at her friend's house for the day, and so Father and I were alone. Instead of fixing a big dinner, Father would prepare us up a couple of tasty snacks that we would nibble on as we listened to a network radio show.

Tuesdays always seemed nice.

I also looked forward to Saturday when we would have a day off from school. This Saturday, in particular, I decided to practice the things that Father had taught me so that Billy and I could have a big game on the following Friday. I felt excited as I thought over my plans. I practiced standing back and then running in for the short stuff.

The big watch felt *right* in my hands. My feeling harkened back to the three previous owners. It called attention to the persistence of memory.

"Rico?" I heard Father calling.

"Yes, I'll be down in a second."

Rico went into the church during the hours posted for Confession. There weren't many people sitting near the confessional. Rico figured out the order and sat down. It had been a while since he had been in a church. He had forgotten the smell of the incense. He had forgotten the sight of the red glass candle holder suspended from the ceiling. As he waited for his turn, Rico felt a sense of peace.

Mother bent over and handed me a soda. "This will make you feel better, Rico," she said.

Rico took the glass and drank it. It was the first time Lita had bought him a drink. Things had changed since the marriage proposal. But Lita hadn't said 'yes' or 'no.'

"There, that's *better*. You'll feel like a new man," said Mother.

And I did.

"Bless me, Father, for I have sinned."

"How long has it been since you've made a confession, my son?"

"Over a year, to be sure."

"Examine your conscience, my son, and tell me what weighs heavily upon you?"

"I am troubled. I've asked the woman I've been seeing to marry me, but she is not so sure. My mother kicked me out of the house and is living on the money my father left for my education. I think she's having sex with her brother."

"This sounds like you have a lot on your soul, my son."

"I'm miserable, Father."

"Do you come regularly to mass?"

"No. I used to before I moved to Dallas, but lately everything seems to be falling apart."

"Do you think you will hurt yourself?"

Rico paused. "No, but I might hurt someone else. I don't know."

"The woman you want to marry?"

"No, I'd never hurt her. She's a saint."

"Then who do you think you might hurt?"

"I don't know. But Father, what can I do? I can't just let the sadness and sickness continue."

The priest sighed. "This is a question about the structure of our secular society."

Rico the Great turned his head to try and understand what the priest was trying to say.

"Since the Holy See no longer has secular power because of the rise of Protestantism, secular problems must be met with secular answers."

Rico pursed his lips as he tried to understand the priest. "So, Father, what should I do?"

"Who did you fight with, Rico?" I didn't know how my mother knew I had been in a fight.

"Johnny Hansen," I replied as Mother put the first-aid cream on the cuts—starting with my forehead.

"You fought with Johnny?" she asked me. I didn't say anything until she started putting on the gauze pads.

"Sure did. It was at recess. I saw him hitting Billy. Billy was on the ground. So, I ran up to help out Billy."

"So, you tried to stop a fight?"

"Yes. I mean, Johnny is a lot bigger than Billy. It wasn't a fair fight. So, I thought I'd get into it for Billy."

Mother finished putting on the gauze pads. As she was washing her hands, she asked, "Did anyone else see the fight?"

"Heck no, they were on the other side of the playground. I just happened to be looking for Billy—that's the only reason that I happened to see him."

"WHAT WAS THE FIGHT ABOUT?" ASKED THE TEACHER. SHE WANTED EVERYTHING TO BE OVER. I KNEW IT. I COULD SENSE IT.

"What's the matter?" asked Dianne.

I didn't want to talk to Di at the moment. I was wrong to have yelled at her, and I knew it. She had a right to know—to hear it from me, and not have to hear it from Uncle Adam.

"Come here, Di," I said.

"Something very bad has happened, Di," I began.

"What?"

"Well, you know what day it is?"

"Yes, Friday."

"Yes," I began. Then I stopped. "Let's go outside for a little while Di," I said, putting my arm around her shoulder.

"They tell me the President is a Catholic."

"Yes, he is; he's the first Catholic President of the United States."

"Is he like the Pope?"

"I don't know what you mean, son."

"Well, John Twenty-Three has shaken things up a bit."

"Yes, he has."

"And so has Kennedy."

"That's true. But how can I help you with your confession?"

"If we render unto Caesar what is Caesar's, then problems in the secular realm flow from the head of the secular realm, correct?"

"Yes, but I'm not sure what you're getting at."

Then Rico smiled, got up, and exited the confessional. It

was late May and he wanted to get his head straight.

"I assume you've come for help on your philosophy essay on 'Beauty'?"

"Yes," I replied.

"Have you done your reading?"

"Was it in the textbook?"

"Yes," said the professor. He was almost sixty but he still had jet-black hair and dark-brown, horn-rimmed glasses. His skin was pale, but largely unwrinkled.

"Plato thought that beauty had to be for a social purpose."

"Yes," replied the professor.

"And what if it wasn't?" I asked.

"Then it had to be stopped."

"Stopped? How?" I asked.

"Well, in the ancient Greek times, there were no police forces. People had to take justice into their own hands."

"What does that mean?"

The professor took off his glasses and polished them with his pocket handkerchief. "It could vary, but it usually meant some violence that would cause the miscreant to leave town."

"And what if he wouldn't leave?" I put to him.

"Then there were other options—the worst being to kill him."

I stopped a minute. I was shaking my head. "You mean it could be noble to murder someone?" I was intrigued.

"If it were for the public good, yes."

"You're lying to me," said Dianne.

I looked down at my sister. Some messages are hard to convey. How could I tell her about what had happened to Father?

On June 4, 1963 Rico saw a story on the front page of the newspaper that caused him to fork over a quarter, drop it in the slot, and pull down the iron and glass door in order to buy the edition.

The Pope had died. What would be next?

"HELLO, MRS. PATRICINI?"

"YES. THIS IS SHE."

"I WONDER WHETHER I COULD SCHEDULE AN APPOINTMENT WITH YOU TO TALK ABOUT YOUR SON, RICO."

"RICO DOESN'T LIVE HERE ANYMORE. WHO ARE YOU, ANYWAY?"

"MY NAME IS FRIEDMAN, I'M AN AGENT FOR THE F.B.I. WE ARE INVESTIGATING A CASE WHICH MIGHT INVOLVE YOUR SON."

"MY SON IS A LOSER, BUT HE'S NOT A CRIMINAL. WHY DON'T YOU GO AFTER THE GUY WHO KILLED PRESIDENT KENNEDY?"

"WE BELIEVE THAT MAN WAS LEE HARVEY OSWALD, AND HE IS DEAD."

"EVERYONE KNOWS THAT THERE WAS A PLOT AND YOU ALL ARE COVERING IT UP."

"SO, WHAT TIME WOULD BE CONVENIENT FOR ME AND MY COLLEAGUE, AGENT WALLACE, TO STOP BY? WOULD LATE AFTERNOON TODAY WORK?"

"The University of Washington," I replied.

"How many years did you attend?" asked the HR officer.

"One year plus one term."

"Why did you leave?"

"Money. My father died and my uncle decided that he didn't want to pay for my education anymore."

"I see," said the HR officer. I hoped that it would not be an impediment for my full-time position—after all, I had worked over the summer for them as a contract worker. And after that as a temp.

HR man asked me to sit where I was while he went into another room to talk about my suitability for working on the assembly line. I waited an hour before the man returned.

The man must have been in his forties. He had a box-shaped head and sported a blonde crew cut with lots of hair gel to keep his hair standing straight up to attention. Before he responded to me, he jutted out his jaw and seemed to be chewing something (though he never swallowed). "Well young man, today is your lucky day. In our new Dallas plant, we have a job for a core cutter and reamer. If you can get down there by Monday, the job is yours."

I didn't know how long it would take for a bus to make it to Dallas. It was Wednesday. That would give me 5 days. I knew I couldn't afford a train ticket, but you can generally get better deals on a bus. "I can get there, sir."

"That's fine, boy." Crew cut was smiling. Then he reached out to shake my hand. I received his iron grip and didn't wince. "I'll call Cal McGill and tell him you'll be there at 8am on Monday morning." Then he turned and picked up a 3x5 card that had the address of the plant written in block letters. Then he wrote something on the other side of the card. He reached out his hand again to give me the card.

I took the card and looked at what he wrote: *$1.50 an hour plus benefits.* Then I looked up and asked, "What are the benefits?"

"You get healthcare and a retirement plan after you've been there for five years."

"Yes sir," I said and bowed my head slightly. Then I turned and left the room.

I decided my next stop would be to the YMCA where I was living on a day-to-day basis to retrieve my duffle, and then to the Greyhound bus station.

"WHERE DID HE GO AFTER HE LEFT COLLEGE?"

"HE GOT A TEMPORARY JOB AT A PAPERMILL IN TACOMA. THEN HE RELOCATED TO DALLAS."

"ARE YOU SURE ABOUT THAT TIME-LINE?"

"WELL, HE DIDN'T COMMUNICATE WITH US, IF THAT'S WHAT YOU MEAN. BUT WE GOT A FORWARDED LETTER FROM THE FLOP-HOUSE HE WAS STAYING AT IN TACOMA. HE HAD GIVEN OUR ADDRESS WHEN HE GOT LODGINGS."

"YOU SAY HE WAS STAYING IN A FLOP-HOUSE? OUR RECORDS SAY THAT HE WAS AT A YMCA."

"YES, THAT'S RIGHT, BUT SOMEONE AT THAT FLOP- HOUSE WROTE ON THE ENVELOPE THAT HE'D GONE TO DALLAS. BUT SINCE THEY HAD NO FORWARDING INFORMATION, THEY'D RETURN ALL MAIL TO THE ADDRESS HE'D PUT AS HIS LAST ADDRESS AND THAT WOULD BE HERE."

"I SEE," SAID AGENT FRIEDMAN.

My last term at UW was my best term. I wish that I could have continued. My favorite class was ceramics. I made several artifacts that I gave to Dianne. I kept trying to repeat my black pitcher but couldn't, so I moved on to other work. And then there was my Asian Philosophy class where we read *The Temple of the Golden Pavilion* and *The Extinction of Desire*. I had taken an earlier class from the same professor that had been on 19ᵗʰ Century European philosophy. In that class we had read *Crime and Punishment*, which was a test of Nietzsche's thesis about the superman living within an uncaring, blind society.

I liked my philosophy professor. He tried to make texts relevant to *today*.

Finally, there was my religion class in which we talked about the Protestant

Reformation. In the process, we also discussed Pope John XXIII and his agenda to revitalize the Catholic Church by making it more friendly to regular people: putting the mass into everyday language and fighting for the poor of the world. There is much resistance to these ideas. But someone had to come forward to set off a firework so that things might change.

"But Father, what can I do? I can't just let the sadness and sickness continue."

Mother wanted to take us out to a diner after the funeral, but neither Dianne nor I felt like it. I think Mother was mad.

Father Weal made a visit to our house. Neither my mother nor Uncle Adam was home. I answered the door. We talked in the front room and sat on the brown leather sofa that seats four. Father Weal sat mid-way and I was at the end. I called to Dianne, but she didn't want to come down.

"What are you feeling, Rico?"

I shook my head.

"You know that *death* is a part of *life*. It's hard to understand that when you are just a child. But God has a plan for us all, and it was time for Rex to join his Father in Heaven."

I shook my head.

Then Father Weal put his hand on my shoulder. I turned to ice.

The next time I could interact with my sister was when I convinced her to fly kites. We had kites that we had put together from kits with Father. It seemed like the proper thing to do.

"Can we fly our kites to heaven?" asked Di.

"If we could, I'd like to climb on board," I said, "then I could be with Father."

"Don't forget me!" pleaded Di.

"What is it with you, Rico?" asked Lita. The two were over at her place. It had been a week since he'd asked her to marry him. "Doesn't it matter to you that I'm a whore?"

"You can stop that whenever you choose to. That's part of what I'm asking."

Lita didn't respond.

"Look, Lita, I earn $50 a week after taxes and my place only costs $45 a month. We could move in together on my salary. We could probably eat on the cheap for $45 to $50 a month and that leaves us over $100 a month for stuff we want to do—like movies or dancing."

"You'd be willing to be seen with me as your woman?"

"Sure, so long as you gave up being with other guys."

God has a plan for us all.

"But how can it be a part of His plan that my father dies?"

"I know it's difficult to comprehend, but sometimes the moment is right in His Divine plan that someone—even someone very important—has to die."

And both of our kites flew so very high into the air!

"WE HAVE PHYSICAL EVIDENCE. WHEN YOUR SON, RICO, WAS BROUGHT IN ON THE RAPE CHARGE THEY FINGERPRINTED HIM. NOW *THAT* CHARGE WAS DROPPED ON THE REQUEST OF THE VICTIM. SO, YOUR SON IS NOT A RAPIST."

JACKIE SNORTED AND THEN SNEERED AT THE F.B.I. AGENT. "I TOLD YOU THAT."

"WELL, THAT'S NOT ALL THERE IS TO THE STORY."

"MY SON IS NOT A RAPIST."

"NO. THE COMPLAINT AGAINST HIM WAS WITHDRAWN. BUT WE STILL HAVE THE FINGERPRINT IN OUR NATIONAL FILES."

After the Pope died and Rico purchased his rifle, he decided that he should practice some so that he might become a good shot when he needed to use it. Rico found the perfect spot. It was a deserted rail yard a couple of miles away.

Rico would walk over there with an empty half-gallon milk carton. Rico would cut the carton flat and set the carton down in front of a derelict wooden wall. Then he would fire six rounds and see how many penetrated the carton. At first, he was not a very good shot, but then he started getting better. Gradually he would move farther and farther away. Soon he had to use the rifle's scope to hit the target.

"I don't believe in God," said Dianne.

"Why do you say that, Di?"

"Why do you think?"

We had been flying kites for some time. We didn't talk to each other except at the beginning. But now this came out. I thought I should say something. So, I repeated what Father Weal had said. "Sometimes good people have to die. It's part of God's plan."

"That sounds dumb," replied Di.

"Well, that's what Father Weal said."

"Then I think Father Weal is a turkey."

"Why a turkey?"

But Di wasn't in a talking mood.

"Look, you're a sweet guy. I had you pegged all wrong. I really like you," said Lita as she lit her Lucky Strike cigarette.

Rico was sitting on a chair in her kitchenette. It was bare bones with only a hotplate and an old ice box (with no ice). Lita didn't do much cooking.

"Want a smoke?" she asked.

Rico shook his head. Rico didn't smoke.

Lita ran her fingers through her straight, black hair. Tonight, it wasn't braided. Then she turned to look at Rico.

"Look. I like you. And I don't much like my job. You say you'd do the work to pay the bills, and I'd go get my G.E.D. Right?"

"Yeah."

"What's in it for you?"

"Companionship. I have an affinity for you."

"What does 'affinity' mean?"

"It means you make me less anxious."

Lita thought a moment and took a long drag on her cigarette. Then she smiled. "You should take-up smoking. It's good for that anxiety."

I received an "A" grade in ceramics. The teacher said that he found my work *inspired*. It was the only "A" grade I was to earn in those four tri-mesters at UW. I only kept the black pitcher. For some reason it was the sole thing I'd ever done that seemed perfect to me. It was *too* perfect. When I moved down to Tacoma to work at the papermill, I took a needle and made a scratch near the bottom of the pot so that it would no longer be perfect. Sometimes a man has to act.

"IT WAS SOMETHING ELSE, MRS.PATRICINI.THE DAY AFTER THE KENNEDY ASSINATION IN DALLAS THE F.B.I. DID AN EXTENSIVE SEARCH OF A ONE-MILE RADIUS FROM THE CRIME SCENE," SAID AGENT WALLACE. "WITHIN TWO BLOCKS OF THE CRIME SCENE THEY FOUND A RIFLE. IT WAS A WORKING WEAPON THAT HAD BEEN RECENTLY FIRED."

JACKIE GOT UP AND POURED HERSELF ANOTHER CUP OF COFFEE—BLACK.

"IT WAS A .22 CALIBER WEAPON. THE GUN WAS TAKEN IN TO THE LAB AND ANALYZED. THERE WERE A NUMBER OF CLEAR PRINTS OF YOUR SON, RICO, ON THE GUN."

JACKIE SAT DOWN AGAIN. SHE SET HER JAW FORWARD. "SO WHAT? HAVE YOU EVER HEARD OF THE SECOND AMENDMENT?"

AGENT WALLACE SMILED. "YES, MA'AM. BUT THE FUNNY THING ABOUT THIS IS THAT TWO 'NON-OSWALD' BULLETS WERE FOUND NEAR THE CRIME SCENE AND THOSE TWO BULLETS WERE SHOT FROM THE GUN THAT HAD YOUR RICO'S FINGERPRINTS ON IT."

"What are you working on?" I asked my roommate.

"Take-home test in chemistry."

"Take-home, eh? That should be easy. Just look up the answers in the book." I grinned on what I thought was a gift from the professor.

"Yeah, that's what I thought, too. Problem is that the prof is not a total dumb ass. He *expects* you to use the book so he creates a test that is based on an *application* of the material. So that he knows we are looking things up, but then we have to apply them in ways only *suggested* in the text." Bill Bonnavert sighed and took a bottle out of his desk and dropped a pill into his palm and then swallowed it with coke.

"You sick?" I asked.

"Yeah. Sick of school. I'd like to tell them all to fuck off."

"Oh, I meant the pill. That for your sickness?"

Bill looked at me as if *I* were the *hick* instead of him. "It's called an *upper.* It helps you stay sharp."

"I always used coffee for that."

"Get the hell out of here, Rico. I'm working. I don't need you around me."

So, I left. I didn't come back to my dorm room until the next day after lunch.

"I'm so sorry, son," began Mr. Souposey. "You've got to go back home now."

I felt confused.

"C'mon," he said, gently putting his hand on my shoulder. "I'll take you home to your mother."

FATHER HAD PREPPED ME ON THE STRATEGY TO BEAT BILLY. SINCE BILLY WAS ALWAYS THROWING THE BALL AGAINST THE WALL VERY HARD SO THAT IT WOULD GO OVER MY HEAD AND THUS GET HIM HOME RUNS, FATHER HAD SUGGESTED THAT I PLAY DEEPER AND OCCASIONALLY RUN IN- AND- OUT TO CONFUSE BILLY.

I REALLY LIKED BILLY. OUTSIDE OF MY FAMILY, HE WAS THE CLOSEST FRIEND I HAD. BUT BILLY *ALWAYS* USED TO BEAT ME. I WANTED TO WIN, TOO. I DIDN'T WANT TO WIN *ALWAYS*, BUT I WANTED TO WIN. SOMETIMES I IMAGINED BEATING BILLY AND HIS FEELING WERE HURT SO BAD THAT HE STARTED TO CRY. I DIDN'T WANT BILLY TO CRY. BUT I WANTED TO WIN.

"SOMETIMES YOU ARE GOING TO HURT PEOPLE. SO LONG AS YOU ARE DOING THE RIGHT THING, THAT'S OKAY," SAID FATHER.

Sometimes you will make people cry.

Lita started to leave when she stopped and turned around. "Rico," she began. Then she coughed several times, requiring her to pull up her handkerchief that she kept in the pocket of her skirt. When she righted herself, she stood like a statue looking at him. Then she approached and put her hands upon his shoulders with her arms straight. "I can't marry you, Rico, because I can't marry any man. I used to think I could— there was this guy named Harvey. But he left for Odessa without a forwarding address. I loved that bastard. But he drove me to the street. Son-of-a-bitch," Lita delivered these words as she walked towards the back wall. Then she paused. Rico stood his ground. Then, she pivoted and said, "But I will live with you if you like under the conditions you set out." Then she returned to him and squeezed his shoulders. "I can move in tomorrow. Let's begin our lives together, tomorrow."

Rico smiled and nodded his head.

"One day Rico the Great met a damsel in distress. She had been bewitched by an evil warlock who had made her into a dragon. Rico wanted to save the damsel. But first he had to discover the source of the bewitchment. In order to discover this, Rico had to climb to the top of a tall mountain to the abode of the sacred sage named 'the Pope.' Rico asked the Pope how he could save the damsel. He was given specific charges that would gain him strength so that he might kill the evil warlock.

"It was not easy, but Rico the Great fulfilled all his tasks and then took a mighty sword and killed the evil warlock. Instantly, the spell was broken and all was blessed in the land of *toujour d'amour*."

When I finished my fall term of my second year in college, Uncle Adam said that he would help me move my things to Tacoma. He gave me a duffle bag and said that I could move anything that would fit. He also helped me by buying me a one-way bus ticket to Tacoma. He even gave me $5 for my first night's lodgings in town. I wanted to say *good-bye* to Dianne, but she was going on a "week-end" with the cheerleaders (of which she was one) and the incoming basketball team. It was all sponsored by the school. We no longer belonged to the same tribe.

"YOU THINK MY SON SHOT PRESIDENT KENNEDY?"

"WELL, IT'S TOO EARLY TO SAY FOR SURE. FORENSICS HAS TO RE-DO THEIR TESTS TO BE TOTALLY CERTAIN. WE ALSO HAVE TO EXAMINE THE WOUNDS FROM THE AUTOPSY PHOTOGRAPHS TO DETERMINE WHERE ALL THE ENTRANCE AND EXIT WOUNDS ARE. WE HAVE SOME WITNESSES WHO THINK THEY

HEARD TWO SHOTS FROM A GRASSY KNOLL
BEHIND A WHITE HALF-
WALL.

"AS YOU KNOW, PRESIDENT JOHNSON,
TWO WEEKS AGO, COMMISSIONED SUPREME
COURT CHIEF JUSTICE EARL WARREN TO
ESTABLISH AN INDEPENDENT COMMISSION TO
FULLY INVESTIGATE ALL OF THIS. I AM PART
OF THAT COMMISSION AND THESE
QUESTIONS AND YOUR ANSWERS WILL
BECOME A PART OF THAT BODY OF
EVIDENCE." AGENT WALLACE PEERED OVER
HIS BLACK, HORN-RIMMED GLASSES AT
JACKIE.

JACKIE STARTED SHAKING HER HEAD. "I
DON'T THINK I WANT TO BE A PART OF THIS."

F.B.I. AGENT WALLACE SAID, "I
RECOGNIZE HOW HARD THIS IS ON YOU MRS.
PATRICINI, BUT THIS INVESTIGATION IS OF
NATIONAL IMPORTANCE. YOU MUST
CONTINUE WITH THE QUESTIONING."

*Lita moved in with Rico in July. Everything that she had
fit into a medium-sized, tan cardboard suitcase with metal
snaps at the top. Rico had purchased another mattress and
some sheets from a store a few blocks away. It was a Salvation
Army second-hand store.*

*When Lita came to Rico's place (it had been the first time
she had gone to his place), the only two things she noted were
that Rico had a working half-sized refrigerator, and a working
gas stove. She said nothing about the rifle that was propped up
in the corner near the two mattresses that were situated next to
each other on the floor. Rico's apartment also had a private
toilet and bath. There was also one closet. Technically, it was
a "studio" apartment, but with sheets that Rico had hung from
the ceiling around the beds, it gave the impression of a one-
bedroom apartment.*

It was certainly a step-up in material comfort for Lita from where she had been.

"SO, IN EVERY GAME, RICO, THERE IS A CERTAIN AMOUNT OF STRATEGY AND A CERTAIN AMOUNT OF LUCK." FATHER HAD JUST GOTTEN ME A COKE OUT OF THE REFRIGERATOR. FOR HIMSELF, FATHER POURED A GLASS OF TAP WATER. HE REACHED INTO A DRAWER AND TOOK OUT SOME SALTINE CRACKERS TO SHARE WITH ME.

I NODDED AND STARTED IN ON THE COKE, BUT STOPPED. "HOW DO I KNOW WHICH IS WHICH?"

"GOOD QUESTION. I'D SAY THIS," BEGAN FATHER AS HE FIT A CRACKER INTO HIS MOUTH AND CHEWED IT CAREFULLY. "WE WORKED OUT OUR STRATEGY FOR THE GAME WITH BILLY. AND YOU CAN FOLLOW THAT. BUT THAT DOES *NOT ENSURE* THAT YOU WILL WIN."

"THEN WHY DO I DO IT?"

"GOOD QUESTION. THE BEST ANSWER THAT I CAN GIVE YOU IS THAT YOU MUST ALWAYS DO YOUR BEST. IF YOU LOSE AND YOU'VE DONE YOUR BEST, THEN THAT'S JUST BAD LUCK. BUT IF YOU'VE NOT DONE YOUR BEST, THEN THE FAULT LIES ON YOU." FATHER FINISHED HIS WATER AND THE TWO REMAINING CRACKERS. "YOU'VE GOT TO HAVE FAITH IN THIS, RICO. MOST OF THE TIME WHEN YOU DO YOUR BEST, YOU'LL COME OUT ON TOP BECAUSE A MAN CAN BECOME ANYTHING IF HE TRIES HARD AND APPLIES HIMSELF CORRECTLY."

"The death of the Holy Father cannot be fully comprehended by us," said the Father confessor. "The Pope certainly had a profound effect on the world. But sometimes the Holy Father has to die for the benefit of us all—just as our Lord Jesus had to die on the Cross."

It was shortly after this interview that Rico went out and purchased his used .22 rifle with scope.

I was not prepared for the ease that I was removed from the family home. Uncle Adam and my mother were in cahoots. They wanted me *gone*. It was barely into the first week in

January that I was on my way to Tacoma with my one-way bus ticket, one duffle bag, $5, and five postage stamps. I was just about to turn 20 years old. I had had 4 terms of college and now I was an entry-level peg in a national paper mill company. The coldness of the process made me think that my mother was dead, too. Though she stood next to her brother as I got on the bus, I had the feeling that she was no longer my mother. She was Adam's wife. CESTIN!

It wasn't long after Lita had moved in (mid-July) that Lita came home after her first day at the G.E.D. study session. Rico had bought her a ten-lesson program. It was the most he felt that he could afford. On her part Lita had come home with a gift for him: a History Comic Book. It cost $.60—almost the price of two McDonald's meals. Rico was thrilled.

The story in the History Comic Book was the story of Oedipus, the King—or Oedipus Rex. The title struck Rico as "Rex" was his father's name. Rico couldn't wait to read it. It rather disturbed him so he tried to read it cover-to-cover every day for a week.

I was happy when my freshman year was coming to an end. My grades were not exactly stellar but I was pulling a "C" average which (if I kept it up for four years) would get me my diploma.

My roommate, Bill Bonnavert, had a higher grade point—and he was taking mostly math and science classes. But Bill had help. He purchased lecture notes and versions of tests that he got from a fraternity that specialized in pre-med students. If you paid enough, you could even get someone to go into the test room and take it for you. Those big lecture sessions had so many students that the teacher didn't have a clue who was or was not one of his students.

"I THINK OUR INTERVIEW IS OVER, MR. WALLACE."

THE F.B.I. AGENT/PSYCHOLOGIST TOOK OFF HIS BLACK, HORN-RIMMED GLASSES FOR A QUICK CLEANING. THEN HE OPENED HIS

BRIEFCASE AND HANDED JACKIE A FORM TO
SIGN.

"IS THIS REALLY NECESSARY?"

"YES, MRS. PATRICINI. THIS
ACKNOWLEDGES THAT YOU AND I HAD THIS
DISCUSSION TODAY AND THAT EVERYTHING
THAT YOU'VE TOLD ME IS THE TRUTH."

"OF COURSE, IT'S THE TRUTH."

"I KNOW, MA'AM. THIS IS JUST ALL
PROCEDURE. SIGN AT THE BOTTOM AND
PRINT YOUR FULL NAME: JOCASTA
PATRICINI."

I started walking downstairs to get a cookie when I
heard my Uncle Adam talking with Mother. I carefully and
silently made my way down and stopped when I could hear
them talking.

I sat down. If I tilted my head slightly, I could see
through the baluster slats that held up the stair railing. I had
a direct view into the kitchen where they were standing next
to each other.

"What am I going to do?" said Mother. "I don't have a
job. How will I pay the bills?" Mother was shaking her head
and lifting her arms in the air.

"Well, I've spent the day on that. With the copy of the
death certificate and your driver's license, the bank bought the
story that I was your brother (which I am, of course). Your Rex
had put away two months expenses in a savings account. I
also got the name of his broker.

"I called the broker. He had heard about Rex's death
from other clients. Apparently, your Rex had been a big deal
in the local business community: president of Rotary, and the
like."

"Yes, he was always going to those meetings. It gave me
some peace to get him out of the house."

Uncle Adam laughed and hugged his sister. She hugged
him back—really hard.

"You should only speak well of the dead, little girl," said Uncle Adam. "The broker told me that your Rex had a $500,000 life insurance policy. That pays off tax-free with a lifetime annuity of $20,000 a year forever until you die."

Mother broke free. "Twenty-grand a year? Wow. That skinflint was putting it all away in his little pots."

"Now you won't have to get a job. That'll be enough for me to move in with you and then neither of us will have to work. Cool."

Mother then did a little dance to a song she was singing. Adam also danced but he didn't sing. When they had finished, Mother hugged Adam very hard again.

Adam broke the embrace and added, "There's also a generous fund for Rico's and Dianne's college education. It's in an aggressive mutual fund that will keep up with inflation. But if things get tough, we can dip into that, too. It's all in your name, as beneficiary."

"Oh, this is so wonderful. It couldn't be better." Mother was shaking her head. "We were so unhappy together, Adam. I can't tell you. He used to tell me that my frivolous spending was driving him to the grave. He said that if I wanted to spend as I liked, that I should get my own job! Imagine that! Suggesting that I get a job. That's *his* role, not *mine*."

Adam came to her and hugged her so that the lower parts of their bodies were connected but their faces were apart. "Jackie, you shouldn't blame yourself for Rex's death. You were just a normal housewife." He paused for a moment. "It's that brat son of yours, Rico. He wanted all of his father's time. If there was an outside cause of the stress that brought him to his grave, it was Rico. *He* killed his father."

My mother put her face on Adam's chest and started crying.

I didn't want to hear anymore. I turned to go when I saw my sister one step behind me. I wondered how much she had heard. Obviously, she heard the part where I was accused of killing my father.

Rico had a hard time breathing. It started in the end of July. Lita said she thought it was all the fine paper particles that floated in the air at his job. She had known a number of men who suffered the same way.

"Give me five dollars," she said to Rico as he was coughing up blood.

Rico waved his hand toward his wallet. When he did this, she could take whatever she needed. She never cheated him.

After a couple of hours, she returned. She carried a brown paper bag. In it was a syringe and a small glass bottle. Lita put the needle into the bottle and drew out the contents. Then she injected Rico into his left biceps. Within an hour, Rico felt better.

"What was that?" asked Rico.

"They call it an 'upper;' it gets the body moving again. I've seen it save more than one life."

Rico was on his mattress and Lita was in the kitchen, sitting at a chair studying for her G.E.D. exam #2. Rico got up and went to Lita. "I'm better. You cured me, Mother."

Lita turned to him and frowned, "I'm not your mother. I'm your lover."

Rico smiled and kissed Lita. "I think you saved my life."

Lita nodded. "No problem. Now, do you want to help me study for my second test?" Rico got a second chair and sat down next to her.

I WAS THE HOME TEAM. BILLY WAS THE VISITING TEAM. I WAS FULLY READY TO USE MY FATHER'S SYSTEM THAT WE HAD PRACTICED. OBVIOUSLY, I HADN'T TOLD BILLY ANYTHING ABOUT IT.

BILLY WAS UP FIRST SO HE HELD THE TENNIS BALL IN HIS HAND, GETTING READY TO THROW IT DOWN AGAINST THE CEMENT AT AN ANGLE BEFORE THE WALL SO THAT IT WOULD SOON BOUNCE UP AGAIN. THEN HE LOOKED BACK AT ME. I WAS PLAYING HIM DEEP, JUST LIKE FATHER SUGGESTED.

"I'M GOING TO START, RICO," SAID BILLY, SINCE I WAS POSITIONED DIFFERENTLY THAN I EVER HAD BEEN BEFORE. I SUSPECT THAT HE THOUGHT THAT HIS INVOCATION WOULD BRING ME UP CLOSE THE WAY I USED TO DO IT.

"READY," I REPLIED. THEN BY INSTINCT, I RAN IN AS BILLY TRIED TO THROW A LITTLE LOOPER AGAINST THE WALL. I CAUGHT IT ON THE FLY: ONE OUT.

ON THE NEXT TRY, BILLY TRIED HIS FAVORITE HOMERUN THROW, BUT I STAYED BACK AND CAUGHT IT WITHOUT MOVING A STEP.

BILLY WAS TAKEN ABACK. THEN HE CALLED "BUNT," WHICH MEANT A VERY WEAK TAP AGAINST THE WALL IN WHICH HE WOULD THEN COUNT "ONE-ONE THOUSAND, TWO-ONE THOUSAND, AND THREE-ONE THOUSAND." IF HE MADE IT TO THREE AND I HAD NOT PICKED UP THE BALL AND TOSSED IT AGAINST THE WALL, IT WAS A BASE HIT.

BUT I WAS RUNNING IN AGAIN AND THE BALL HIT THE WALL AT 'TWO.' SCORE AT THE TOP OF THE FIRST—'0 TO 0.'

WE WERE SCORELESS UNTIL THE FOURTH INNING WHEN I GUESSED ON RUNNING IN, BUT BILLY SENT ONE OF HIS SIGNATURE HOMERUNS OVER MY HEAD. I IMAGINED SEEING MY FATHER ON THE PORCH IN HIS CHAIR, SHAKING HIS HEAD, "THAT'S NOT THE WAY WE PRACTICED IT, RICO."

I COULD JUST SEE HIM WAGGING HIS FINGER AT ME. I WAS DETERMINED NOT TO LET HIM DOWN.

It was early September, just after Rico had come home from work, that Lita opened the door and ran over to him and put her arms around him to kiss him. "I passed," she said.

"The G.E.D.?" asked Rico.

"Yes, now I'm a high school graduate! Isn't that wonderful?"

"It certainly is. Let's go to McDonald's and celebrate."

"Wonderful!" Lita gave Rico another kiss and hugged him around the neck.

Cindy had wanted our relationship to progress faster than I was prepared to do. Why couldn't she just talk to me?

Instead, I discovered we were over, and she was far along with someone else. It didn't seem fair.

Because Rollo and his crowd all told the same story, they never got into any serious trouble—only some community service. I had terrible pictures in my mind of Virginia and Rollo kissing and him unzipping her dress. She seemed to be enjoying herself so much. But then why didn't she just go to the prom with Rollo? Maybe her parents knew what kind of guy Rollo was? *At the McDonald's, they had a machine that would take your picture (3 shots) for fifty cents. After they ate, Rico convinced Lita to pose with him for two pictures of themselves together and one of Lita, alone. Rico put in the quarters and within a few minutes they had their pictures. When they got home, Rico cut the pictures apart and kept one, gave one to Lita and put the one of Lita alone onto their refrigerator. It was the end of a wonderful day.*

IN THE FIFTH INNING I GOT THE RUN BACK. I HAD A RUNNER ON FIRST WITH TWO OUTS AND I DECIDED TO TRY THE SCREW BALL MY FATHER HAD TAUGHT ME: "THE BALL WILL CURVE AFTER IT HITS THE WALL IF YOU THROW IT HARD ENOUGH—BUT BE CAREFUL BECAUSE THE TWISTING OF YOUR WRIST WILL BE HARD ON YOUR ELBOW. ONLY USE THIS TRICK ONCE A GAME." I TRIED IT, AND IT WORKED. WHEN IT WENT PAST BILLY, HE COULDN'T GET IT TO THE WALL BEFORE I COUNTED TO "NINE" (WHICH MEANT A TRIPLE IN OUR NEW SYSTEM)—MY RUN SCORED. IT WAS A ONE-TO-ONE TIE. I FELT THAT GOOD TIMES WERE ON THE WAY.

I didn't know why I suggested that Dianne and I fly kites. While it was beautiful to see them flying away, I was reminded of how Father's soul had flown away from us. How lucky the kites were to be near Father.

Sometimes the pain inside is beyond tears, and you can only watch what you love flying high in the sky—far, far away—never to return.

When Rico got home from work, he opened the door expecting to see Lita. Rico had purchased the tickets for a Halloween party that Lita had told him about at the Lone Star Tavern. It was supposed to be a surprise, but when he got home the only evidence of Lita was a piece of paper on the kitchen table:

"I know this will sound rotten to you. But I've quit my new supermarket job and have decided to go after Harvey. He was my first love, and he broke my heart when he left me for Odessa. I figured that since he's a car mechanic that there aren't a million car mechanics in Odessa and I might find him. It's something I just have to do. Sorry, Rico, you've been very straight with me—the G.E.D. and everything. You're a great guy and deserve someone better than me. I hope you find her. Love, Lita."

Her picture of Rico and Lita was also on the table. Rico picked up that photo and tore it in two. He also took the photo of the two of them from his wallet and tore it in two. He threw the torn pictures into the waste can. Then he went over to the refrigerator and took down the photo of Lita alone and put it in his wallet.

Adam came to her and hugged her so that the lower parts of their bodies were connected but their faces were apart. "Jackie, you shouldn't blame yourself for Rex's death. You were just a normal housewife." He paused for a moment. "It's that brat son of yours, Rico. He wanted all of his father's time. If there was an outside cause of the stress that brought him to his grave, it was Rico. He killed his father."

My mother put her face on Adam's chest and started crying.

IN THE SIXTH AND SEVENTH INNINGS THERE WAS NO SCORE. BUT IN THE EIGHTH I GOT A SINGLE AND THEN ADVANCED THE RUNNER WITH A BUNT: ONE OUT—RUNNER

ON SECOND. I TRIED FOR A BIG PLAY. I THREW THE BALL AS HARD AS I COULD, BUT BILLY HAD ME OUT-FOXED. HE RAN BACK ON THE PITCH, SEEING HOW HARD I WAS THROWING IT. HE GOT IT. AND THREW IT AGAINST THE WALL BEFORE THE COUNT OF THREE SO I COULDN'T CLAIM A TAG-UP. NOW IT WAS TWO OUTS AND A RUNNER ON SECOND. THEN I REMEMBERED THE SECOND TRICK PLAY MY FATHER HAD TAUGHT ME. "YOU HOLD THE BALL JUST ON YOUR FINGERTIPS (DON'T LET THE OTHER GUY SEE HOW YOU'RE HOLDING IT THAT WAY) AND THEN YOU THROW THE BALL AS HARD AS YOU CAN, BUT THE BALL WILL BE RATHER WEAK BECAUSE OF YOUR GRIP. IT WILL TRICK THE OTHER GUY SO THAT HE RUNS BACK WHILE THE BALL IS A WEAK SINGLE. THIS ALSO MIGHT HURT YOUR ARM SO SAVE IT FOR THE KEY MOMENT." NOW WAS THE KEY MOMENT. I DID IT, AND IT WORKED. MY RUNNER SCORED. I WAS AHEAD BY ONE GOING INTO THE TOP OF THE NINTH.

I really didn't understand why fixating upon the noble and the beautiful (what my philosophy professor called "*to kalon*") had to do with creating a home for nihilism. I was thinking about writing my paper on this theme, but I wasn't sure I really understood the process very well. I'm a very straight forward guy. I'm not full of the many twistings of Raskolnikov's mind so I do not understand why this nihilism caused him to act as he did. Our professor also said that a general social acceptance of nihilism in Russia was a precursor to the Bolshevik Revolution. Was this what Nietzsche meant about re-making the moral code? It all passed by my brain at a dizzying pace. I was very attracted to philosophy, but I always seemed to be missing something because it never completely came together for me—at least according to my midterm paper grade.

I was very lonely for those three weeks after the senior prom and the ending of the term. Officer Guttman believed my story and the fast crowd had to agree to do a certain number of community service hours in order to avoid a court hearing and a bad mark on their permanent record. I guess we're born to be social animals. It's hard to be excluded. I remember how much I liked going to the Catholic Church with my father. In the communion line everyone was together. Father used to say that the mystery of communion made the church one—all together.

When I had to go to Protestant church with Uncle Adam and Mother, the whole thing was different. The sermon was a half-hour: it was like going to school—all by yourself. There was no communion except at Easter and then it was grape juice in tiny glasses served in a round silver tray that was passed down the pews. There was no line. No one had to leave his seat.

Rico the Great was confused. In the land there was sickness and sadness. Rico wondered what he could do. So he went to the priest and asked him. The padre looked sad and shook his head. "I'm sorry, my son, but this is not the work of God. God only wants good for His children." Rico the Great was anxious with this response.

"'But Father, what can I do? I can't just let the sadness and sickness continue."

The priest slowly shook his head. "This is a question about the structure of our secular society."

Rico the Great turned his head to try and understand what the priest was trying to say.

"'Since the Holy See no longer has secular power because of the rise of Protestantism, secular problems must be met with secular answers."

Rico the Great pursed his lips as he tried to understand the priest. "So, Father, what should I do?"

"Who rules the secular realm?"

"Why the King, of course."

"And the King is in charge of the secular realm."

"Yes."

"So, if He isn't doing his job, what should happen to him?"

Rico the Great took his index finger and ran it across his throat as if he were killing someone.

The priest smiled.

I WAS NOT CERTAIN WHAT I SHOULD DO. THERE WERE RUNNERS ON FIRST AND SECOND BUT THERE WERE TWO OUTS. BILLY WAS STARING AT MY POSITION. HE STOOD ALERTLY, ON THE TIPS OF HIS TOES, HIS KNEES SLIGHTLY BENT, AND HIS ARMS POISED FOR THE INEVITABLE MOMENT. THE GAME WAS ON THE LINE. MY FINGERS BEGAN TO SWEAT. *It seemed heavy in his arms. Every moment the weight seemed to increase.* I felt separated *it was as if he were watching a movie or maybe, he felt it was closer to a dream that you try to control, but can't. His eyes were fixed on the hand* THAT HELD THE BALL

BILLY WAS GOING FOR IT ALL WITH A HOMERUN THAT WOULD PUT HIM ON TOP FOR THE FIRST TIME IN THE GAME. I FAKED LIKE I WAS RUNNING IN AND THEN I BACK PEDDLED. BILLY GAVE IT HIS BEST SHOT, BUT I WAS READY AND PLENTY DEEP TO TAKE IT *into his sight and pull the trigger for the first shot.*

IT WAS OVER. I HAD WON THE GAME. I'D BEATEN BILLY FOR THE FIRST TIME. I RAN HOME TO TELL FATHER.

Rico looked through his rifle scope after his second shot. Perhaps his second shot hit Kennedy? At least the President leaned forward. His blood spilled on Jackie. It was time to escape.

HE HAD DONE IT! BILLY HAD FINALLY LOST A GAME! THE FIRST TIME.

A man can be anything

> **Or nothing**

and with God's help

you'll get

Our Father who art in heaven

DID BILLY LET ME WIN THE GAME? Then I saw Mr. Souposey. He came to me. Was he going to hit me? "Rico," he said. His voice sounded gentle. "Don't be afraid. I won't bite you. You'd better get home, son. I think your mother would like to see you."

White wheel covers; it was a strange car—kind of like a boxed rectangle and all black except for I was hungry. It was as if I were watching myself in a movie. Rollo was right about Virginia. C i n d y w a s   r i g h t   a b o u t   m e. *Rico took out his picture of Lita. It was all he now had of her.*

Rico ran from the scene and ditched his rifle in the nearest receptacle. He made his way to the bus station. He had already purchased his ticket to Odessa. His bag was in a locker. The key to the locker was in his pocket. Rico took out a Lucky Strike and lit it. Did he really know where he was going? No. His job was over. His life in Dallas was over. But he had a ticket for Odessa and $200 in his wallet. Time was melting the family watch away I WAS NOT CERTAIN WHAT I SHOULD DO *besides getting on a bus to nowhere.*

א

The Long Fall of the Ball from the Wall

Other Novels by Michael Boylan

Rainbow Curve (2014) Fans of baseball's history will appreciate this compelling tale about race, politics, and corrupting power; and one's man's courage to stand-up. *De Anima #1*

The Extinction of Desire (2007) What would you do if you suddenly became rich? *De Anima #2*

To the Promised Land (2015) Are there limits to forgiveness: personal, corporate, and political? *De Anima #3*

Maya (2018) Follow the fate of an Irish-American family through three generations in the U.S.A. It's the story of immigrants, and an account of History. *De Anima #4*

Naked Reverse (2016) There is a backdoor to the ivory tower. Find out what happens to one college professor who escapes. *Archē #1*

Georgia: Part One (2106), Part Two (2017), Part Three (2017) A novel told in three parts. Explore racial identity and themes of social justice through a murder mystery set in the early 20th century. *Archē #2, 3, 4*

T-Rx: The History of a Radical Leader (2019) An epistolary novel about radicalization in the Vietnam-era. What are and what are *not* legitimate tactics for social/political change? *Archē #5*

Made in the USA
Columbia, SC
06 January 2020